PRAISE FOR K

"Thriller fans will enjoy the action and suspense."

—*Publishers Weekly*, on *The Devil's Daughter*

"This cross-genre mystery/romance is fast-paced and suspenseful, with zesty dialogue and likable characters."

—*Kirkus Reviews*, on *The Devil's Daughter*

"Robert shows off her impressive versatility in this fast-paced and inventive new Hidden Sins series."

—*RT Book Reviews*, on *The Devil's Daughter*

"Robert combines strong chemistry, snappy plotting, and imperfect yet appealing characters . . . This installment is easily readable as a stand-alone, and it's a worthy addition to a sexy series."

—*Publishers Weekly*, on *Undercover Attraction*

"Robert easily pulls off the modern marriage-of-convenience trope . . . This is a compulsively readable book! It's more than just sexy times, too, though those are plentiful and hot! . . . An excellent start to a new series."

—*RT Book Reviews*, on *The Marriage Contract*

"*The Marriage Contract* by Katee Robert is dark, dirty, and dead sexy. I want a Teague O'Malley of my very own!"

—Tiffany Reisz, author of the Original Sinners series

"A definite roller coaster of intrigue, drama, pain, heartache, romance, and more. The steamy parts were super steamy, the dramatic parts delivered with a perfect amount of flair."

—*A Love Affair With Books*, on *The Marriage Contract*

"The series is a hit all around, and I'm already loving it."

—*The Book Cellar*, on *The Marriage Contract*

"If you like angsty reads, this book is right up your wheelhouse."

—*Heroes & Heartbreakers*, on *The Wedding Pact*

"I loved every second."

—*All About Romance*, on *The Wedding Pact*

THE SURVIVING GIRLS

ALSO BY KATEE ROBERT

The Hidden Sins Series

The Devil's Daughter

The Hunting Grounds

The O'Malleys Series

The Marriage Contract

The Wedding Pact

An Indecent Proposal

Forbidden Promises

Undercover Attraction

The Bastard's Bargain

The Foolproof Love Series

A Foolproof Love

Fool Me Once

A Fool for You

Out of Uniform Series

In Bed with Mr. Wrong

His to Keep

Falling for His Best Friend

His Lover to Protect

His to Take

Serve Series

Mistaken by Fate

Betting on Fate

Protecting Fate

Come Undone Series

Wrong Bed, Right Guy

Chasing Mrs. Right

Two Wrongs, One Right

Seducing Mr. Right

Seducing the Bridesmaid

Meeting His Match

THE SURVIVING GIRLS

KATEE ROBERT

This is a work of fiction. Names, characters, organizations, places, events, and incidents are either products of the author's imagination or are used fictitiously.

Published by Montlake Romance, Seattle

www.apub.com

ISBN-13: 9781503902442
ISBN-10: 1503902447

Cover design by Mark Ecob

Printed in the United States of America

To the survivors

CHAPTER ONE

Lei Zhang had never trusted the woods. Not from the first time her parents dragged her on a camping trip when she was seven in an effort to do what *normal* people did. Certainly not now, when she knew all too well what the evil forests were capable of hiding. The trees had a way of closing a person off from the rest of the world, even a few hundred yards from a well-traveled road. Out here, one could almost believe their actions didn't have consequences—that nothing they did would ever be discovered.

Secrets. The forest is full of secrets.

It was her job to help uncover those secrets.

Penance, some called it. Lei just called it her job—her purpose.

She forced herself to drag her attention away from the lake her German Shepherd–Great Pyrenees mix, Saul, had led her to. He'd found something, which meant it was time for his reward. Saul was smarter than any dog had a right to be, but that didn't mean he cared about the conflicting feelings that rose in her with every search they did.

A successful search meant there was a body at the end of it.

She crouched down and stroked Saul's dark fur. "You did good, boy." Because of him and Lei, there would be a family who got closure.

She didn't have to wait to see what the divers would find to know that. Saul was never wrong.

Lei, on the other hand, was wrong far too often.

Not this time.

She threw the ball for him; the joyous wiggle his big body gave lightened her mood a little bit. It didn't quite make her forget the divers slipping into the water or the uneasy murmur of the cops gathered on the shoreline, but her search was over. Right now, her only priority was rewarding her dog for a job well done. He didn't care that a successful hunt meant someone had been brutally murdered and had their body dumped. For Saul, the joy was the search—and playing with his ball afterward.

He dropped the bright-red globe at her feet and turned in a quick circle, a doggy grin on his face. Lei picked it up and tossed it again, careful to aim well away from the lake and the path she and Saul had taken here.

Evidence.

Technically, she could leave at any time—her report would be filed later—but she needed to confirm they brought up a body. Needed to know the job was fulfilled. Needed to bear witness.

Sometimes it felt like she'd been bearing witness for twelve long years, ever since she opened that window . . .

Saul whined, and Lei gave herself a sharp shake. "You're right. No use thinking about that. Not now." Not when they had a hike back down the trail ahead of them. It would take less time to hike out than it had to hike in because Saul wasn't tracking.

The sheriff strode over, looking ten years older than when he'd initially contacted Lei for her help. He yanked off his wide-brimmed hat and scrubbed a hand over his thinning gray hair. "That girl deserved better than this."

"They always do."

He frowned at her, as if trying to decide if she was joking. Seeming satisfied she wasn't out of line, he hooked his fingers into a belt almost hidden by his overflowing stomach and huffed out a strained laugh. "Figure you're used to it by now, huh?"

Lei tensed. It never failed; someone always brought up her past during these searches. Cops had long memories, longer by far than the even more dogged media cycle or true-crime fan. She worked hard to ensure that the legacy she left behind wasn't that of a victim. It seemed like every time she turned around, she faced down some mention of the night her life had taken a hard right turn into a nightmare there was no escaping.

But she *had* escaped.

She hadn't let that bastard win. She hadn't curled up in a ball and let life go on without her, or slipped into a drugged haze and become a living zombie. She'd *lived.*

She was a goddamn survivor.

But then the sheriff's words processed, and she forced herself to relax. *He's not talking about* that *past. He's talking about Saul.* "It is what we do." Find the lost ones. Give closure. Do their part to battle the evil that seemed to crop up in the most unexpected places.

Like a cute fraternity boy . . .

Stop it.

He replaced his hat, still looking uneasy. "You're going to want to head back to the road. It'll be dark before long."

She ignored that. Cops usually fell into two camps when it came to cadaver dogs: they saw the search team as a tool to be used, or they considered the dog damn near a miracle worker. Sheriff Joffrey fell into the latter category, though he'd probably label it witchcraft before he went with something as benign as a miracle.

Lei picked up the ball Saul dropped and threw it again, though not as far this time. "How long will the divers take?"

"Hard to say." He cast a sorrowful look at the lake. "It's not particularly deep, but the currents run a little funny—or so my men say. The search area is a little wider than they expected."

The unnamed little lake sat smack-dab in the middle of Colville National Forest. Murderers always thought they were so clever, hauling bodies into national forests and burying them or tossing them into lakes like this one. And sometimes that was even true.

There weren't that many cadaver dogs out there, when all was said and done. Not nearly enough to make up for the sheer number of bodies. Especially when some police departments weren't keen on bringing them in.

Saul came bounding back with his ball, and Lei slipped it into her pack and patted his head. "We'll wait."

He hesitated. "Suit yourself."

It took longer than she would have liked. Several hours passed before the signal went up that they'd found something.

She forced her body to relax, banishing the tension from her fingertips to her tight shoulders. This was always the hardest part, though water searches were the worst by far because they took longer. There was something invariably terrifying about death rising from the deep.

She and Saul moved closer, staying well outside the circle of activity. The body was wrapped in tarp and tied with thick rope. Weights had been attached to the rope—more than enough to keep it submerged indefinitely. With the tarp, even as the body decomposed, it would remain in its final resting place.

Not final.

You're going home.

My job's done.

Exhaustion pulled at her, the aftereffects of her adrenaline high. "Come, Saul."

He trotted at her heels, ears up and alert as they hiked slowly back to the road. Lei's truck sat at the makeshift trailhead—the same place

Mark Jones's truck had been spotted after the disappearance of Shelly Jones. For all his apparent preparation, he hadn't realized he'd been seen, or expected the cops to call in someone who could track where he'd dumped his wife.

She still had almost a three-hour drive ahead of her. It was tempting to plan to stop off somewhere and take a nap, but Emma would worry.

It was easier to put her friend and roommate's worry at the forefront, but the truth was that Lei didn't sleep any place but in their little fortress of a house. She'd tried. Even twelve years later, when a job forced her to stay overnight in a hotel, fear kept bolting her awake hour after hour, and even Saul's presence wasn't enough to change that. She'd tried pills and therapy—she was the child of a psychologist, after all—and she'd even gone so far as to attempt to numb the memories with whiskey. None of it ever truly got her past her own frequent personal nightmare.

Once they reached her truck, she took a few minutes to set out Saul's food and water in a pair of bowls. He could eat on the go, but they weren't so pressed for time that she had to rush him.

Lei checked to make sure he was good and then dug out her cell phone. There was only one text from Emma. Call when you're done.

She dialed from memory. The phone barely rang before her friend picked up. "How'd it go?"

"We found her."

Emma hissed out a breath. "Good. That's good. I was tracking your location. Why is it always a lake?"

"Because *CSI* doesn't cover the fact that dogs like Saul can track a scent even over running water. And how many books did we read in school, and after, where a person crosses a river to confuse a trail?" It might confuse some dogs, but cadaver dogs' training meant it would take a whole hell of a lot more than that to lose a trail. It also meant that strange things like underground streams or inclement weather could lead to an unfollowable trail. *Life is never boring.*

"Good point. I guess I shouldn't complain. It makes our job that much easier."

"Yep." Saul had finished eating, so she wiped down his bowls, tossed the remaining water, and tucked them back into her pack. "How are things going?"

"Nothing catastrophic happened while you were gone. We got a few more requests for searches—the springtime surge is in full effect—and Isaac offered us a job. Again."

Isaac Bamford being the sheriff of their small town, Stillwater. Lei smiled despite the absurdity of it. "He does realize that cadaver dogs aren't very useful in a town where the last murder was fifty years ago, right?"

It was glaringly clear to anyone with eyes that Isaac cared less about having Lei and Emma on staff and more about spending time around Emma. He'd held a flame for her for years, ever since she and Lei bought the house. The only person in Stillwater who *didn't* know that was Emma herself.

"He's persistent. I'll give him that."

"That he is." Though if he'd just ask Emma out, they could be done with all the nonsense of him offering them a job. Again. They were independent contractors for a reason. It gave them the freedom to do the most good possible—and to turn down jobs that didn't measure up. They had an excellent system. Lei and Saul traveled, while Emma worked remotely using her technical skills to do everything from finagle grids to researching to hacking—though that last skill was one they left off their résumé.

They were a good team. One of the best.

"When will you be home?" Emma's question snapped her out of her musing.

"I'm leaving right now. Two and a half, maybe three hours." She glanced at Saul and held her phone out. "Saul, say hello to Prince."

Saul barked, and almost instantly a tinny bark responded. Lei originally got the Golden Retriever to act as backup to Saul, but he'd bonded with Emma instantly. He had basic training for simple searches, but in practice he functioned more as a therapy dog. Lei was just grateful her friend had bonded with *something* not connected to the trauma they'd survived. *Someone beyond me.* Dogs were better than people most of the time anyway.

"Prince is missing Saul. Drive safe."

"I will."

"I'll keep the light on."

"You always do."

That was the other reason she couldn't stay out overnight. Lei had done it before—and would again—and both she and Emma had survived just fine, but neither of them had handled it well. After hours of sleeping like shit, she would come home and find Emma curled up with Prince on the couch by the front door. Waiting to see for herself that Lei was alive and well.

A shrink would have a field day with their friendship. Lei's parents had thrown the best therapists in the country at her—and at Emma by association—in the years since the Sorority Row Murders. It never failed to disappoint them when psychologist after psychologist failed to *fix* their damaged daughter. They were happy she'd survived, of course, but every strained phone call reinforced the fact that she'd never be their darling daughter again.

Even for all that, at least they tried.

They were a far cry better than Emma's parents, though that wasn't saying much.

She put her broken pieces back together in a way they didn't recognize—couldn't recognize, because then they'd have to face the depth of the terror she'd lived through. Easier for everyone if they kept their distance, aside from the expected monthly phone calls.

That monster . . . No. She was stronger than that. Refusing to name him gave him power and turned him into a bogeyman. Hadn't Lei learned that through watching Emma over the years?

Travis Berkley. The Sorority Row killer.

Even if Lei and Emma had *technically* survived that night, Travis had killed the innocent girls they'd been in the same way he'd cut down twenty-one of their sorority sisters.

And Lei was the one who'd unwittingly given him access to the house.

Saul nudged her leg, a clear sign to get her ass in gear and stop wallowing in guilt over something that happened more than a decade ago. For all her claims about being as well adjusted as someone who'd gone through that level of trauma could be, and her lack of fear in facing the world after she'd seen the worst it could offer, Lei's life had jumped the rails that night, and she'd never quite reclaimed her path.

She'd made her peace with that.

Mostly.

"Up, Saul." She waited for him to jump into the truck and then shut the door firmly. It was time to go home.

◆ ◆ ◆

Dante Young knew it would be bad the second he saw the officers' grim expressions. To a man, they were trying to tough it out, but they all looked green around the gills. Seattle might not have the highest crime rates in the country, but it saw its fair share of murders. For something to affect the cops this thoroughly, it was going to be a rough one.

Then again, he wouldn't be here otherwise.

He held the police tape out of the way for Clarke Rowan, his partner. She shot him a sharp look, but it was half-hearted at best. In the years they'd worked together, they'd learned to pick their battles. Clarke put up with his "macho blue-blood bullshit," and he didn't take the chip on her shoulder personally.

She ducked under the tape. "Figures that we're not getting two cake cases in a row."

"Not sure the last one qualifies as a cake case."

"It was as open-and-shut as they get. Husband cheats on wife with yoga instructor. Wife kills husband and yoga instructor and, since she happens to be an avid Stephen King fan, tries to put a ritual spin on the murders to point the cops in a different direction. It took us twelve hours to figure out."

"Because you're an avid reader of horror, and those cops weren't."

Clarke's fascination with all things macabre qualified as one of those things he'd never understand, no matter how long they were partners. Working for the FBI—and the Behavioral Analysis Unit, specifically—meant they saw the worst humanity had to offer. After the cases he'd worked, he needed the mental break that comedy or even action provided. Horror didn't fit the bill.

But Clarke never bothered to fit into any expectations.

Dante nodded at the detective standing outside the front door. It was rare that the BAU was called in before the scene had gone cold, but he and Clarke had already been in the area for the aforementioned murders about an hour south of here. "Detective Smith?"

"You BAU?"

"Agents Young and Rowan."

He eyed them, and Dante found himself holding his breath. Seattle was known for being forward thinking, but that didn't mean it extended to Detective Smith. He and Clarke were quite the pair, and he knew it. A big black man and a tiny little redhead with freckles who looked about sixteen didn't exactly scream *Feds* to most local cops. It was why Britton Washburne, their boss, usually kept them to cases in bigger cities unless he felt an exception needed to be made.

Finally, Smith sighed, and his shoulders dropped half an inch. "Might as well take a look." He motioned to a scrawny brunet standing by. "Mitch, get them booties and gloves."

Dante exchanged a look with Clarke. Booties weren't a good sign. The bodies had already been carted off by the coroner, and the preliminary forensics scan was complete. There was less worry about contaminating the scene now, but if they needed to cover their shoes, that meant the scene was just as bad as he'd expected from the cops' faces.

He pulled on the plastic shoe covers and followed Smith into the apartment. They were in the university district, which meant the victims were likely students. "Where did they attend?"

"University of Washington. All three were graduating this year."

"Bummer," Clarke muttered.

Smith shot her a sharp look but didn't comment. The main floor of the apartment didn't appear to have anything out of place but for a single lamp knocked over. Dante moved to the sliding glass door overlooking the street. They were on the second floor, which was high enough to give the occupants comfort, but it wasn't much of a deterrent if someone was determined to gain access. He tried the door. "Unlocked."

"You think he came in there?"

Dante was already moving again, circling through the kitchen. A knife was missing from the block. *Not enough to break in. Have to kill them with a weapon from their own apartment.* Something about that pulled at him, like he'd seen or heard of it before, but he set it aside.

This pass was for first impressions. Later he'd go through second impressions and see what else popped.

"That way." Smith pointed up the stairs.

"Not joining us, Detective?" The edge in Clarke's voice spoke volumes. She'd seen that initial hesitation and resented it. She always did—as much on his behalf as on her own.

"I've seen it. No need to see it again."

Dante braced himself. He already knew the bare minimum—three female victims, all stabbed to death—but there was stabbed and then there was *stabbed*. For the BAU to be the first call the locals made . . .

Walk up the damn stairs and see for yourself.

He followed Clarke to the second floor. For a second, Dante thought the carpet had changed from the nondescript beige to a shocking crimson, then his mind caught up with his eyes, and he realized that it was soaked with blood. It started just before the first door, and even after several hours, spots gleamed wetly in the light.

"Fuck," Clarke breathed. "This is worse than the last one, and that chick was *trying*."

"Yeah." He edged around her and walked carefully down the hall. There were several sets of footprints in the liquid, but there was no telling which belonged to the unsub—the unknown subject—and which to investigators.

The first door was cracked open, and he touched it with a gloved finger to push it the rest of the way open. Where the downstairs looked almost eerily idyllic, all the violence had been saved for this floor of the apartment.

Judging from the shredded state of the mattress and the blood spatter on the wall, the unsub had caught a victim here in her room and then dragged her into the hallway. "Where were the bodies found?" He raised his voice just enough to carry down to Smith.

"Office up there. All three were laid out." Smith sounded vaguely sick to his stomach and pissed off about it.

The other two rooms were variations of the same. Slashed beds. Blood everywhere. A trail leading into the hallway and then farther down to the fourth door. "Lots of work. How'd the others sleep through their roommate being stabbed to death?" Clarke grimaced at the blood on the floor. "This is a shit-ton of trauma. No one sleeps through that, even if you're drunk as fuck during spring break."

"Time of death and a tox screen will tell us a lot." He followed her into the office. It was the biggest of the rooms, and it was more rec room than office. A desk with an iMac was set up in the corner, as well as a printer and some other tech. A second desk held a charging station with two computers; headphones in pink, blue, and red, respectively; and a tablet. The couch was old and threadbare, but clean. Or it had been.

There was enough blood on the floor that he could see the faint impressions where the bodies had lain until the cops were notified by a friend of one of the girls who'd come over for a study session but found that no one answered the door or their phones. The landlord had let her in, and they'd found the carnage. The girl'd had the foresight to call the police and stay out of the scene—a small miracle.

But Clarke was right. There was something off about the timing. Dante turned a slow circle, taking in the room again. "Phones."

"What?"

He strode to the desk with the charging station. Tucked in the drawer were three phones, all crushed.

Clarke leaned around to get a look at them. "Why crush the phones if he sneak-attacked them in their rooms? For that matter, how the hell did you know they were here?"

The memory that had bothered him downstairs solidified. *I know this case. I've seen this before, if only in case files.* "You're, what, twenty-five?"

"You know damn well that I'm twenty-nine, asshole."

He gave her a brief smile despite the scene around them. "Right around the time you were graduating high school, there was a case like this. Bigger. Flashier. A higher body count. The Sorority Row Murders."

"No shit? I vaguely remember that." She frowned at the room. "That guy killed like thirty women. Even as far away as Chicago, that was big news. Weren't there survivors?"

"He killed twenty-one, and yeah, there were two survivors." He'd been going through the academy at the time, and one of his instructors had used the case as a teaching point. Those survivors—their names escaped him—were key witnesses in identifying Travis Berkley as the man who killed their sorority sisters, but local cops still had to build the case against him.

As the only son of billionaire Gerald Berkley—along with being a football star, holding a 4.0 GPA, and volunteering at a homeless shelter in his free time—Travis was borderline untouchable. The girls' accusations initially brought only disbelief.

But as more and more evidence was collected, it became increasingly clear that he was just as much a monster as they'd accused him of being. It had been one of the most sensational cases in the last decade or so, and Dante had found the whole thing fascinating, in a horrifying kind of way. To him, it just went to show that good police work could bring down even the smartest and most privileged of killers.

"Don't tell me he got out on parole?"

Dante shook his head. "He's still locked up, last I heard." He eyed the phones. "He locked the girls in their main room and then took them out one by one. At first, he told them he was letting each girl go, but eventually the carnage was too much to hide, and he stopped pretending he was doing anything other than murdering them."

"Jesus, Mary, and Joseph."

"Yeah." The stuff of nightmares. "But if this guy is following that MO, then that explains why the women didn't hear their friends being murdered—they didn't sleep through it. They were locked in here."

"Which invites the question—who's using Travis Berkley's playbook?"

And where would he strike next?

CHAPTER TWO

The coroner represented Dante's least favorite stop in any murder investigation. There was no escaping the smell he always associated with death—cold and clinical, with the underlying base of shit and blood. No amount of sterilization could cover up the fact that the row of square metal doors on the far side of the room contained any number of bodies.

But only three bodies brought them there today.

Detective Smith had escorted them down to the morgue. He didn't look any happier to be here than Dante was. The older man held himself straight and looked pointedly at the medical examiner instead of the corpses. "What have you got for us?"

The ME had the physique of someone who ran regularly—thin and ropy in his midfifties. His dark hair had a smattering of gray at the temples, but he wasn't slowing down anytime soon, if Dante didn't miss his guess.

The medical examiner raised his thick eyebrows. "Feds? Already?"

"You've seen the bodies. You know why I called them in."

Dante exchanged a look with Clarke. They'd been under the impression that it was the state of the crime scene that prompted BAU's involvement. Obviously Smith had held back something important.

"Point to you." The ME turned to them. "Dr. Jordan Franco. I'd say it's a pleasure to meet you, but no one comes down here for the pleasure of my company."

"Get to it, Franco."

Dr. Franco smirked. "Put on your big-boy pants, Smith. This is going to be a bad one." He moved to uncover one body after the other.

Two Caucasians and one African American. Pretty girls, though that was the only thing they had in common. The first was tiny and dark haired. Her skin would have been pale even before the multitude of stab wounds drained the blood from her body. The black girl was tall and lean with well-defined muscles that spoke of many hours in the gym, and probably some kind of sport. Her neatly cornrowed hair supported that theory. The final girl, a blonde, was curvy with shoulder-length hair. She had bright-red nails, which drew the eye in a room devoid of color.

Each girl's torso was a mess of wounds, ranging from the throat to just above the pubic bone. Dante tried to count, but it was impossible—especially since some of them ran into one another. "How many?"

"Fifty-one, twenty-seven, sixty-two." Dr. Franco pointed to each body in turn.

"That's a lot of frenzy." Clarke moved closer to the brunette. "Did he rape them?"

"It appears he tried but wasn't able to complete the act."

Was the frenzy because he was unable to perform? Or did the frenzy come first? Dante joined his partner at the edge of the metal table. "How close were the deaths, timewise?"

"It's hard to get a good gauge, but they were all killed within a two-hour window from one a.m. to three a.m." Dr. Franco hesitated, looking less than sure of himself for the first time since they'd walked into the room. "This is where it gets weird."

Clarke barked out a laugh. "It wasn't weird before? We practically needed waders to walk through the blood in that apartment."

The ME pulled back the coverings that had hidden the girls' lower bodies. Dante froze. It took him precious seconds to make sense of what he was seeing. "He wrote on them."

"He *carved* words into them." Dr. Franco paled slightly. "These wounds happened before the stabbings."

Dante shifted to read the words better. "'For Trevor,'" he read aloud. The same phrase on all three bodies.

Clarke whistled. "If he's that much of a fan, you'd think he'd get the name right. You said the Sorority Row Killer was *Travis* Berkley?"

"Yeah." The message could be meant for someone else entirely, but that didn't seem to jibe with the details they'd come up with so far. This had all the elements of a tribute, but the obvious target for the obsession was the Sorority Row Killer. To have a different—similar—name on the bodies . . . It didn't make sense.

"Do you see what we're dealing with now?" Smith finally moved forward. "I remember the Berkley case back in the day. I had a friend who worked it, but I'd left California by that point." He shook his head. "I don't want a copycat fucking around in my city. I don't have any use for the Feds normally, but this is bigger than a pissing contest over jurisdiction."

Dante didn't take the detective's dislike of Feds personally. It was a viewpoint that a lot of cops shared. The media liked the FBI. The second they discovered the Feds were on the scene, they focused on the agents rather than the local police. If and when the case was solved, the glory often went to the FBI as a result, despite their best efforts. He focused on Smith. "You think he's linked to Travis Berkley." Dante believed as much, but he wanted to hear the detective's thoughts.

"I looked up the details of that case to refresh my memory the second I realized what these murders reminded me of." Smith squared his shoulders, as if preparing to walk into a fight. "The details match, though we can't be sure if this guy was let in by one of the girls or if he broke in. But the process of hauling them to the office and then taking them out one by one to rape and kill matches. Though Berkley was able to perform the rape itself, and he only stabbed about half of the victims."

Dante remembered. The other half were bludgeoned, strangled, or shot. Berkley had worked his way up to stabbing the last fifteen girls. This unsub had started right in with it.

Fewer girls means less warm-up time. The thwarted rape would enrage him, too. All that planning and careful execution, and he couldn't perform. "Berkley killed those girls in California. What's linking Seattle to LA?"

"That's the question, isn't it?"

Clarke crossed her arms over her chest. "We know where the survivors are? If this guy is a fan, he might take it into his head to finish what Travis Berkley started. Berkley might even be encouraging him to do exactly that."

Which meant they were going to have to talk to Travis Berkley.

It also meant they were going to have to see how easy the survivors were to track down. If this unsub was writing love notes on the bodies of his victims, this wasn't something that was going to stop. Whatever the source of the obsession—whether romantic or adoration or something else altogether—he would only escalate, either to provoke a response from Berkley or to prove his devotion. Neither option was good for his future victims.

◆ ◆ ◆

Lei took Saul for a quick walk around the property before she went into the house. Theoretically, it was to give him some exercise after the long car ride before they settled in for the night. In her heart of hearts, though, she could admit that what she really wanted to do was make sure everything was as it should be.

All the cameras were working, and nothing had been disturbed, but that didn't stop the hair from rising at the nape of her neck. She stopped in the middle of the lawn and turned to face the trees that edged the area. If there was someone out there, the cameras would have caught them, and Emma would have called the cops. Saul would already be on high alert, rather than sitting next to the front door and patiently waiting for her to let him inside.

Yet the heebie-jeebie feeling raised goose bumps along her exposed skin.

Lei gave herself a shake and took the porch stairs two a time. She unlocked the front door and held it open for Saul. "Rest, Saul."

He nosed her hand and then trotted down the hall to the kitchen where they kept the dogs' food. Lei shut the door and locked both dead bolts behind her before she called out, "I'm home." Even as she said the magical words, the tense thing inside her slowly uncoiled. *Another one down.* She wasn't sure she believed in karmic balance, but after everything, the only thing Lei wanted was to put out some good in the world.

"In the kitchen," came the reply.

She followed Emma's voice and found her friend pulling a rack of cookies out of the oven. Chocolate chip, from the smell. Her friend looked much the same way she had on that first day of rush for Omega Delta Lambda—beautiful and blonde and curvy. Back then, they'd both smiled a lot more and laughed about nothing and had secretly believed they were immortal. Their friendship might have survived that horrible night—but not much else of their respective personalities had.

Lei leaned against the doorframe. "What's wrong?"

"Why would anything be wrong?" Emma set the cookie sheet on the stove and then popped a second one in the oven and started the timer. All while not looking over.

"Because you're baking cookies while on a no-carb diet." She kept her voice low and even. Once upon a time, Emma had been a social-justice warrior who was all too willing to step to the line in any argument, while Lei shied away from that kind of confrontation because it reminded her of her parents' constant arguing. These days, they'd flipped. Lei jumped headfirst into every confrontation in an effort to conquer the fear she never quite escaped, and Emma curled up like a wounded animal at the first sign of raised voices.

"No-carb diets are torture. I'm done with it."

Good. In Lei's opinion, Emma's insistence on ping-ponging from diet to diet, each more extreme than the next, was survivor guilt in the form of self-punishment. But what did she know? She wasn't a shrink, and Lei had fired every one she'd had.

None of that changed the fact that something was most definitely wrong. "While we're in agreement about the diet, you haven't looked at me once since I got home. What's wrong?" She thought hard. It was the wrong time of year for the holiday-card Christmas spiral—nothing like seeing her family move on with life without missing a beat to really kick Emma in the teeth—but there might have been a birthday Lei forgot about. Emma's mother might have been happy her messy daughter moved away, but she still twisted the knife every chance she got.

Bitch.

Lei didn't let any of it show on her face. She just waited her friend out.

Emma sighed, her bottom lip quivering. Her long blonde hair was pulled back into a messy bun, and she wore yoga pants and a flowing shirt with thick wool socks to combat the relative chill of the house. She was always cold, no matter that the temperature of this old house never dropped below seventy-one.

Thankfully, her friend didn't make her wait long. "We got a package this afternoon. No return address."

Not from her family, then—*they never send anything other than a card.* Lei pushed off the doorframe. "Where?"

"Front table."

She must be more tired than she realized if she'd walked right past it without seeing it. Lei turned on her heel and marched back down the hall. Saul's nails clicked on the hardwood as he followed. He always knew when something was wrong—or about to go wrong.

Lei picked up the box. It was a standard priority flat-rate box. The only real thing of note was the lack of return address on the label—and that it'd been addressed to both her and Emma. *Goddamn fan mail.*

More than a decade later, one would think the true-crime groupies would have found someone more interesting to send shit to. Lei and Emma weren't exactly hiding, but they also didn't advertise their presence. Most of the people who lived in Stillwater knew who they were, but they didn't bring *the incident* up.

Or at least most of them didn't.

Lei pulled her knife from her boot and cut open the thick packaging tape. The box was light enough that she had half a second wondering if it was empty.

But when she dumped its contents onto the small square table next to the door, two things fell out. One was a postcard for the University of Washington, showcasing a bookstore with a jaunty font proclaiming it was located in Seattle. She flipped it over, finding a carefully printed note in block lettering. SEE YOU SOON.

"What the fuck?" The second item was a square cardboard box that looked like something that would house cheap jewelry. She opened it, and all the breath rushed out of her lungs. "Shit."

"What is it?" Emma's voice seemed to come from the other side of a long tunnel. Saul barked once, a warning that something was wrong, and her voice went panicky. "Lei, talk to me."

She turned to face Emma, her hand spasming from how tightly she held the box. "It's hair." Three little bundles of hair that looked like they'd been clipped off the end of a ponytail, each tied neatly with a red ribbon. Blonde, brunette, black hair.

Just like the little clippings that had been found in Travis's apartment when he was finally arrested.

Saul barked again, quickly echoed by Prince. "It's okay." She spoke through numb lips, but the alternative was not speaking at all and having Emma lose her shit. Lei forced herself to move. She set the box back on the table and carefully replaced the lid. Her knees gave out and she sank to the floor. Saul was instantly there, nudging closer until she wrapped her arms around him and buried her face in his shoulder.

Emma walked around her, and she listened to her friend look in the box, gasp, and set it back down. "It's him."

"It's not him." She spoke without looking up. "He's still in prison." She knew because Emma called once a month to check, a compulsion she couldn't seem to stop. Lei let herself hold Saul for three more seconds, and then she lifted her head. "His last appeal was denied."

It wouldn't stop Travis from appealing again. His family had the money and the influence to keep hiring lawyers to try to change the guilty verdict, which meant that once every few years, she and Emma would be dragged before a new judge in a dog and pony show. So far, every appeal had been denied, but in the darkest part of her soul, she didn't think they'd win forever.

And when Travis walked free again, he'd be coming for her and Emma. She knew it, and Emma knew it.

They'd done everything in their power to ensure they were ready when that time finally came. Their house had top-of-the-line security and two safe rooms, one on each level. They had cameras set up across their property so no one could approach without being seen. And they'd both taken a multitude of self-defense courses and were damn good with the handguns they had stashed around the house. Short of purchasing a tank, they were as prepared as they could be.

"I need my phone." She climbed to her feet while Emma retrieved it. It took a few seconds to find his number, but she didn't hesitate to call. This wasn't the time to talk herself out of how serious this was. If they were getting some kind of message, Britton Washburne needed to know about it.

He answered his phone, just like he had every time she'd called over the years. "Lei, how are you?"

For the first time in ten years, she didn't have her normal answer. "I think we got a calling card or a threat or something."

"Slow down." His voice was deep and low and designed to calm. "Start from the beginning and tell me everything."

Lei took a breath and then another. She gave in to the need to sit on the floor and lean against Saul. There was a time for strength, and now wasn't it. No one could see her except Emma, and she and Emma had already seen each other at their worst.

This wasn't even close.

"I got back from a job tonight. Checked the inner perimeter. Sometime this evening, a package was delivered—flat-rate box, no return address. It's got a postcard from UDub Seattle with a note written on the back that says 'See you soon' in block lettering. And a box with three things of hair, all tied with red ribbon."

"Blonde, brunette, and black hair?"

Her heartbeat kicked up a notch. "Yes." She didn't ask how he knew, and he didn't make her wait to answer the unspoken question.

"There's been an incident in Seattle. I have two of my people on the ground there currently."

It couldn't be Travis. As she'd just told Emma, he was in prison and would remain there. Even as rich as his family was, his reach only went so far.

Which left two options. "Copycat or fan?" A copycat would retrace his steps. A fan, on the other hand, would be trying to get Travis's attention directly with the murders. Two sides to the same coin, perhaps, but the distinction was important.

Britton hesitated. "We think the latter, though it may be too soon to tell."

Lei dropped her forehead to rest against Saul. "He killed three girls." That was what the hair meant—three lives taken. And the sick bastard had sent them to this house. To Lei and Emma. She lifted her head. "One minute."

She pressed the phone to her shoulder and met Emma's blue gaze. "Check the security cameras while I get my gun. We're sweeping the house."

Emma flinched, but nodded. "Prince, come." The Golden Retriever followed at her heels as she hurried to the office they had set up on the main floor.

Lei put the phone back to her ear as she followed her friend. "We need to clear the house. If he sent a package here, he knows where we live." If he was a fan, like Britton suspected, then at some point he'd take a shot at them. The surviving girls. The ones who got away.

To his credit, Britton didn't tell her that she was being paranoid. He knew better. "Call me as soon as you're finished. I'll send the local PD to you in the meantime."

Lei didn't know what Isaac was going to do, but he was the local sheriff, so calling him in was the right step to take. "Okay. I'll call soon." She hoped.

She hung up as she reached her room. She'd left her gun there for the search, just like she always did. Technically, she was licensed to carry, but Lei didn't make a habit of bringing her gun on searches. It made the cops edgy, and edgy cops tended to be assholes and make her job harder. She paused to check to make sure it was loaded and the safety was on.

No more weakness. Emma could defend herself in a pinch, but this was Lei's home, and whoever this bastard was had infiltrated it—even if the package was only the first step.

Back downstairs, Emma met her at the office door. "Security cams are clear. The motion-sensor cameras have been going nuts all day, which makes it impossible to track them one hundred percent, but it's that time of year with all the animal traffic through our property. Nothing popped except your circuit around the lawn when you got home, and the mail guy. And before you ask, the mail guy was our regular one. I didn't answer the door, but I still checked."

Just because he was the regular guy and had lived in Stillwater his entire life—they'd checked that, too, when they moved in—didn't mean the mail guy wasn't a psycho. Better to be safe than sorry, which was why Emma didn't open the door for anyone. Ever.

Stop it. You're being paranoid.

Damn right I am.

"Okay, so he's probably not in the house." She double-checked the gun to ensure that the clip was in and there was a bullet in the chamber. "Stay in here and keep watch on the monitors."

"I will." Emma touched Prince's head. "Prince, protect." The dog moved with her into the room and set himself up watching the door while Emma took her chair in front of the half a dozen monitors set up on the wall above the desk.

Lei shut the door behind her and then looked down the hall. Saul remained at her side, alert and ready to do whatever she asked of him. They'd done this drill more times than she could count. She was an imperfect searcher, but nothing would get past Saul's nose. Not the dead, and certainly not the living. If there was someone here, her dog would find him.

"Saul, search."

CHAPTER THREE

"I need you to go to Stillwater."

Dante blinked sleep from his eyes and checked the clock. Five in the morning. He fumbled the phone as he sat up and had to make a fast grab before it hit the floor. "Now?"

"Yes. Immediately."

What the fuck? Anything that put *that* tone of worry in Britton Washburne's voice was enough to have him dropping everything. "What's going on?" Dante grabbed his clothes and pulled them on without missing a beat. He'd barely had a chance to unpack, so it was just a matter of throwing a toothbrush and razor in the beat-up old bag.

"You linked the Seattle murders to Travis Berkley."

"I haven't had a chance to report that to you yet."

"I know the bare details, courtesy of Detective Smith's request for assistance."

"Then how did you make that jump? I had to see the scene before I put two and two together." And he hadn't had a chance to report his findings yet. Dante double-checked to make sure he hadn't forgotten anything and walked out the door and down to the room where Clarke was. He knocked on her door.

"Stillwater is approximately three hours from you. Lei Zhang and Emma Nilsson are there. I'll text you the address."

"The same Lei and Emma who were the only surviving women of the Sorority Row Murders?" He didn't ask how Britton knew their address. Britton seemed to know a whole lot of shit that he shouldn't. It had awed Dante when he was a rookie. These days, he just took it for what it was—an edge.

"Yes. They received a gift last night, likely from your unsub. I need you to talk to them, get a feel for how much immediate danger they're in, and then proceed accordingly."

Clarke opened the door and turned back into her room without saying anything. Dante walked inside and faced the window while she put on pants. "We're not babysitters, Britton. This guy is going to move again. We don't know a damn thing about what his cooling-off period might look like, because even if he's mimicking Berkley, that was a one-off, so to speak."

"Correct. But you're going to have to leave anyway to talk to Travis Berkley. You want to see the girls before you do." This wasn't a suggestion—it was an order.

He considered that. Britton had a point. If this unsub was a devoted fan, he was obsessed with Travis Berkley's previous murder spree. Those girls knew Berkley better than anyone, and not just because one of them had dated him prior to the murders.

That didn't mean he wanted to drive three hours to talk to women who no doubt wanted to do anything but have a walk down memory lane, where Berkley had stalked the Omega Delta Lambda halls. "We're leaving in thirty."

"Good. Fill me in afterward."

"Will do." Dante hung up and cursed. "We don't have time for this."

"For what?" Clarke took in his suitcase at a glance and quickly packed her own. "We're leaving already?"

"Apparently the two sorority girls who survived Travis Berkley live three hours from here." Hard to think of that as a coincidence. He used his phone to do a quick search on Stillwater, Washington. Ten thousand people, if that. Just big enough to have a couple of little stores and a single stoplight.

Exactly the town where a person would settle if they wanted to fly under the radar.

A place equally difficult to produce a sorority, since it didn't even have a high school, let alone a college.

Clarke took the phone out of his hands and eyed it. "Seattle is about as close as you can get and still follow Berkley's MO."

"That's what I was thinking." Dante shook his head, trying to chase away the last bit of sleep clinging. "Fuck. Britton is right. We need to talk to them before we do anything else." The victims here mattered, but if this was all some kind of love note to Berkley, then the case would hinge on Lei Zhang and Emma Nilsson.

They were at the center of this, whether they wanted to be or not.

"Be pretty shitty to think you got out and survived and then have some fanboy hunting you down to finish the job."

"I don't think 'shitty' begins to cover it." He led the way down to their rental and held the door for Clarke. She rolled her eyes, but after seven years as partners, she didn't waste the breath to bicker about it. Dante got in the driver's seat, plugged the address Britton had texted him into the GPS, and started the long process of escaping Seattle's city limits.

Clarke typed away on her phone, her brows drawn. He let her have the uninterrupted silence to do whatever research she'd set her sights on. It was too fucking early to hold down much in the way of conversation anyway. Thirty minutes and a large coffee later, Clarke set her phone down and twisted in her seat to face him.

Dante glanced at her. "What did you find?"

"Lei Zhang and Emma Nilsson both graduated UCLA after a year's sabbatical—during which there isn't much information at all, so I'd guess it included a whole lot of therapy and antidepressants—and went on to form their own business. They train cadaver dogs and contract out to find bodies—both for government agencies and private parties."

"No shit?" If someone had asked him to make a list of what he thought their jobs would be, cadaver dogs wouldn't have been on it.

"Well, Lei contracts out. Emma is a tech geek who invented some kind of program where you can plug in the evidence about a potential burial site and it spits out a grid of the most likely locations. She patented it a few years ago but hasn't offered it for sale despite rumors of the government offering a significant amount of money for the program." Clarke propped her feet on the dashboard. "Lei handles the dog and the actual feet-on-ground part of the search. She's got an eighty percent success rate, which is pretty damn impressive. Not too shabby for sorority girls, huh?"

"You do realize that sororities are more than what you see in the movies, right?"

"How would I know that?" Clarke propped her hands behind her head. "I'm not the one with a rich daddy and society-darling mommy."

FBI agents came from a variety of backgrounds, but his and Clarke's were a study in opposites. She'd come up in foster care and managed to beat the odds stacked against her as a result. Dante had gone the other way. His parents were good people, and all they'd wanted was for him to follow in their footsteps. College, either med or law school, and a career helping people—and making bank while doing it.

He preferred to help people without a price tag attached.

"And miss out on giving you shit for being born with a silver spoon in that pretty mouth of yours? Never." She closed her eyes, basking in the pale morning sun like a cat. "I'll admit that sororities aren't all fluff. Those girls wouldn't have survived the night, let alone be showing signs of flourishing, if they didn't have a core of steel."

"Indeed." He didn't bring up the fact that pledging Omega Delta Lambda hadn't helped their sorority sisters. Twenty-one killed, and they didn't go easily. They'd all suffered horribly. He'd done some reading last night to refresh his memory of the case, and it was worse than he'd remembered. Berkley made their current unsub look like an amateur. That alone seemed to indicate Berkley had killed before the night of the murders, though no evidence had been found to support that theory.

Their current unsub didn't have quite the same finesse, so there was hope he'd left behind trace evidence that would lead them straight to him.

He refocused on the road. "The women can't bring in much money with the searches."

"They don't." Clarke didn't open her eyes. "They won a civil suit against Travis Berkley about a year after he was convicted of the murders."

Now she had his attention. "And they escaped in the first place—bet that really stung him." From all accounts, Travis Berkley was a textbook sociopath, and his parents and his money had only encouraged that. His mother and father's parenting style could be summed up with benign neglect—his father had worked eighty-plus hours a week during the majority of his childhood, and his mother had done the equivalent via a full social schedule as well—and they'd thrown money and toys at him to compensate for the lack of time and attention they dealt out. Travis was brilliant enough to keep himself occupied, and to cover up his less conventional entertainments. The end result was a man who ruled his own little part of the world and felt perfectly entitled to do so. "It must have burned every single day in court to see them there, defying him and his so-called perfect plan to walk away from this crime with none the wiser."

"Yep. Though you'd think he wouldn't wait ten freaking years to get his revenge."

Dante had thoughts about that. He also had thoughts about the fact that Britton had been called in to consult on the case when the girls pointed the finger at Berkley. The cops had wanted every t crossed and i dotted, so Britton had drawn up a blind profile—without knowing there was a suspect, let alone their identity.

He'd described Berkley right down to the Jaguar he drove.

The fact that Britton was apparently still in contact with the survivors was something Dante would have to bring up when he had a free moment. The head of BAU had invaluable information, and he needed access to it.

But he wanted to go into meeting the women without anything coloring the first impression.

The drive went quickly. It helped that western Washington was gorgeous, especially this time of year. The mountain pass and thick forests gave him plenty to look at while Clarke dozed in the passenger seat.

The sun had risen well into the sky by the time he followed the GPS's instructions to a gravel drive that wound off the main road. "Clarke."

She opened her eyes, instantly awake. "This looks like the intro to a horror movie. We'll drive down there, the car won't start when we try to leave, and then the nice sorority girls will kill us and cook us in soup."

"Woman, you have *got* to stop reading all those horror novels." Dante leaned forward and examined the surrounding trees as they crawled forward. "You see that?"

"Cameras."

About a half a mile in, the trees fell back to reveal a charming two-story house with a big lawn and decent-size kennel behind it. Dante stopped for a few seconds, taking in the whole picture. Cameras dotted the front porch, decorative bars covered all the windows, and the front door looked sturdy enough to survive a siege. The house was a couple of decades old, but someone had put a lot of money and effort into turning it into a fortress. "Interesting."

"Those cameras are different. The ones on the trees are motion activated, if I don't miss my guess. These are on constantly."

It made sense from a tactical point of view. The other cameras were an early-warning system. These were a last line of defense.

Since there was no way the women didn't know they were here by now, he pulled onto the paved driveway and parked. "Be nice, Clarke."

"I'm always nice." She caught his glance and sighed like a kid who'd been lectured by a parent. "Fine. But I get to be bad cop when we get the first suspect."

"You're always bad cop."

"Good to know you're seeing things my way." She hopped out of the car and headed for the front door.

Dante allowed himself to curse for a full five seconds. He adored her, but these women would require careful handling, and Clarke was about as subtle as a two-by-four to the side of the head. It meant she and Dante worked well together and could adapt to any situation, but sometimes it took everything he had to reel her back in. He did *not* need today to be one of those days.

He took a calming breath and followed Clarke to the front door.

"Incoming," Emma called from the office. "Front door."

She didn't sound worried, so they must be the Feds Britton had promised to send. Lei touched Saul's head. "Saul, stay." He sat a few feet back while she answered the knock that came a few seconds later.

Lei hadn't slept much, which was her only explanation for staring like an idiot when she opened the door. The two people on the porch screamed *federal agent* so strongly that she would have had them pegged even without Britton's warning, but that wasn't what had her fighting to drag her jaw off the floor.

The woman had to be in her late twenties, though she looked younger because of her wide blue eyes and the smattering of freckles across her nose and cheeks. Or maybe it was the mass of curly red hair barely contained in a messy bun at the nape of her neck. Either way, she might be nontraditional, but she didn't hold Lei's attention.

No, that was all reserved for the man. He wasn't particularly tall—probably topping out around six feet—but his shoulders were wide enough to fill the doorway. His warm dark skin contrasted against his white button-up shirt, and his dark eyes took her in the same way she was taking him in.

Or not the same, since I'm ogling him like an idiot.

Lei didn't move, and the redhead seemed to realize they were all staring at one another. She snorted. "You must be Lei Zhang. I thought you'd be taller."

"They all say that."

"Agent Clarke Rowan." She jerked a thumb at herself and then her partner. "Agent Dante Young. Britton said you'd be expecting us."

They had all the right information, but that didn't mean she was just going to let them into her house. Lei eyed them. "Badges, please."

"Oh, for God's sake."

"Clarke, if you were in her position, you'd do the same damn thing." Agent Young passed over his badge.

"If I was in her position, I would have moved to fucking Antarctica." She handed over her badge as well.

"Antarctica is rather cold this time of year." *And I'd never be able to look at myself in the mirror if I spent the rest of my life hiding on another continent.* Some—namely, her parents—might call what she did now hiding, but Lei knew better.

She took a picture of both their badges and information and handed them back. She didn't get any weird vibes off them, and if they weren't who they said they were, she'd find out soon enough. She texted the pictures to Emma with a request to follow up to make sure they were legit. "You can come in."

"Thanks."

She led the way into the sitting room off the foyer. It wasn't a room she and Emma ever used, mostly because they avoided company whenever possible, but it was useful to have when guests were unavoidable.

Like now.

Saul waited for her to sit in the single chair by the window and then took up a spot at her feet, eyeing the newcomers with polite curiosity. It could turn on a dime if she needed it to, but Saul wasn't a guard dog. He was a cadaver dog who could also do search and rescue in a pinch. It wasn't in his nature to attack, but he was still protective of her. "I'm assuming you did your homework."

Detective Young nodded. "I'd like to see the box, if it wouldn't be too much trouble."

She raised her eyebrows at the politeness of the question, especially considering the circumstances. "The local sheriff requested I keep it until you two showed up." She took it out of the cabinet she'd stowed it in after Isaac had left last night, and passed it over.

Dante examined it and then handed it to his partner. "I know you've gone over this already, but please walk me through what happened."

He had a nice voice—nicer even than Britton's. It kind of reminded her of the tide, slow and steady and totally able to pull you under if you were unwary. *Stop that.*

Lei went over it all. Again. Her job yesterday. Coming home to the package having been delivered by mail. What she found when she opened it. "It's not particularly helpful, I know."

"No way to know."

Agent Rowan rolled her eyes. "Bullshit. You know damn well that the unsub covered his tracks. If the package had a postmark from Seattle, he must have sent it the second he had a chance for it to show up the same day."

"Clarke."

She blatantly ignored the warning in his tone. "I'm stating a fact. And the *fact* is that Lei has gone through enough crap that she won't appreciate me sugarcoating facts. Right?"

Lei smiled despite the situation. She'd met more than her fair share of Feds over the years, but Clarke was definitely unique. Normally they were better at dissembling, but the redhead didn't seem interested in trying. After all the careful handling she endured at the hands of most people she met, it was a breath of fresh air. "You wouldn't be wrong."

"See."

Dante turned those captivating dark eyes on her. "Where's Emma?"

"Emma is right here." She made her entrance like she'd been waiting for her cue—which she probably had.

Lei bit back a sigh. Her friend exerted control over her surroundings in any way she could, usually by eavesdropping. It went hand in hand with Emma's hacking—what was hacking but a different kind of eavesdropping? But the way the Feds' eyes narrowed showcased their dislike for that little stunt.

Emma crossed to perch on the arm of Lei's chair, Prince on her heels. He took up a spot opposite Saul, and Lei watched the agents note the proximity of both dogs and the women. Emma crossed her arms over her chest—or under, since she had the body of an old-school pinup girl. "You've heard the story. What are you going to do about it?"

Lei nudged her. "Shut up. They're here to tell us about the murders."

Agent Young raised his eyebrows. "What makes you think there were murders?"

"Don't play with me. One—Britton already told me there were murders, because apparently unlike you, he isn't concerned with hiding information to prove that he has the biggest cock in the room. Two—hair is a traditional trophy of quite a large number of serial killers and serial rapists, and it was delivered to *our* house. And, finally, three—BAU wouldn't be here for something as mundane as stalking.

Stop playing coy and give us the information we need in order to keep ourselves safe."

Agent Rowan blinked and then grinned. "I changed my mind—she's exactly the right height."

Agent Young shot her an exasperated look. "Knock that off." He turned to face Lei and Emma. "There were three women murdered last night—and their coloring matches the hair delivered to your home, though we'll have to test to ensure that it's a true match."

That was bad—and it had to be bad for it to be connected to them—but he was holding something back. Lei leaned forward and pinned him with her best take-no-shit look. "The other shoe—drop it now, please."

Agent Young spoke softly, almost cautiously. "All three women were members of the University of Washington chapter of Omega Delta Lambda—your sorority. Whoever this unsub is, he's following in the footsteps of Travis Berkley."

CHAPTER FOUR

Lei couldn't breathe. Her chest closed painfully as if she'd been knocked flat on her back, and her lungs burned with the need for oxygen. Somewhere in the tiny rational corner of her mind, she knew there was nothing *really* wrong with her, but rational thought had no place in the midst of her panic.

He's back. Emma was right all along, and he's coming for us.

Stop.

You're spiraling.

Travis Berkley is still in jail. This is a copycat, and no matter how bad a copycat is, he can't be worse than Travis. You survived before. You will this time, too.

A whine cut through her thoughts, and then Saul was there, nudging her hand with his cool nose. She inhaled sharply, suddenly aware that everyone in the room was staring at her. The Feds had the blank-slate expression she'd come to associate with cops when they were in a difficult situation. Emma looked at her as if she was on the verge of her own panic attack.

Lei stroked her hand over Saul's head, forming a wall of indisputable facts in her mind to keep the fear at bay. She wasn't twenty-one anymore, only a couple of years out of the stifling family home she'd grown up on, still drunk on freedom and the realization that she could do anything she wanted to with her future.

She'd been an idiot. A child who was playing dress-up without realizing the pitfalls of adulthood.

Though most pitfalls don't come attached to a knife.

Lei wasn't that girl anymore. She'd seen the worst Travis Berkley could offer and had the scars to show for it. She could shoot. She could fight. She'd worked with enough cops over the course of her career as a trainer and as part of a search team that she had an inside view as to how their minds worked.

She would *not* lose herself to terror.

Another stroke to Saul's head and she was able to speak. "How close to the original murders are the details?"

Agent Young exchanged a glance with his partner and leaned forward, bracing his elbows on his knees. His big hands dangled between his legs, and she distantly noted that he had really firm thighs beneath the expensive slacks. He spoke slowly, as if gauging her response. "We haven't had a chance to check the original case files, but the big details are almost identical. The murders were performed in the same way—girls kept in a main room and taken out individually. We think he entered through the sliding glass door, because their condo was on the second floor and he used a knife from the kitchen."

She could almost hear Travis's voice in her head, even after all these years. *Let me in, Lei-Lei. I have a surprise for you.* Stupid. She'd been so incredibly stupid, swayed by a pretty face and a boy her parents would approve of who made her *feel.* Smart, athletic, the right dollar amount in his family's bank account. Someone bright and colorful and checking all the right boxes.

Since she couldn't bring herself to ask if one of the girls had let him in, she focused on the rest. "If this is a fan, he must have been in contact with Travis at some point." She put her hand on Emma's leg when her friend flinched at his name. The Feds didn't react, which made her sigh. "But you already knew that. You don't need me telling you how to do your job. What *is* it you need?"

Another loaded look between them. They'd obviously been partners for a long time, because they managed to convey an entire conversation's worth of talking in a single look.

Again, it was Agent Young who took the lead. "We can find the details of the case easily enough, along with your accounts, but what I'd like to know is your take on Travis."

"Because I dated him." She stated it baldly, as if the fact she'd slept with a murderer was something she'd dealt with and moved on from. As if the fact didn't still keep her up at night, moving beneath her skin until she wanted to take a wire brush to her body. There weren't enough hot showers and bleach baths in the world to change the fact that she'd willingly been with him. She could never take that back.

"Because you—both of you—have known him longer than anyone."

"Agent Young—"

"Dante."

She stopped short. *Dante.* It fit him somehow—strong and a little bit intense. He masked it well, but there was fire lurking in the depths of his dark eyes, in the way he clenched his fists as they spoke about Travis. She shouldn't be forming personal opinions about any man, let alone one connected with the case. Lei's track record had more than proven *that* fact.

While she was still trying to process her strange and seriously inconvenient reaction to him, Emma had found her voice. She spoke softly, her southern accent giving her breathy tone a pretty lilt. She had a Dolly Parton thing going for her—at least before Dolly got a little crazy for plastic surgery—and Emma wasn't above playing up the sweet-southern-belle thing when it suited her. "Travis Berkley is a sociopath with a healthy dose of narcissistic personality disorder—which you already know because you read the file. *Everything* is in the file. We have been doing our best to get past what he did to us—to our sisters—and that means forgetting as much as possible."

Maybe for Emma. Lei couldn't afford to forget. It had been her mistake that tipped the first domino that destroyed so many lives. While it was possible Travis could have gotten into the house on his own, she'd been the fool who let him in her window.

The knowledge made her hands shake. Emma might want to do everything to avoid that gory walk down memory lane, but Lei didn't have that option. Guilt wrapped around her throat, tightening, ever tightening. "You have something specific you're here for."

Agent Rowan leaned forward, a clear indication that she'd take it from there. As much as Lei wanted the calming force Dante—Agent Young—seemed to emanate, she turned almost gratefully to the redhead. She eyed her as if Lei was a particularly interesting bug. "We're theorizing this fucker—"

"Clarke."

She didn't look at him. "These women have seen enough, Dante. You know as well as I do that a few choice curse words aren't going to have them scrambling for their sniffing salts."

Lei understood now why Britton had paired these two together. Clarke was the blunt force designed to set a person back on their heels so they were too busy reacting to her foul mouth to stop and think that there might be a shrewd mind behind those deceptively big blue eyes. Dante, on the other hand, was a cool summer mist, unruffling feathers and putting everyone in the room at ease with his calm presence. Both agents would be underestimated in different ways, which was only to their benefit.

Clever.

She eyed the dogs on the floor. Neither of them seemed overly concerned with the Feds in the room. *Good.* Lei had more than proved that she could be fooled, but Saul couldn't. Every time he reacted poorly to a person, she paid attention—and most of the time something eventually came to light to prove her dog's instincts correct.

Clarke followed her gaze and then refocused on Lei and then Emma. "A lot of sociopaths think they're smarter than everyone else in the room—some of them are even right—and Travis sure as hell falls into the latter category. His IQ is 167, and from all accounts, prison hasn't broken him. What we need to know is if he'd encourage a fan to take these steps."

"Of course he would. He's a fucking psycho," Emma snarled.

"What do you think?" Clarke was looking at Lei.

Because, why not? Even now, cops thought Lei had some kind of inside track to the way Travis's mind worked. She'd dated him for months, had slept with him countless times, and so she must have some insider knowledge to explain how the golden boy went so very, very wrong.

She hadn't been able to give them a satisfactory answer then. She didn't have one now, either, but she could try. "Travis liked to be the smartest person in the room, mostly because he liked the attention. I could see him being amused by this fan, but if it gets to the point where he feels like he's been upstaged, that could change on a dime."

Dante nodded as if she'd confirmed something he expected. "I know this is painful, but we need you to walk us through what you remember of that night."

"Why?" Emma slid down onto the chair next to Lei, wedging herself in until they were pressed tightly together from knee to shoulder. This close, the tiny shakes she'd been hiding until now came out, and Prince shifted closer to lay himself over Emma's feet. But she wasn't done. "You have the case files. You have the new murders. Why do you need us?"

Lei clasped her friend's hand. She didn't want to do this. She didn't want *any* of this. They'd come here to be left alone, to do some good in the world to balance out Lei's karmic debt and to help with Emma's crippling anxiety. Nothing in the plan involved being forced to confront those horrific twenty-four hours that had changed everything. She squeezed Emma's hand. "Because we're the only ones who survived."

◆ ◆ ◆

Watching the women interact was fascinating on a level Dante wasn't prepared for. He'd known Lei and Emma lived together, but he hadn't had the opportunity to take a step back and consider the implications of that arrangement. Emma teetered on the edge of a breakdown and used Lei to pull herself back from the ledge . . . everything made a lot more sense.

They'd formed a symbiotic relationship, of sorts.

There wasn't much data concerning situations like this one, mostly because they rarely arose, and each case was too individual to tie together with nice, easy studies. It stood to reason, though, that coming out of that sorority house as the only two survivors would send these women into one of two futures. In one, they never saw each other and pretended the other didn't exist rather than be faced with the perpetual reminder of what they'd gone through.

In the other, they realized that no one would ever know what they'd gone through as intimately as the other person who'd survived—so they leaned on each other as a result.

Lei was the one who finally met his gaze, and hell if her inky-dark eyes didn't take his breath away despite the circumstances. Clarke had pulled both women's photos on the way over there, but they were old—from their sorority days. Both beautiful in their own way, though they were a study in opposites. Emma had the sweet southern thing going for her, all blonde hair, big innocent blue eyes, and curves that suggested southern cooking. He couldn't tell if her soft tone was practiced or natural, but it pricked at him every time she spoke.

Lei . . . She was something else altogether. She was petite in a way that should have read *frail* but reminded him of a blade waiting to be unsheathed. There were muscles beneath her light-brown skin, and he guessed that she'd have no problem keeping up with the monster dog at her feet during a search. Her straight black hair was pulled back into a no-nonsense ponytail, which left her features in stark relief. *Beautiful, but doesn't like to draw attention to it.* Might as well have tried to hide the sky.

Fuck, get it together. You're here to interview them, not to lose your damn mind over Lei Zhang.

Yes, she was beautiful, but he'd dealt with beautiful women before without jeopardizing his professional persona. Dante didn't know what it was about this woman that called to something in him, but he had to shelve it.

He couldn't afford to be distracted.

Lei clasped Emma's hand but turned her body to face him more fully. "The night of the murders, I let Travis Berkley into the Omega Delta Lambda house. We'd been dating four months, and he told me he had a surprise." Her lips twisted. "It was against the rules, but girls broke the rules all the time."

Dante noted her knuckles whitening where she held Emma's hand, but her voice maintained its steady tone. "We had sex. Approximately an hour later, something changed. I still have problems putting it into words. Travis just . . . shifted. It was like he'd taken off a mask and I didn't recognize the man beneath. He hit me. A few times." She absentmindedly touched the little hooked scar on her cheekbone. *From Travis's ring.* "I passed out. When I woke up, he'd barricaded my door shut and I could hear their screams."

Lei's breath hitched, and it was almost as if she inhaled and Emma exhaled. The blonde lifted her chin. "I was in the basement studying when it started. Finals were coming up, and I was struggling in history and needed the extra study time. The first sign of something wrong was Travis hauling Sarah—" She cut herself off and flinched. "I'm sorry. It's hard to say their names, even now."

Clarke huffed out a breath. "You don't have to name every single girl he killed. We know their names. We know their stories. We just want to hear how it all went down from your perspective."

They wouldn't find anything new here. Dante knew it, and he suspected Clarke knew it, too. These two women had told their stories countless times over the years, and if there was information they hadn't shared before now, he highly doubted this would be the time it'd magically come out.

Hearing the story through their own voices was a whole hell of a lot more jarring than reading it in the file, however.

Emma took them through it. How Travis Berkley brought the entire house of girls into that basement, how he was charming and terrifying and told them that he'd let them go one by one . . . if they did exactly as he asked. It wasn't until the night was over and no one had come to save them that the remaining girls realized what was happening, and even then, they were too afraid to try to overpower him.

Herd mentality. Travis had to have known he could manipulate the whole group as long as he got them scared and in a single place. They believed the pretty lie because the truth was impossible to wrap their minds around.

Emma's voice shook. "There were still . . . ten of us left when I realized I wasn't getting out of that house alive—that none of the girls had gotten out alive like he'd promised. When he took the next girl, I hid under the couch."

"None of those girls saw you hide?" Clarke frowned. "I find that hard to believe."

"I don't know. I don't . . ." She dropped her gaze as if she couldn't bear to hold up her head any longer. "We were in shock at that point—just sitting there, lost in ourselves. We didn't talk. We didn't even look at each other. We just sat there and . . . contemplated the fact we were going to die. I don't know if they even noticed I was gone. I hid until every single one of them was gone. And he just . . . walked out."

"He came for me. I guess it was then." Lei didn't shrink in on herself. She seemed to grow taller, sit straighter. "I heard him removing the barricade, and I panicked. After listening to that all night . . ." She shook her head. "I knew what would happen if he got back into my room, so I climbed out the window."

Clarke went still. "I saw the list of your injuries. You had a broken arm, your knee was so fucking swollen you shouldn't have been able to walk, and you had several head wounds and a handful of broken ribs on top of that. How the hell did you climb out a window?"

Lei shrugged one shoulder. "He would kill me if I didn't. I figured falling to my death was preferable to letting Travis have me, so I took my chances."

It was only sheer dumb luck that it was late enough in the morning that a student jogging past saw Lei. By the time he'd come back with help, Lei was unconscious in the flower bed, and Travis was gone.

Dante sat back, going over the story again in his head. As he suspected, there was no new information, but they'd be remiss if they didn't go over it one more time. He exchanged a look with Clarke. The killings in Seattle held some key differences. He didn't think any of the girls had willingly let the unsub in, and he had carved his message into their bodies when he was through.

A message that may or may not have been meant for Travis Berkley. Hard to believe that someone who'd gone through the trouble of researching the murders would get the killer's name wrong, but the alternative was that the girls' deaths were meant as a tribute to someone *else*. Both possibilities stretched the realm of belief and didn't make a damn bit of sense.

The tension in the room grew like it was a living thing, coiling and snapping among the four of them. Once Dante and Clarke left, things would move quickly. They had to talk to Berkley. They had to head back to Seattle to go over things again with Detective Smith and the ME.

They had to track down this bastard before he continued with whatever plan he'd begun with those girls' deaths.

Dante, at least, would have the comfort of motion to keep him distracted from the scenes that he'd witnessed. Lei and Emma wouldn't have even that. He leaned forward, catching Lei's attention. "We can assign a protection detail. I don't think you're in any immediate danger, but if it would help ease your mind, I'll make some calls."

Lei's lips quirked up at the edges, but the smile never came close to reaching her eyes. "Dante—Agent Young—we were in immediate danger the second that asshole singled Travis out as someone he wanted to emulate. We're more than capable of taking care of ourselves."

CHAPTER FIVE

There wasn't much to say after that. The agents took the evidence and left. Lei was only slightly sorry to see them go. Maybe in a different situation, she would have liked to have spent a little more time with them. *With Dante.* It didn't matter. Too much had happened in too short a time, and she felt like she'd just been told the monster lurking beneath the bed was real—and coming for her.

She had more important things to worry about than how well Dante Young's shoulders filled out his suit. *If I'm attracted to him, it means he's got some horrible skeletons in his closet.* She hadn't been a saint for the last twelve years, but there was something fundamentally wrong with her, because the only guys she seemed to be attracted to had something wrong with them. Her mother liked to theorize that her sad attempts at dating were just as self-defeating as Emma's diets. None of them came close to replicating Travis, but they ranged from being a generic asshole to a narcissist with abusive tendencies. So she'd stopped trying.

Maybe I'd try again for the right man . . .

She shook her head and moved to the window to watch the agents' car disappear down the driveway. Now that the strangers were gone—and the potential danger with them—Saul gave her a sniff and headed for the kitchen and his lunch, Prince following close behind. As the taillights disappeared through the trees, Lei transferred her attention to the trees themselves. She and Emma had the best security money could buy set up around the house and the outlying property. No one should be able to approach without their knowing it.

Should left a lot of room for error, though. Plenty of terrible things in this world happened despite the fact that they *shouldn't*. Fear tried to flare, but she muscled it down, beating it back into place with cold, hard facts. She took a deep breath and ran through the worst-case scenario again.

Even if someone *did* approach their house, they only lived fifteen minutes from town, and Lei was confident in her abilities to hold off a threat until the police arrived. If, for some reason, they couldn't get a call out, they had enough guns to staff a small armory and a secondary phone line, which was connected to two safe rooms with a router that couldn't be cut from the outside.

Paranoid? Yes, extremely. Her and Emma's safety precautions might teeter toward doomsday prepping, but if it meant they walked out of a conflict alive, it was more than worth it. No one could really guarantee safety, but they'd come as close as humanly possible.

She tapped her finger on the glass—reinforced so that it would crack instead of shatter, one degree down from actually being bulletproof. She *knew* there was no one standing just inside the tree line. Watching. But that didn't stop the small hairs from rising along the nape of her neck. Someone could be out there, and she'd never know.

Except for the cameras.

The motion-sensor cameras were more a pain in the ass than helpful this time of year. They didn't pick up animals smaller than forty-five pounds, but this area was thick with deer, and they set off the sensors often enough that Lei regretted installing the damn things.

But the cameras around the house *were* reliable.

And the fact that I do regular circuits with Saul. If someone was hiding just out of sight, he'd know.

Though he wasn't as good with live scents as he was with decomposition. If someone knew that—and knew how to use the wind against them—Saul might not be able to sound the alarm until it was too late.

Stop that.

She blew out a breath. This was what the killer wanted—for them to feel hunted again, scared and helpless and waiting for the next blow to fall. *To be frozen, ears pressed to the door, listening for the creaky floorboard down the hall, because we knew what it meant . . .*

Emma came to stand next to her, the brush of her shoulder banishing the ghost of memory holding Lei hostage. Emma sighed. "We're going to help, aren't we?"

"We don't have a choice. We're in this. *He* brought us into it." Whoever this person was, it wasn't Travis, but the situation had that prick's fingerprints all over it. The Feds might not be able to prove that he'd written the killer with the intent to resurrect the nightmare, but he was responsible. She knew it in her very soul. "Whoever this guy is, he isn't going to be content with us staying on the bench. The Feds might think they can keep us out of it, but eventually he'll force their hand. I'd rather take the offensive than let him have control."

"I thought you might say that." A tremor worked its way through Emma, so small that Lei barely felt it where their shoulders touched.

Lei turned and leaned against the wall next to the window. All the color had leached from Emma's already sun-starved skin, leaving her looking more wraith than human. Fear. They reacted to it differently—they always had—but that didn't stop Lei from wanting to wrap her up and ship her off to somewhere safe to ride this out. "If you don't want to—"

"That's not it. I just . . . We have a life that we've worked really hard for. The house. The dogs. The business." She stirred, some color returning to her cheeks. Emma motioned at everything and nothing.

"I know it's probably giving the killer too much credit, but it feels like he waited until we finally felt safe to strike."

"You're safe. *We're* safe." She didn't believe it any more than Emma did. They'd both worked hard to get past what had happened to them—what Lei had opened the door for—and now they were being dragged back in. It didn't matter how much therapy they had, how many steps they'd taken to feel in control. In the course of twenty-four hours, their illusion of safety had been ripped away as if it'd never existed.

Well, fuck that. She was taking control back in the only way she knew how.

Emma took a deep breath and pulled the curtains shut. She went to each window on the ground floor and repeated the action, blocking the view of their nonexistent watcher. Lei wasn't about to admit how spooked she was, not with Emma showing burrowing tendencies. The last thing her friend needed was Lei tipping her into a full-blown panic attack.

The closed curtains should have left the house feeling claustrophobic, but although Emma was agoraphobic, she hated to feel closed in. She'd done extensive research when they were renovating this house, and they'd settled on a floor plan that passed as open, but still had enough rooms separated that they could retreat from each other as necessary. They spent an entire week painting all the walls in soothing blue-and-cream tones that made the rooms feel larger than they were. Combined with the cozy furniture and careful lighting choices, the house could be closed up completely and still feel open and welcoming.

Lei shadowed Emma's path, double-checking each lock on both the windows and doors. They hadn't done a full sweep like this in a long time, and it comforted her even as she mourned the necessity. *He knows where we are.* It wouldn't have taken a tech whiz to figure it out. They weren't exactly hiding, but though they were downright notorious in California, up in Washington with the years padding people's memories, they'd become Lei and Emma, cadaver-dog search team and researcher extraordinaire first, and victims second.

That was about to change.

It wouldn't be long before the murders of three pretty sorority girls started making headlines, and then it was just a matter of some ambitious and creative reporter connecting the dots and realizing that this case shared shockingly similar details with one twelve years ago in California. The Internet was forever, and a search of Emma's and Lei's names would bring up their history and their current business.

Maybe they should have tried to hide more. New names, a state farther away—hell, a new country. Something to make it a little more challenging for some sick sociopath to hunt them down.

Careful, there. You're thinking like a victim. This guy wants a piece of you? Let him come. You'll put him in the ground the way you weren't able to with Travis.

The thought rang hollow. Lei was capable, but she wasn't an international badass. She was only human, and humans made mistakes. *Mistakes are something I'm good at.*

They ended up in the kitchen, and Saul instantly left his comfortable place on the cool tile floor to come to her. He always knew when her emotions were getting the best of her, even if she'd perfected her poker face a long time ago. Lei crouched down and wrapped her arms around him, giving herself five seconds to lean on him.

Warmth. Comfort. A steady presence that calmed her racing thoughts.

She inhaled deeply. His doggy smell was comforting even as she wrinkled her nose. "You need a bath." *Four, three, two, one. Move.* She scratched him behind his ear and stood. "You might as well get some sleep, boy. We're going to be a while."

Emma grabbed two cookies and tossed her one. "Let's get started."

They headed for Emma's office, which doubled as a secondary safe room. It had no windows, and they'd had a contractor come in from out of state to reinforce the walls with steel plates so no one could chop their way through. Emma had set up a network that couldn't be cut from outside the room, and she had a phone line routed to both safe rooms—the only one in the house. The safe next to the couch held a small arsenal, their bugout bags, and two first-aid kits.

The room wouldn't hold up against an assault indefinitely, but it would keep them safe until reinforcements arrived.

The actual safe room was upstairs, and they could access it from either of their closets. Someone would have to know it was there to find it, and even if they did, no one was getting inside that room with anything short of serious hardware.

Emma dropped into the fancy chair in front of her computer setup. Three massive monitors were arranged on the sturdy desk, and she immediately started clicking through things fast enough to make Lei's brain hurt.

Hard to believe that when she was in Omega Delta Lambda, Emma's major had been nutrition science. These days she spent as much of her time on the dark net as she did anywhere else. Her program made a big difference in helping find the lost ones—the people who up and disappeared one day. It cross-referenced their information with Jane and John Does that were reported over the years. The numbers on both sides of things were astronomical, so it would never have an end, but Lei suspected that was part of what drew Emma to the task in the first place.

They both needed purpose.

Emma put names to the ones who had been found. Lei found the ones who had been hidden.

They were doing good work, though no one attached to their old lives saw it that way. *Penance,* Lei's parents called it. *Disturbed and disgusting,* from Emma's mother. It shouldn't matter what they thought. It *didn't* matter most days.

Her friend cursed, and Lei spun to find her glaring at the monitors lining the wall adjacent to the desk. There were twelve of them—six on the right only lighting up when movement triggered the cameras sprinkled throughout the property, six on the left showing strategically placed cameras that were recording at all times.

Lei recognized the battered old Jeep pulling up the driveway and sighed. *Should have expected this.* "You know he won't leave until he sees that you're okay." Sheriff Bamford—Isaac, as he insisted they call him—wasn't a bad guy as such things went, but he'd run Stillwater for the last fifteen years, and he took any threat against its citizens personally. They were all under his protection by virtue of being part of the town. He hadn't known what to think of Emma and Lei when they first moved into this house, but once he realized they weren't romantically involved, he'd developed something of a crush on Emma.

Calling it a crush felt juvenile, but the description fit. Isaac orchestrated reasons to come out to the house to "check on" them regularly, and he always seemed to pop up when Lei went into town. She knew Stillwater's gossip mill was to blame for *that*, and they found the sheriff's interest in Emma as fascinating as the most recent season of whatever dating reality show was on TV. Attractive and in his late thirties, Isaac was one of the only eligible bachelors in the area, which meant speculation ran rampant about when Emma would finally settle in and make an honest man of him.

Lei could have told them it was a lost cause. Emma preferred her relationships through the safety of the computer screen. Lei didn't ask too many questions about the semantics behind that because it wasn't her business. They both had their own way of dealing with the crushing loneliness that breached their defenses in moments of weakness. They had each other, but there were still gaps that neither could fill for the other. Nor should they. They were already too codependent. *Unhealthily so,* according to the last therapist her mother had thrown their way.

Lei had fired him after a month. After he went through what they had, he could talk shit about being unhealthily codependent.

Emma clicked something that had her computers going blank and pushed to her feet. Her shapeless sweater covered her to just above her knees, and her knitted socks left only a sliver of black leggings showing, but she could have been wearing a paper bag and still look beautiful. It was something her friend used to know and capitalize on—she'd loved her curves and loved showing them off.

But that was Before.

Then again, Lei was hardly the same bright-eyed, naive coed she'd been Before, either.

They met Isaac at the front door. He could have been pulled from the pages of a hiking magazine—all rugged good looks, broad shoulders, and close-cropped ginger beard. He was handsome enough, but Lei wasn't remotely attracted to him—the only sign she really needed that he was a good guy.

"Ladies. The Feds called me on their way out of town." He stepped into the house and raised his eyebrows when Lei leaned against the wall and Emma took up a position in the doorway leading to the sitting room. "I take it this won't be a long talk." His voice sounded a bit like he'd gargled gravel. It made Lei think he must have been a smoker at some point in his life.

Emma crossed her arms over her chest. "We have a lot of work to do."

Lei shot her friend a look. It was one thing not to be interested, but they didn't need to piss Isaac off. He didn't *seem* the petty type, but if he was so inclined, he could become a royal pain in the ass. "What Emma means is that talking with the Feds was exhausting, so we're both tired. Is there something we can help you with, Sheriff?"

His hazel eyes flicked from Emma to Lei and back again, and his voice softened. "I came by to make sure you were okay."

Lei and Emma both trained regularly in jujitsu, and she dragged Emma out to their makeshift shooting range on the property once a week. She didn't know what kind of training was required for someone to be sheriff of a tiny town, but she'd wager they were better prepared than Isaac was. "We're fine."

"Fine and dandy," Emma quipped.

Isaac cursed and yanked his hat off. "Even if you weren't, you wouldn't tell me, would you?"

No. There was exactly one person Lei could rely on in this world, and she was standing in that room. Everyone else was expendable—and a potential enemy. Including Isaac. She wouldn't tell him that, because it would hurt him, and it wasn't personal. The frustration rolling off him in waves made her relent, despite herself. "There's nothing to say, Isaac. Three girls died, and whoever did it has some kind of fascination with us. How do you think we're doing?"

He scrubbed a hand over his face. "Yeah. Okay. Yeah, I get it. I'm sorry. I didn't think." He straightened, layers of professionalism sliding into place like unruffling feathers. "If you want a security detail, let me know and I'll get one of the boys out here. Doesn't have to be in the house." He paused, looking at each of them in turn. "You get in over your head, there's no shame in calling for help. I'll make sure someone's close enough to get here in time. You might not see it that way, but you're one of us in Stillwater. We take care of our own."

Emma flinched as if he'd reached out and struck her. "Thank you." Her words were stones dropped into a still pool, and Lei couldn't help thinking they'd regret the resulting ripples.

Paranoid. Without a doubt. She preferred it that way.

Her long-held nightmare had returned, and this time it didn't wear a face she recognized. *Anyone* could be the killer—except Travis Berkley. He was safely behind bars and would remain there for as long as she had any say in the matter. Lei didn't care if she was eighty years old, she'd still be sitting in that courtroom and recounting her own personal horror story to ensure he stayed safely in that six-by-eight cell. *If only he hadn't dodged the goddamn death penalty.*

She blinked, realizing that Emma had ushered Isaac out onto the porch. Their soft good-byes were different, a change from Emma's normally clipped tones. Lei shifted, trying to get a better look at them. *Maybe I was wrong all along about her not being interested . . .*

Her friend closed the door and locked it. When she turned around, resolution firmed the lines of her face. "Let's get to work."

Or maybe Emma was just doing what needed to be done to get him the hell out of here.

CHAPTER SIX

California State Prison looked like every other prison Dante had ever had cause to visit. Massive fence overlooked by watchtowers. Everything vaguely dusty, as if it was a place time had forgotten, and as beige as if the color had been slowly leached from it.

Dante parked but made no move to get out of the car. He drummed his thumbs on the steering wheel, turning over the facts the same way he had on the flight down here. They had plenty of evidence, but nothing resembling a suspect. Detective Smith and his people were interviewing friends and known associates of the girls, but if this was a love letter to Travis Berkley, the sorority had more significance than the identities of the victims.

He hated that.

Three girls were dead. They should be at the center of this all, rather than a footnote in a tragedy that started twelve years ago.

"Prisons creep me out."

He glanced at Clarke, finding her peering out the windshield at the tall stone walls surrounding them. Two men watched from each of the towers. She shuddered narrow shoulders. "You ever feel like one of these days, we'll go interview a monster and they'll decide we're more suited to being locked up, too?"

Dante chewed on that for a moment. "We're the good guys."

"Roll in the shit long enough and you're no different from the pigs."

He leaned back and looked at her—really looked at her. "This one's getting to you more than the others. Why?"

"It's getting to you, too. You haven't said more than a word since we booked the tickets. You're not the chattiest of assholes, but you don't do the silent thing unless you're worried." She dug through her purse and yanked a hair tie out to pull her red curls back from her face.

Damn it, she's right. He rubbed the back of his hand over his mouth, but there was no overriding the bad taste this whole thing left. "I read the news articles from back when the Sorority Row Murders happened. I hadn't realized how beloved Berkley was." It defied comprehension that not only had Lei and Emma gone through that horror show but that initially they'd also been met with disbelief and downright amusement when they'd accused Berkley. That monster had almost walked free by virtue of his family, money, and reputation. Judging from Britton's profile, if Berkley *had* gone free, he would have tracked down Lei and Emma and finished the job.

Similar to what someone was doing now.

He kept picturing Lei, the way her lips tightened when he'd delivered the news. That was it. The only reaction she'd allowed. Dante didn't have the same hang-ups some men did about pretty women being fragile—he was partnered with Clarke, after all—but Lei was a civilian. She didn't have to spend every day peering into the darkness to get a better look at the monsters who moved within it.

She didn't have to, but she'd chosen to.

What kind of woman survives a massacre and spends her life hunting dead bodies?

He didn't have an immediate answer to that, and it intrigued him more than it probably should have. Lei would have been more than entitled to break down in shock—to cry—but she'd just nodded as if she'd expected something like this to happen all along. "Those women deserve better."

"Those women . . . or Lei?" She held up her hands when he shot her a look. "Come on, Dante. Give me a little credit here. I'm a fucking FBI agent. You and Ms. Zhang's chemistry sparked hot enough that I was about to go looking for a fire extinguisher." She reached for the door. "I'm not exactly a stickler for the rules—"

"No shit, really?"

"Shut up." She waited until they strode through the main entrance to continue. "The kill count surpassed twenty last time something like this happened, and even if it's playing out differently now, we can't afford for either of us to be distracted. Your attraction to that woman is a distraction."

"It's nothing." The words tasted like a lie, but he didn't correct them. He might admire the hell out of Lei Zhang, and she might be one of the strongest and most beautiful women he'd ever seen, but finding the unsub was more important than anything else. It had to be.

"If you say so."

They went through security with little fuss and met the warden on the other side. Geoffrey Franklin had been in charge of California State Prison for thirty years, and he looked like he could go another thirty without a problem. His close-cropped gray hair, combined with the set of his shoulders and the purposeful way he moved, had Dante marking him as former military. Franklin nodded as if they'd said something and turned. "This way."

Dante fell into step next to him, leaving Clarke to bring up the back. She preferred to let him do the talking—he preferred it, too. Even when she wasn't going out of her way to play bad cop, oftentimes Clarke rubbed people—especially men—the wrong way. "Berkley's in solitary?"

"Usually. He doesn't play well with others." Franklin's gruff tone spoke of how much he liked *that*.

"Fights?" It didn't fit the profile of the guy he'd read about up to this point, but prison changed people—usually for the worse.

Franklin shook his head. "Nothing like that. He likes games. He riles up one inmate and sets them on another. Nothing we can officially trace back to him, but when he gets tired of the games, he'll do something to cross the line and get back into solitary. It's a pattern that's repeated itself regularly since he showed up here."

That sounded more like what he'd expected.

Travis Berkley was pure predator, and being in prison and surrounded by other predators wouldn't be enough to force him to change his nature. If anything, prison sharpened those instincts. "Is there someone he's interacted with named Trevor?" A long shot, but he had to ask.

Franklin frowned. "Name's not familiar, which only means he wasn't cell mates with this guy. I can talk to the guards. They'd know better than I would."

"Appreciate it." Sometimes serial killers gained fans through the media, and sometimes they influenced other inmates to do their bidding. Unlikely given Berkley's profile, but stranger things had happened. "We'll need access to his mail."

"I'll have my guy put it together for you. We check it all before it gets into Berkley's hands, and my guys personally went through it a second time after your call yesterday." Franklin's lip actually curled. "There's a large amount of it."

Unsurprising. Serial killers held a kind of fascination for society. For most people, it was a morbid feeling that intrigued them even as they were horrified. A real-life scary movie—something they could research and read about and share with their friends.

For others, the fascination went much deeper. They wrote. There was a whole subset of people who fantasized about killers romantically. From Travis's pictures, Dante imagined he got a whole hell of a lot of mail of that variety.

Franklin led them to a door. "He's in there. Question him as long as you need to, and knock when you're finished. I'll be in my office if you want to talk further."

"Thank you." He waited for Franklin to walk away before turning to Clarke. "You want in the room or out?"

"In," she responded promptly. "If he focuses on me, that will free you up to ask questions that might get something resembling an honest response."

"You know better." They were mostly here for the mail. Britton had pegged Travis as a sadistic sociopath. He had a borderline-genius IQ, and he liked to play games. The only reason he'd talk at this point was because he was bored out of his damn mind. That still didn't mean they'd get anything useful. "Let's do this."

Dante let Clarke go first and followed her into the room. Travis Berkley looked up and smiled when he caught sight of them. "The FBI. Lucky me."

He really was a handsome bastard. Even sitting there, dressed in orange and handcuffed to both the table and the floor, Berkley looked exactly like what he had been before he murdered twenty-one girls in cold blood—the star football player who was well liked by everyone and spent weekends on his family's yacht. His blond hair was a little shaggier than it had been in his pictures, and his shoulders and body were corded with more muscle, but those amused blue eyes were the same.

A pretty college girl wouldn't stand a chance.

Lei hadn't stood a chance.

It was hard to picture the woman he'd met the day before being tempted by something as superficial as good looks, but twelve years was a long time. Dante took a seat next to Clarke.

Berkley flicked a glance over her and focused on Dante. "You look suitably glowering. Who died and brought the Feds to my door?" Something like lust flickered across his face. "Was it Lei?"

Dante caught himself leaning forward and forced his posture to relax. The hungry way the man said Lei's name had him clenching his fists beneath the table. "You get a lot of fan mail, huh?"

The interest in Travis's blue eyes sharpened. "Someone's left me a love note, didn't they?" He leaned forward, the chain of his cuffs clinking. "Has someone been naughty, Agent? Did they sneak into a sorority house and stab those sluts to death? Tell me the details and I might have some information for you."

Dante held himself perfectly still, his expression bland. "You have a wild imagination."

"Yeah, well, I don't get much in the way of entertainment." His gaze slid to Clarke. "You're pretty enough. Pickings are slim here, you understand."

She huffed a laugh. "Prison has dulled your skills, Berkley. I heard you were a charming fucker, but all you've done in the few minutes since we arrived is verbally jack yourself off." She leaned back and dropped an arm over her chair, every inch of her posture screaming belligerence. "This is a waste of time. He doesn't know anything useful."

Dante picked up where she was headed with that and shrugged. "Crossing t's and dotting i's."

Berkley raised his eyebrows. "Does that dog and pony show actually work on people? You're Feds. You don't just drop by out of the goodness of your heart. Something happened, and you think I might know something. Considering my skill set and history, that something is pretty little sorority girls getting sliced up in the night." There was that flicker again, the one far too close to lust for Dante's liking.

It wasn't unexpected. Obviously Berkley got off on murder or he wouldn't have done it. Most sadistic killers had a degree of sexual deviancy involved, and Berkley was no different. The thought of women being hurt aroused him. Frankly, Dante had seen worse.

But those other murderers hadn't victimized Lei Zhang.

Get a hold of yourself. You met the woman once. You don't have a right to feel protective of her, and it's fucking up your ability to do your job. You have to maintain distance.

Easy in theory, but something about Lei had gotten under his skin.

Clarke must have seen something on his face, because she leaned forward, drawing Berkley's attention. "Fine. I'll play. Have you been talking, Travis?" She almost purred his name. "Have you been spilling all the dirty details of that night to your fan club?"

"And let every asshole with a knife think he can replicate what I did?" Berkley snorted. "Not likely. Copycats are for losers."

"Copycats are for losers," Clarke repeated slowly, sinking a world's worth of derision into the four words. "Travis Berkley, you're wasting my time. Though, I have to say, your fan club leaves something to be desired. They couldn't even get your name right."

"You're looking for something specific." He shifted again, eyes narrowing. "What name did they use?"

It wouldn't hurt anything to tell him the truth—and it might just rile him up enough that he told *them* something useful. "A fan left a very specific love note—for Trevor. Not Travis."

Berkley went completely still, the very essence of a predator sensing prey. Only for an instant, and then he was back to the belligerent asshole. "Shame they couldn't manage one thing right."

They wouldn't get anything from him. If Berkley knew something, he wouldn't share it with them, if only to dangle the knowledge of how fucking superior he was over them. He wasn't really why they were there anyway. Dante pushed to his feet. "I think we're done here."

"How's my Lei-Lei doing these days?" The amusement disappeared from Berkley's face, and the mask dropped fully for the first time since they walked into the room. "I hear she spends her time hunting corpses with a little doggy friend. Fitting. Lei-Lei always was a bitch."

Dante held open the door for Clarke and stalked out of the room behind her before he could do or say anything to feed into Berkley's ego. They found Franklin back in his office. "We need to see his cell."

Franklin raised his brows. "Let's go."

Ten minutes later, Dante was looking at the space where Berkley spent most of his time. There was no clutter. The only thing nonregulation was a stack of books next to the bed and a picture taped to the wall. Dante riffled through the books. Two thrillers that had obviously been read a few times, judging by the broken-in spines. There were no papers inside or writing in the margins, so he set those aside. The third book made him stop cold. *Cadaver Dogs Handbook.* This one, too, had the markings of being heavily read. He looked up to find Clarke holding the photograph. "What is it?"

She tapped it against the back of her free hand. "Polaroid. Looks like some random clearing in some random woods, except . . ."

"Except?"

She flipped it around. Two numbers had been written in pen on the back. "Call me crazy, but these sure look like they could be coordinates."

He looked at the numbers. "We're going to need to bring this with us." Dante was hardly an expert, but he'd bet his badge that those numbers pointed to a place somewhere within driving distance of Stillwater, Washington. Berkley was too damn smug for it to be anything else.

Coordinates. A book on cadaver dogs. Taunting comments about Lei Zhang.

It all added up to a shitstorm of epic proportions.

CHAPTER SEVEN

"Pick her back up."

Luna Henderson had no more tears left. No more horror. No more strength. She knelt in the damp underbrush and stared into the blank gaze of her dead best friend. No more. *He'd* made sure of that.

She reached out a shaking hand and covered those unseeing blue eyes. *I have to run. I have to get help.* She managed to lift her head enough to look around. He'd taken them from the city and into the mountains, but she'd lost all sense of direction in the darkness, and when dawn finally came, she might as well have been on the moon.

And Jennifer was still dead.

All her friends were still dead.

"Pick her up, love."

She couldn't bring herself to look at him. Hated the voice that poured over her like honey, the same one that had coaxed her into one drink and then another. *Just one more, love. Take me home with you. No one has to know.*

She'd done this.

It was all her fault.

A rough hand gripped her hair and forced her head up. "Look at me. You pick up that bitch or you drag her, I don't care, but move her body now or I'll kill you where you kneel."

If she gave up, there would be no chance of escape, no opportunity to survive. Luna sucked in a breath and used the exhale to shove to her feet. She could do this. She *would* do this.

She gritted her teeth and hooked her hands under Jennifer's armpits and began to drag her. Luna's world narrowed down to each step she took. *Step. Breathe. Drag. Repeat.* Time lost meaning. The trees blocked the sun's path from view, so it might have been one hour or seven before he finally called a halt to her progress.

"Nice job, love. Great job. Now, on your knees like a good girl."

She stared down the barrel of a gun, and the strength went out of her legs. This was how it ended. There would be no chance to run, no way to get help.

No justice.

His lips pulled into a smile that made her skin crawl. "Good-bye, Luna."

Dante's phone had half a dozen missed calls on it when they exited the prison. He dropped into the driver's seat and turned the engine on, letting the AC get started while he waded through them. "Look up those coordinates."

"Already on it, boss."

He shook his head at Clarke's sarcastic tone and scrolled through his phone. Two calls from Detective Smith. Two from a number he didn't recognize, and two from Britton. He considered and called Detective Smith first.

The gruff man answered almost immediately. "We have a problem."

Not words anyone wanted to hear in the middle of a murder investigation. "I'm listening."

"Our three victims weren't alone in the house. We thought it was mostly empty because of spring break, and a lot of kids go home or travel or do whatever the fuck college students do with a week off. But there are two girls unaccounted for. Jennifer Baldwin and Luna Henderson."

He slumped back against the seat. Damn it. Making sure those three girls were alone in the house was the first thing they should have done. He'd taken it for granted that the PD had cleared it first. *Sloppy on my part.* With the girls being scattered to the winds, he should probably give them a break, but there were two girls who had been missing for well over twenty-four hours at this point. If they were alive, it was a goddamn miracle. "Any idea how our guy got them out of the house without someone seeing?"

"No." Detective Smith spit the word like something foul tasting.

Fuck. Dante pinched the bridge of his nose. "We're catching the next flight back to Seattle. We'll start from there."

"See you then." He hung up.

"Shit," Clarke breathed.

More bad news. They weren't going to catch any breaks on this case—*that* much was clear. "Where do the coordinates lead?"

"An access road in Mount Baker–Snoqualmie National Forest. It's roughly two hours from Seattle—and about an hour from Stillwater."

Dante cursed. "We have jack shit. Berkley is clearly involved, but there's nothing obvious in his mail, and it'll take weeks to wade through it to figure out if he was talking to someone in code. We have three dead girls, and now we have two missing girls from the same sorority. All within easy driving distance to Lei Zhang and Emma Nilsson."

"Think they have something to do with it?"

He threw the car into gear and backed out of the space. "We can't discount anything. Considering the rape aspect of the murders, it's more likely the unsub is a man—"

"Except the unsub couldn't follow through on the rape, so there wasn't anything left behind that couldn't have been done by a woman."

He couldn't argue that point. His gut said Lei had nothing to do with those girls' deaths, but if he told Clarke that, she'd accuse him of thinking with the wrong head. Better to discount Lei and Emma in the normal way. "We need to figure out where they were during the time of the murders."

"Oh, that's easy. Lei and her dog were in Colville National Forest on a search for the victim of a murderous husband. There are half a dozen witnesses that were with her at any given time, and she wouldn't have had the opportunity to slip away to Seattle."

He growled. "If you already looked up her alibi, why the song and dance about her possibly being guilty?"

"Because you need to face the fact that something about this woman is throwing you off your game. I don't know what it is about her, because I've never seen you go all googly-eyed." She shuddered. "It's creepy as fuck."

"Clarke."

"I'm serious." She held up a hand. "She's more likely to be the victim than the killer, but we can't take anything for granted."

Damn it. She was right. He'd taken one look at Lei's big, dark eyes, and some part of him had wanted to shield her from what was coming. She'd gone through the worst the world had to offer, and instead of letting it beat her, she'd come back swinging. She hadn't let Berkley break her—not in that sorority house, and not during what came after.

He knew he had a white-knight complex—one didn't end up in the BAU without at least a dose of it—but it'd never hit this hard. *Though my parents might disagree with that.* There'd been comments about his "bleeding heart" for as long as he could remember. Dante blew out a careful exhale. "Noted."

"Good. Now that we got that out of the way . . . I might have found the alibi for Lei, but I don't have one for Emma." Clarke settled back in the passenger seat and propped her boots on the dashboard. "I chatted up Stillwater's sheriff when I called to request a follow-up, and from what he let drop, Emma doesn't leave the house."

"Ever?"

"Ever."

He'd noted that the blonde seemed skittish having them in her home, but he'd chalked it up to the fact that they were delivering unwelcome news. It was possible that was actually guilt . . . He shook his head. "It's possible. At this point, anything is possible. That said, the semantics of it are complicated. I only saw one vehicle out there. If she was hiding another one, wouldn't Lei know? Unless you think Lei is part of it?"

"I don't know what to think—which is the point."

He drummed his fingers on the steering wheel. They wouldn't figure out any answers on this drive. There were too many questions in this case, and even the answers they came up with just spawned more questions like some kind of hydra.

Dante switched gears. "I don't like the access road being part of this. That picture doesn't show any kind of road, and it looks like it hasn't seen human interaction in years—if ever."

"He's playing games." Clarke twisted to face him. "Want to bet that if we took Lei and her dog out to that point, they'd pick up on the scent of a body—and *that* would lead us to the two missing girls?"

"I'm not taking that bet." It seemed like exactly the sort of thing Berkley would orchestrate. Except . . . "It's too easy."

"Easy?"

"Yeah, easy. Berkley plays games—"

"I just said that."

"Right, but this is a guy who dated a girl for months before he even tried to get her to break the rules to bring him into the sorority. Berkley gets off on getting away with murder—not on being a criminal mastermind who likes to lead the cops around by their noses. It doesn't jibe. It's too heavy-handed, too attention grabbing. If all he needed before was to get away with murder to get off on his superiority, why is he throwing up these 'Look at me' signs now?"

Clarke shrugged. "Maybe prison changed him. It tends to do that."

"Yeah, maybe." It still didn't sit right. Something about this scenario wasn't adding up. Unease slithered through Dante, leaving him cold. They were playing on someone else's game board, to someone else's timetable. The only way they had a chance of solving this was to get ahead of the unsub and anticipate his moves.

Something they hadn't managed to do in the twenty-four hours since they'd gotten the case. That had to stop. Now.

Drip. Drip. Drip.

She leaned against the door with everything she had, blood making its way lazily down the bridge of her nose to bead and drop to the ever-growing puddle on the hardwood floor. He's coming back. And when he does, he'll kill me just like he's killed the others. *The screams had stopped some time ago. It might have been seconds; it might have been hours. Lei had no concept of time anymore. The sky on the other side of her window remained dark no matter how long her friends suffered. Unrelentingly dark, just like the house after the power went out.*

Travis. Travis did that.

He'd done all of this.

Her arms shook from holding the door shut. Or holding herself up. She didn't know which was which anymore.

On the other side of the thin wood, down the hallway in the direction of the stairs . . . a floorboard creaked. Even though she braced for it, his voice still jarred a small sob from her lips. "Lei-Lei, it's time. Open the door and let me in."

Lei shot straight, her scream firmly on the inside of her lips. Sweat made her tank top cling to her body and plastered her long hair to her head and neck. She reached out, and then Saul was there, jumping onto her bed and licking her face. "It's fine. I'm fine."

I'm not fine. I'm not anything resembling fine.

She didn't have nightmares now as often as she used to, but she'd trained herself years ago to keep her screams silent. Better that than have Emma rush in, see the memories lurking too close to the surface, and be dragged down in the process. No, Saul knew, and that was more than enough.

She rested her forehead against his shoulder, letting his steady breathing soothe hers out. There would be more nightmares before this thing was done, and not all of them would happen while she slept.

Saul whined again, and she sighed. "Yeah, let's get you out." Lei pulled on a pair of shorts, her running gear, and slipped into her holster. She usually settled with pepper spray, but normally the only thing she was worried about was a cougar getting too frisky. *I could just stay inside and use the treadmill.*

But that felt too much like hiding.

Hiding worked for Emma. It was how she dealt with stress and her complete lack of trust in anyone who wasn't Lei. Maybe it would have been different if either of their parents was more supportive. At least Lei's parents *tried*, even if they missed the mark by a mile. Emma's mother just devolved into a strange kind of psychological warfare via holiday cards. No wonder Emma shut herself off from the world if that was the only model she'd had growing up.

That wasn't how Lei functioned, though. If she walked into this house with the intention of never coming out again, she might as well put a bullet in her brain and bury herself right then. "Come, Saul." She grabbed her nine-millimeter off the nightstand and slipped it into the holster, twisting a little to ensure the fit wouldn't hinder her movements. Thirty seconds to pull on her shoes and key the alarm and she was out the door, Saul at her heels.

Lei kept her pace nice and slow as they headed across the yard and into the trees. She'd beaten down half a dozen trails over the years, and she aimed for one that would be a nice five miles. Enough to burn off some of her anxiety without tiring her out too much.

After the first mile, her shoulders relaxed. By the second, her mind had cleared. There was only the pounding of her feet to the ground and Saul's happy panting next to her. He loved running. It was one of the few nontracking activities that he did with total abandon, and it chilled him out the same way it did Lei. Nothing mattered except their next breaths, the next footfalls, the next mile.

She caught sight of something bright pink through the trees and stumbled to a stop. "What the hell?" They were still well within the property line, and one of the first things she'd done when they'd bought the house was go around to all the potential access points and post **No Trespassing** signs. A fence would have been nice, but the property was too heavily wooded and too large an area to make that a feasible option. They'd never had an issue with trespassing before, though once a lost hiker had wandered in. The poor woman was so relieved to see another person, she'd burst into tears on the spot. Not exactly a threat.

This was something else.

"Saul, heel."

He responded instantly, taking up position approximately six inches off her left foot. She watched him closely, looking for the telltale signs that he smelled someone else. There was nothing but attentiveness as he waited for her next command.

The pink thing hung at eye level against a tree. It had to have been nailed there, because she didn't see any way it was being held up. Lei stared. She should walk away. *Hide. Pretend this isn't happening.* Instead, she carefully picked her way through the underbrush to its position. All the while, she kept one eye on Saul and one on the area around her. There were too many trees for a long-range attack to be effective, but she didn't expect this killer to employ sniper tactics. No, he wanted to be up close and personal when he killed.

But there was no wind to hide his scent behind. If he was close, Saul would smell him and give warning. She stopped in front of the tree, her mouth going dry. The pink thing was a purse. Pink and glittery and something a college-age Lei would have loved. It hung on a nail that had attached a plastic Ziploc bag to the bark. The bag held a generic-looking card envelope with her name scrawled on the side. *Lei-Lei.*

"Saul, guard." His primary skill set wasn't to be a guard dog—not like Prince—but he knew the command well enough to watch her back. Lei dug out her phone with shaking hands and took a picture of the purse and the bag. She should wait for the cops but . . . She dialed and held the phone to her ear.

"Lei? The damn motion-sensor cameras are going crazy." Emma's voice went shrill.

"I'm close to mile marker three. I found something."

"What the hell are you talking about?"

"A purse. Someone left it and a note for me. I have to come back for gloves and something to put it in that won't contaminate the evidence." Whatever evidence was left after sitting on a tree for God knew how long. She didn't have high hopes that the killer had managed to prick his finger and leave some convenient blood for them to trace. "Someone came here, so there's video of it. You just need to find it." The problem with the damn motion-sensor cameras was that they really needed a full-time team to filter through all the input. "Shut off all the cameras except this one. I need you to watch it."

The thought of the killer coming in behind her and snatching the purse made her skin crawl. He could be watching her *right then*, and she wouldn't . . .

Stop that. I would know. Emma would know. The cameras would pick him up. Whoever this guy is, he's not a freaking ghost. He's just a man.

A man can be killed.

"Lei, if I shut off the other ones . . ." Emma took a shuddering breath. "No, you're right. Even if he didn't orchestrate the other ones going nuts, he definitely took advantage of it. I still have the normal ones around the house up and running, and that's enough. I'll watch this one until you can get back there."

"Thanks." She hung up and started back toward the house, already dialing a second number—one she'd put in her phone after the Feds left yesterday.

"Agent Young."

Something in her chest threatened to relax as his smooth voice came over the phone. She gritted her teeth and picked up her pace. "It's Lei Zhang. We have a problem."

"Lei? What's wrong?" A pause. "We're less than thirty minutes away."

That almost brought her up short. Last she'd heard, they'd been headed for California and Travis and . . . *They found something.* She knew they'd be back eventually because the killer obviously had plans for Lei and Emma, but she hadn't expected them here so quickly.

She gave herself a shake and kept jogging. "I found something on our property. A pink purse and what looks like a greeting card or something with my name on it." *With the name Travis used to call me.* "I was going to get gloves and—"

"We're on our way," Dante spoke firmly. He didn't try to tell her not to worry or snap that she didn't know what she was doing. He just stated that they would be there in that calm and soothing voice of his. "Go back to the house and lock the doors. We'll be there in twenty."

She started to tell him she was more than capable of retrieving a purse without screwing up evidence, but . . . he was right. She might work with cops regularly, but she wasn't a cop. More than that, even if she *was*, she would have been yanked off this case the second they realized how connected she was.

Ignoring that order was stupid. This killer was focused on her, and as much as she'd like to just duke it out and be done with it, letting the Feds do their job was the only real option. "Okay. I'll meet you back there."

"Thank you." There was something like relief there. As if he thought she'd go rogue and tell him to fuck off.

Considering that was exactly what she wanted to do, she didn't blame him for assuming the worst. She hung up and picked up her pace.

CHAPTER EIGHT

Dante tore up the driveway, the tires of the rental sending gravel flying. He slammed to a stop as soon as he saw Lei jogging out of the trees on the other side of the little lawn. Clarke smacked him. "Fuck, man, you aren't in NASCAR. She's fine. Calm down."

"I am calm."

"No, you're not. You have a wild look in your eyes, and you're going to scare the shit out of her if you get out of the car right now. Leash it, Dante. This girl is either a suspect or a victim, and you can't run out there and start yelling at her because she went for a jog on her own damn property."

Considering that was exactly what he was in danger of doing, he paused and took a slow, measured breath, striving for calm. He didn't have a claim on Lei. He didn't have anything *resembling* a claim on her. They'd had exactly one conversation. "I'm sorry. I don't know what's wrong with me."

"Don't sweat it. Just maybe wait to ask for her number until after you've caught the guy that wants to make her into a human pincushion."

He shot Clarke a look. "That's not helping."

"Sure it is." She climbed out of the car before he could form a response, which was just as well.

Dante watched his partner cross to Lei, still fighting for control. Part of him wanted to haul her into her fortress of a house and tell her to stay there until they caught this guy, but it wouldn't work.

Get out of the car. Act normal.

It wasn't a problem he'd ever had before. Dante was professionalism personified. It was how he operated. How he'd *always* operated. He'd never come across someone who'd gone through quite as much as Lei Zhang, but that didn't mean he had an excuse to act like a damn caveman. Since cleansing breaths weren't doing a damn thing, Dante shut off the car and joined Clarke and Lei out on the lawn. "How far out?"

She raised her eyebrows. "Hello, Agent Young. Nice seeing you again."

Damn it, he was making a mess of things. He ran a critical eye over her, searching for any sign of distress. Nothing. Nothing but strong legs leading up to criminally tiny shorts and a fitted tank top that showed off surprisingly toned shoulders and arms, considering her small stature. *She's no victim.* He knew that. Of course he knew that. "Are you okay?"

"Yes." She paused and blew out a breath. "No. I'm not okay. Every single year, I swear we're going to take down those goddamn motion cameras, and every year I put it off because I'm afraid that when we really need them, we won't have them. Now, we needed them, and they didn't even function properly. It pisses me the fuck off."

Clarke nodded. "I'll go see how Emma's coming with the videos. Grab the gear and get the purse."

Subtle, Clarke. And then she was gone, leaving them alone. Well, them and the dog. Dante nodded at it. "What breed?" He'd been curious before, but it hadn't seemed like a good time to ask. No reason not to now—especially if it gave the added bonus of distracting Lei a little. The dog looked like something out of a nightmare, its black-and-gray fur covering a body that was too big to be a German Shepherd. If he met it in the middle of the night, he might start to believe all those old legends about black dogs that his nana used to tell him when he was a kid.

"German Shepherd and Great Pyrenees." She ruffled the dog's massive ears. "Saul's parents had a fling, and it was me or the shelter. We decided we're suited, and the rest is history."

He highly doubted that it was as simple as that. Dante didn't know much about the training that went into a cadaver dog—at least not outside theory—but it was a whole hell of a lot of work. *And you're stalling.* He walked back to the rental and grabbed a pair of gloves and a plastic Ziploc bag. "Show me the purse, please."

"Let's take the four-wheeler." She spun and headed for the small lean-to situated near the back of the house. There was a single four-wheeler tucked there, along with a variety of lawn-care stuff, tools, and a gargantuan stack of firewood. She grabbed the keys off the hook on the wall and shrugged when she caught his surprised expression. "We have a whole hell of a lot of security. No one is going to hike up here to begin with, and even if they did, we'd know they were there long before they got this far." A shadow passed over her face. "At least, that's what we thought."

He reached out before he could tell himself it was inappropriate and touched her arm. "We'll get to the bottom of it."

"Yeah, I know." She swung a leg over the four-wheeler and started the engine. "Come on."

Dante didn't let himself think too hard about it. He just swung up behind her. The move plastered him to her back, sealing them together from shoulders to thighs. He froze for one eternal second. *Move, damn you.* She felt . . . soft and supple, and he had no business thinking any of that. Dante shifted back to grab the metal rack behind him. He couldn't keep from touching her completely, but at least he maintained some distance.

Lei gave herself a little shake and twisted to look at Saul. "Saul, home." The dog whined, obviously not liking the command, but she narrowed dark eyes and pointed at him. *"Home."* He whined again, but this time he trotted to the back door, shooting wounded looks at her every few feet as if he expected her to change her mind and call him back. She pulled out her phone, and a few seconds later the back door opened, and Saul slipped into the house with one last mournful look over his shoulder. Lei sighed. "Sometimes when he thinks I'm being stubborn, he tries to disobey like he knows better." She shook her head. "Damn dog."

There was such fondness in her tone that Dante found himself leaning forward. "Does he think he knows better . . . a lot?"

"Every damn day." She threw the four-wheeler into gear and edged them out of the lean-to. From the tension in her narrow shoulders, she would have liked to have torn back to where she'd found the purse, but she took them down the narrow path at a reasonable speed. The trees reaching over the path discouraged any speed close to sprinting, and Dante still had to duck to avoid getting clocked.

"You run out here a lot?"

"It's our property." Again, that thread of anger and fear was present in her voice. The unsub hadn't invaded her home, exactly, but he'd dirtied what was once a safe place for her. Knowing what he did of Lei, Dante suspected she'd be out on that path again within a day, just to prove to herself that she wasn't terrified out of her mind, but she wouldn't lose herself in running. She'd be on alert and ready for confrontation.

Instead of grilling her, he satisfied himself with studying the trees as they cruised by. Dense forest. They were right on the foothills of the Cascade Mountains, and since the closest pass was Loup Loup Pass, time had left Stillwater mostly untouched. The town was too far for Seattle residents to live and commute, but just close enough so that people fleeing city life skipped right over it in favor of Wenatchee or Bend or Spokane.

Lei and Emma had chosen well.

He mulled that over as Lei took a turn, tension bleeding back into her body as they traversed the last mile. "Why cadaver dogs?"

"Because no one deserves to stay lost." She barely spoke loud enough to be heard over the engine. "Most of them didn't turn up dead of their own volition. Someone killed them and dragged them out into the middle of nowhere in an attempt to keep their deeds hidden." Lei glanced over her shoulder at him and brought the four-wheeler to a stop. She turned it off. "Those victims deserve to come home. Their families deserve closure. And the monsters who put them in the ground deserve to be brought to justice."

Just like Travis Berkley was. "You don't have to feel guilty for what happened. It wasn't your fault." Again, against his better judgment, he reached out and touched her arm.

Her dark gaze flicked to where he'd touched her. "Thank you, Agent Young. I've spent the last twelve years just waiting for a man to come along and let me know that it wasn't my fault that my psychotic boyfriend raped and killed twenty-one of my sorority sisters. Now I can move on with my life and take up charity work, get a corporate job, marry some handsome former football star who's started to let himself go, and have three-point-two kids. How did I ever survive this long without your permission?"

Dante jerked his hand back. "That's not what I meant."

"Isn't it?" She climbed off the four-wheeler and started into the trees. "I've met men like you before. They see a broken, fragile thing in need of protection. I don't need your permission to move on. I know it wasn't my fault. Even if I was suffering from crippling survivor guilt, the work I do helps people. Discounting that with some bullshit pat answer that I've heard a thousand times is not helpful. I expected better of someone on Britton's team."

Shit. He *did* know better. Dante sat there for several precious seconds, calling himself seven different kinds of a fool. He was a goddamn professional, and he'd been after Lei like some lovesick puppy. He scrubbed a hand over his face. "You're right. I'm sorry."

She stopped and seemed to really look at him. "I mean, I get it. You're a profiler, and it's your job to psychoanalyze everyone around you, but do me a favor and shelve that crap while we're together. I've had enough of shrinks crawling around in my head. I don't need you there, too."

"I admire you, to be honest." He joined her on the ground and followed her through the gap between two trees. Their destination was obvious—a bright-pink purse nailed to a tree. "Not many people would have survived what you did. Not only survived but flourished." He still sounded like he was babbling, but there was no help for it. He wanted to repair the damage he'd done with his careless comment. "My question about the cadaver dogs wasn't rooted in why you felt the need to help find the lost ones—it was the method. There are a lot of jobs, both in police departments and in the private sector, which would accomplish the same thing. Your friend holds one of them."

Lei stopped a few feet from the tree and took a deep breath. When she released it, she rolled her neck. "Damn it. Look, I'm freaking out right now. We were safe. We moved on, as much as you can ever move on. I'm used to people looking at me like a circus sideshow freak, so I snap back first and ask questions later." She gave a half smile that didn't reach her eyes. "Shall we collect the evidence?"

"Yeah." Dante dug his phone out of his pocket and snapped pictures from every angle. He noted the card with Lei's name written on it in the same careful block lettering that they'd found on the postcard. There wasn't a chance in hell of keeping her and Emma out of things, not with the unsub sneaking onto their property and delivering gifts. If they ignored him and the bread crumbs of evidence found in Berkley's cell, he would just get more aggressive. That might be the right play in some situations, but this wasn't one of them. The chance they had to save the two missing girls meant the whole situation required careful handling. He didn't like playing by this unsub's rules—the good guys weren't likely to come out ahead as long as they did—but their priority had to be keeping the kidnapping victims from becoming murder victims.

A chance, no matter how small, was something they had to pursue.

He pulled on a pair of gloves and passed the Ziploc back to Lei. "Hold this, please." They'd go through the purse once they were safely back at the house. Stillwater's sheriff should be there at that point, and he could officially process the evidence and see that it got to the Seattle PD. Dante was authorized to do it himself, but he needed this to be as official as possible. He wanted this case wrapped up in a goddamn bow once they caught the unsub.

Dante extracted the purse and the bag with the card in it and put them into the Ziploc Lei held. The purse looked like one that would be owned by a college girl, and he suspected it would lead back to one of their missing victims. Once Lei sealed the bag, she passed it back to Dante.

Neither of them spoke as they climbed back on the ATV and headed for the house. What was there to say? He didn't have comforting words to cover up the truth—the unsub had made this into a game, and Lei was at the very center of it.

◆ ◆ ◆

Lei didn't draw a full breath until the house came into sight. She wished she could blame her nerves on Dante's comment, but it wasn't the truth. The safest she'd felt since she found the purse was with him behind her on the four-wheeler, his big thighs bracketing hers even as he tried to be polite and give her space. She knew better than to rely on a man to take care of her—she *did*—but there was something just soothing about his presence, as if he'd sanded down the jagged edges inside her simply with his proximity.

She'd bet he could walk into the middle of a brawl and have both sides talking about their problems over a beer inside of fifteen minutes.

Isaac's cruiser was out front as she pulled up, and she battled the nearly overwhelming urge to sprint into the house and make sure Emma was okay. With a sheriff and an FBI agent keeping her company, Emma was as safe as a person could be. Lei was the one traipsing out into the woods where the killer had lurked.

And recently, too.

She'd had time to think about it while she was driving back. She'd taken that same route the day before yesterday, though she'd veered to the ten-mile loop instead of turning back at three. He could have been out there, watching her, waiting for the opportunity. She shivered despite herself and shut off the engine.

"Lei."

She turned and found Dante's fathomless dark eyes threatening to pull her under. She knew his type. He wanted to protect everyone from the darker threats in life. If she let him, she had no doubt he'd do whatever it took to keep her and Emma from harm, including taking over.

Which was the one thing she couldn't let him do, no matter how tempting she found the idea.

She took a deep breath. "Yes?"

"We'll find him." He climbed off the ATV and offered her a hand.

For a second, she actually considered ignoring it just to prove a point, but Lei didn't have the energy for pissing contests to prove what a badass she was. She'd made her point back there in the forest, and Dante seemed to have paid attention. Being petty now wouldn't do anything but make her look like a dick and potentially damage their working relationship with the Feds.

Or that was what she told herself as she took his hand.

Her reasoning sure as hell had nothing to do with the insane desire to feel Dante's skin against hers. He helped her down but didn't immediately release her. His calluses were twin to hers—courtesy of weight lifting and too many hours with guns in their hands. He opened his mouth, and she just reacted, snatching her hand from his and taking two large steps back. "No."

He raised dark eyebrows. "I didn't say anything."

"But you were about to." The words sounded stupid when she said them aloud, but Lei didn't have the capacity to put her anxiety into coherent sentences. The strange spark between her and Dante was trouble in the worst way. She didn't *think* Britton would allow a sociopath onto his team, but Travis had fooled everyone around him until the very end.

You know damn well that Dante isn't Travis. You're using that as a shield to keep him at a distance.

Yeah, I am. So sue me.

Dante looked at her for a long moment, and she had the crazy suspicion that he could see down to the heart of her and know that the thought of letting someone new close to her—even a little—scared the shit out of her. Finally, he nodded. "Another time." He headed for the house before she could ask what he meant by that.

It didn't matter.

They'd get through the case, find the killer, and they'd both go back to the lives they were living before meeting each other. Simple. Lei turned and looked at the tree line, forcing herself to take a mental sidestep. She and Emma had worked too hard to survive to be brought down by some half-assed version of the original. Fanboy letters. Threats. All that relatively harmless bullshit, they could deal with. Someone actually going so far as to murder . . .

No, they would get through this.

She turned slowly, dragging her gaze over each individual tree, her fingers itching for the gun in her holster. No stranger jumped out to present a target, and she wasn't paranoid enough to carry her gun around in her hand . . . yet.

The day's still young. Anything could happen.

That's what she was afraid of.

CHAPTER NINE

By the time Lei made it into the house, everyone had congregated in the kitchen. Someone—probably Emma—had cleared off the small kitchen table they rarely used for anything other than a place to pile junk mail en route to the trash can. Now, it held the purse they'd retrieved.

Clarke had her phone out and was clicking pictures as Dante removed each item from the purse and laid them in a neat little row on the shining wood of the table. Lei walked over to stand next to Emma, silently cataloging each thing he set down. Gum. Six different lip glosses. Three tampons. Birth control pills. A hairbrush. A half-empty bag of Rolo candies. An overfilled key chain with keys, knickknacks, pepper spray, and a fluffy pink feathered thing. And, finally, her wallet.

Dante flipped through it, his curse low enough that Lei was half sure she'd misheard him. "Luna Henderson." He said her name like it was familiar to him, which didn't make sense . . .

Lei crossed her arms over her chest. "Who is Luna Henderson?"

Clarke shook her head. "One of the missing sorority girls."

The walls came crashing down around her. Lei blinked, half expecting to find the house a crumpled ruin. "That's not how it works," she whispered. There were no missing girls. They were all accounted for.

That was part of the nightmare, the truth she had to live with. This killer was supposed to be a copycat, which meant the killing should have stopped the second he left that house. There was no room for *missing* in that scenario.

Isaac shifted closer to Emma and Lei, as if he could step between them and the truth she saw brimming in Dante's dark eyes. *Reality is never pretty. But just once, I'd like the silken lies instead of the barbed truth.* Wanting the comforting lie just delayed the moment when she'd have to face reality. Lei pressed her lips together but finally made herself speak. "Please tell me what happened." There. That sounded tight and professional and not at all like she was in danger of spinning out of control.

There were rules, rules she'd lived with since the night when everything changed. The night that had never really ended. Not for her, and not for Emma.

As if sensing her thoughts, Emma found her hand and clasped it tightly. Whatever it was, they would face it together, just like they always had.

Dante set down the wallet. "On our way back to Washington, we got word that there were two missing girls from the Omega Delta Lambda apartment. The PD didn't realize they were gone because half the campus goes home or travels for spring break. Luna Henderson is one of those girls."

There was more. She could see it. "And what else?"

"Berkley left us a little bread-crumb trail to follow, and we think it's connected to the missing girls." Clarke held up a photograph. It could have been any clearing in any forest in ten different states. Lei leaned forward, automatically categorizing the trees, looking for turned earth or any other indication of a recently dug grave. There was none . . . but then, there wouldn't be.

"We have no proof other than the photo and coordinates, but there's no denying Berkley is involved. Whether the copycat sent him the photo on his own or Berkley orchestrated the whole thing is up for debate. Ultimately, it doesn't matter right now. What matters is finding those girls."

They had to have been in contact before the most recent murders. It was the only thing that made sense. Which made it that much more plausible that they were partners, rather than the killer acting as a devoted fan.

Clarke flipped the photo, revealing two numbers scribbled in black ballpoint pen. "The coordinates are for an access road in Mount Baker–Snoqualmie National Forest. It's about—"

"An hour and a half from here." The pieces clicked into place, faster and faster. Lei suspected she wouldn't be allowed to sit this one out, even if she were so inclined, but now Travis and his pet had made sure of it. If those coordinates led to an access road close enough to drive to, it couldn't have been a clearer invitation if he'd . . . She stopped. "Let me see the card."

Dante hesitated, but something on her face must have convinced him, because he passed over a pair of gloves and the card, still in its bag. Lei pulled on the gloves, her mind going perfectly blank, as if she'd shut off the last light and stood alone in soul-sucking darkness.

Open it.

It looked like any card envelope found in grocery stores across the country. A tasteful blue of thick paper. The letters of her name looked similar to the block lettering on the picture—and on the postcard that arrived with the hair—but Lei was no handwriting expert. She opened it carefully, but the flap had been tucked down rather than licked. *No DNA samples there.* Inside, there was a card with a picture of two puppies sprawled in the middle of a pristine green lawn. The text read Missing you.

Her stomach lurched, and she had to stop and take several careful breaths to fight down the nausea. It was just a card. It wasn't going to release a cloud of anthrax and kill her. That wasn't Travis's style. No, this was pure psychological warfare, and she was better than this, damn it.

She gritted her teeth and flipped the card open. *Come play with me.* Followed by the same coordinates written on the picture.

It took her two tries to speak past her dry throat. "Someone wants to be sure I'm part of this."

"Don't go." Emma spoke so softly it was almost a whisper. "He already did so much damage. Let the cops handle it. It's their job."

She looked at her friend and saw the same trapped-animal feeling reflected back from those blue eyes. Emma had to know that trying to stay out of this—to stay safe—was futile. They would be drawn in one way or another. Better to start now, on her own terms, than have the bastard force her hand later on. At least if they moved quickly, she had a chance to save those girls.

Even if, in her heart of hearts, Lei knew they were both already dead.

She checked her watch. "Are the local police going to organize a search? We need to start moving now." It hadn't rained in the last week, so that was at least something they had going for them. Saul could scent through pretty serious weather conditions, but it was distracting for both him and her.

"They're already on their way. We were coming here to get you."

Before they were distracted by the purse. She nodded. "Give me a few minutes to change and get my things together and I'll be ready. Emma?"

"Coming."

They strode upstairs and into Lei's room without a word. The dogs were nowhere to be found, so Emma must have put them in the kennel on the back porch when Isaac arrived. "Give me two." She went into her bathroom, stripped out of her sweaty running clothes, and took a fast shower. There was no point in drying her hair, so she threw it up into a ponytail that would keep it out of her face while they searched. Next, she dressed in a pair of jeans and a tank top. Shorts would be better, but there were blackberry bushes and brambles littered all over these mountains, and she liked her skin right where it was. Next came thick socks and her hiking boots.

Common knowledge said that most killers wouldn't haul a body more than one hundred yards from any given access point, but this guy wasn't most killers. He'd issued a challenge directly to her, which meant he knew he'd be tracked by Saul and had planned on it.

She stopped in the middle of lacing up her boots. It could be a trap. It probably *was* a trap.

It didn't matter. She had to go.

Lei found Emma perched on the edge of her bed. Her friend burst to her feet the second she opened the door. "You can't go."

"I don't have a choice."

"That's bullshit. There's always a choice." She clenched her hand so tightly that Lei had no doubt there would be half-moon imprints from her fingernails. Emma lifted her chin. "He's going to try to kill you."

"He's going to try to kill both of us." She said it gently, but now wasn't the time for pretty lies. The thought of losing Emma, of her delicate life force being snuffed out . . . It stole Lei's breath. She pressed her lips together in an effort to get control. *Focus on the facts. No matter how this plays out, you were always prepared for Travis to come for you someday.*

Yeah, but it was supposed to be theoretical.

She swallowed hard. "You'll be safe here. You have Prince, and you have the security and the safe room. He can't get you."

"You think I'm worried about *me*?" Emma looked like she wanted to shake her. "I'm not the one traipsing out into the woods the second he called. Even with the cops and Feds, he knows you're coming, and he's prepared. All it would take is you getting separated from the rest of them, and he could take you—"

"He won't take me," she cut in. Lei crossed to her friend and gripped her shoulders. "We survived the worst he could offer, Em. We lived. He didn't win then, and he won't win now."

Emma's lower lip quivered, but she made a visible effort to hold herself together. "I can't lose you."

"You won't. If he comes for me . . . I *will* kill him." Truth. Cold, hard truth. It should have made her feel better, but she couldn't shake the feeling it wouldn't be as simple as pointing a gun and pulling the trigger.

Emma covered her hands with her own. "Promise me. Promise me if you see that son of a bitch, you won't hesitate. No jury in the country would convict you, Lei. You know that. I couldn't stand it if you died. *Promise me.*"

"I promise."

Dante spent most of the ride on the phone with Detective Smith. Smith was just about as thrilled as one might expect about the idea of a search and potential rescue. It was outside his jurisdiction, but if they found bodies, they would be sent to Seattle rather than the little local hospital. He sent two men to assist, but that was all he claimed he could spare.

It irritated the fuck out of Dante.

Jurisdiction mattered—it had to—but there were two girls missing, and with each minute that passed, it became less and less likely that they'd find them in time.

"Calm, Dante." Clarke spoke from the driver's seat.

He realized he was holding his phone in a white-knuckled grip and forced himself to set it down. "That's rich coming from you."

"Yeah, well, only one of us can be the emotional one, and I called dibs."

To distract himself, he twisted around to look at Lei. She sat behind the driver's seat, her dog curled near her feet. The massive beast took up most of the space and appeared to be asleep. Lei, on the other hand, looked just as tense as he felt. Tension lines bracketed her mouth, and she held perfectly still, as if any movement might start a domino effect of fidgeting and worry.

"We'll find them," Dante said. He didn't know what it was about this woman that made him want to step between her and the rest of the world, but it went beyond white-knight complexes. His early dating history was full of damsels in distress—soft women who needed him, who wanted nothing more than to rearrange their lives around his. It never worked out, and usually ended badly in the process.

After a while he'd stopped trying.

Lei was as different from his exes as a Pit Bull from a show Poodle. So damn strong, but brittle around the edges. Scarred beyond the extensive list of physical damage Berkley had dealt. Those scars hadn't stopped her any more than her fear had—from what he could tell, it hadn't slowed her down in the least. If anything, it seemed to fuel her forward, a warrior goddess who wasn't quite at home in her own skin.

She glanced at him, and her lips twitched in what was probably supposed to be a reassuring smile. "Yes, we will find them. Whether we find them dead or alive is something else altogether."

"Does it make a difference for the search?" It was something he should have asked before now, but she'd been so confident her dog could do the work, he hadn't questioned it. It wasn't false confidence—she had the track record to support it—but her track record featured heavily in the dead rather than the living.

She reached down and petted her dog's head. When she looked at the beast, her features softened, and he got a glimpse of the woman she might have become if life had put her on a different path. "It makes a difference. Saul is better with the dead, but if I have something from one of the girls, he can track it." She met his gaze, once again the woman who'd been to hell and back and lived to tell the tale. "The dirty clothes you requested should work fine."

He'd anticipated that request, so the detectives from Seattle were bringing something from both girls. "Good."

Clarke took a turn, following the sheriff's car in front of them. He led them off the main highway and onto a pitted asphalt road on a sharp incline. Dante leaned forward to look out the windshield. Trees converged on the road, creating the feeling of driving through a tunnel of reaching arms that only waited for the moment they stopped to snatch them up and drag them into the greenery. His skin prickled at the thought.

One would never know they were only an hour from Everett, and slightly more from Seattle. It looked like a different world out here.

Sheriff Bamford pulled onto a shallow shoulder, and Clarke guided their car in behind him. She glanced at her phone. "This is it."

Dante climbed out and walked around to open Lei's door. She gave him a look but didn't say anything as she exited the car, quickly followed by Saul. Clarke walked over to talk to Sheriff Bamford, which left them the illusion of privacy. "How does this work?"

Lei pulled her bag out of the car and went through it, checking it with the methodical movements he'd seen in soldiers about to leave on a mission. "If this isn't all a red herring, then the target parked his car here and either walked or carried the girls into the trees. Even if he carried them, Saul should be able to catch the scent. Most bodies are left or buried within a hundred yards of the access point, but we can't assume that's the case since the whole point of this is to make me jump through hoops like a dancing monkey." She set the backpack on the ground next to her and turned a slow circle. "There are a couple of potential access points. There, there, and there." She pointed to each of them in turn.

They didn't look like much to Dante. One was definitely a hiking trail leading north from the shoulder. The other two could have been animal trails or just some flattened-down brush, but this was Lei's expertise—not his. He nodded. "What do you need from us?"

"Space to work." She glanced over as another car crawled up the road. "Saul's smart enough to know your scents aren't the ones he's looking for, but there's no reason to muddy the water." Lei gave something resembling a smile. "And, really, the only one who's likely to be making mistakes is me. I need to be able to focus on him with minimal distractions. Normally, I request the other searchers give me a good fifty feet."

"That's not an option this time." Fifty feet might not seem like a lot, but with bushes and tree roots and the trees themselves blocking the other searchers' views, the unsub could stage an ambush and hurt or kill Lei before Dante could reach her.

She nodded. "I know."

Two men got out of their car. Even in hiking clothing, these two wouldn't be mistaken as anything other than cops. It was in the tight set of their shoulders and the coldness of their eyes as they took in everything and processed it. The taller one, a black man with a shaved head, stepped forward and held up two sealed bags. "We have the requested clothes."

"Hold tight on that." Lei gave herself a shake and stepped forward. "Those are a backup. Wait here, please." She shot Dante a look. "This might take a while, and it'll probably be boring."

"We'll follow your lead." And they'd keep her safe in the process. He didn't think for a second that they'd find live women at the end of this search, and from the tense expressions on every cop there, they all agreed with him.

It's not always about happy endings. Sometimes it's just about getting closure for the families left behind and ensuring the unsub isn't free to kill again.

Cold comfort, if ever there was such a thing.

Cases like this—with high kill counts and exceedingly manipulative unsubs—were almost enough to make Dante second-guess his decision to join the FBI. They made him wonder if maybe he should have followed in his father's footsteps and gone to college to be a brain surgeon.

Lei turned to where Saul lay and shrugged into her backpack. Instantly, he went from being a bored dog to high alert, his eerie gray eyes focused entirely on her. She moved off the road and toward the first access point. "Saul, search."

CHAPTER TEN

There was nothing quite as pure as a search. Lei's entire world narrowed down to Saul, watching his body for his sign that he'd caught a scent. Decay worked in strange ways, the chemical breakdown starting roughly four minutes after death. There were a lot of factors that went into how fast a body would decompose, but it hadn't rained in a week, and it wasn't nearly warm enough to speed up the process, either. The initial murders had taken place two days ago, which meant if these two girls had been killed with the first three victims, the bodies were still plenty fresh.

Saul's nose was good enough to pick up the scent regardless, but an extra couple of days would have made a big difference in the strength of the odors. Ultimately, it didn't matter. The killer had two girls, which meant it wasn't as simple as tossing a body over his shoulder and hiking in the woods. He had to have traveled the same path a few times, and even with planning, that would leave evidence.

It also meant at least one of the bodies would have been left for a period of time.

Saul scratched at the dirt near what looked like a game trail. His sign. She motioned to the cops and then moved to him. "Search, Saul."

He trotted into the woods, his body language intent. What little hope she had of finding the girls alive died. They were gone, and their killer had brought their bodies this way. She followed Saul, keeping one eye on him and the other on the surrounding area.

There were plenty of popular hiking trails in the area, especially considering how close they were to the coast and the massive population that sprawled from Seattle up to Bellingham. This wasn't one of them. They were too far from any kind of view, too deep into the Mount Baker–Snoqualmie National Forest to interest even the most avid hikers. The only people who came out here were park rangers and people up to no good.

The trees crowded her, and even though she could hear the footsteps and low murmurs of the cops behind her, the feeling of being well and truly alone permeated the area. It could have been just her and Saul out there, doing the one thing they were trained to do. She checked her watch. Saul had to take regular breaks, but they were covering ground faster than she'd anticipated.

Too easy.

Sweat beaded along her hairline and made her shirt cling to her skin. Tension bled into her body as she turned a slow circle, surveying the area. "Saul, hold." They were at a bottom of a shallow ravine, the ridges rising roughly ten feet on either side of her. It wasn't a great distance, but the incline was sharp enough so that she couldn't see much over the top. A great spot for an ambush.

Saul whined, ready to get back to the search. Lei turned and met Dante's gaze. "It's not likely that he could have hauled a body up there, even if he wanted to." The job would take two people and waste a whole lot of energy. "But . . ."

"Nothing to stop him from doubling back." Dante nodded. He spoke softly to the rest of the cops. The other four backtracked to where the ravine started and split, the detectives from Seattle heading up one side and Clarke and Isaac going up the other. Dante rejoined Lei and nodded. "We can keep going."

It was possible they were trampling evidence, but she hadn't been lying when she touted Saul's skill. If the killer *had* doubled back with the body for some reason, he'd find the trail. *All these games. All this wasted time.*

She wanted to call Emma and check in. Hearing her friend's voice would go a long way to reassuring her that this wasn't some kind of bait-and-switch trap designed to separate and destroy them.

Focus on the search. Focus on Saul. Emma can take care of herself.

She had to believe that. Any other possibility would cripple her, and there were two missing girls who depended on her to bring them home—one way or another. *Stop being so goddamn selfish for once in your life.* She took a breath and then another. She despised that snide voice, hated that it dragged out the dark poison inside her and forced her to acknowledge it.

Easy enough to comfort herself with the good she was doing in the world when there was nothing at stake. She might make a living out of finding the dead, but the dead would never hurt her. They wouldn't barricade her in a room and do unspeakable things to the people she cared about. They wouldn't hunt her down and try their damnedest to kill her.

The first time she was faced with real stakes—real danger—and all she wanted to do was rush back to the fortress she and Emma had created to reassure herself that the one person she cared about in this world was safe. The only person who really knew what she'd gone through that night and the months—years—afterward when she'd crawled her way back to something resembling normalcy. Her parents didn't get it, though they tried their best, and she never doubted their love for her. Emma's parents didn't even try. All she and Emma'd had in those darkest of days was each other, and their easy friendship had deepened into something true and lasting.

And maybe more than a little codependent.

Focus.

"Saul, search." She spoke through gritted teeth. They were well past the hundred yards from the access point. She'd known it was a possibility, but every step they took ratcheted up her tension and threatened to distract her.

Saul didn't have that problem. He followed the trail through the ravine, and when it ended, he led them north. Lei fell back a little, her paranoia fluttering in time with her breath. "It's too easy. Saul's good, but he usually loses the trail a time or two in the process. It's like this guy dragged her on the ground to ensure we went exactly where he wanted us to, like good little pawns." She *hated* feeling manipulated. This bastard had them backed into a corner, and there was no way out but through. They couldn't abandon the search just because he *wanted* them to search.

The girls. Remember the girls.

Dante touched the gun he had tucked into a shoulder holster. "Feels like we're a day late and a dollar short."

"Yes. And there's going to be hell to pay as a result." Lei kept following Saul, forcing her leaden legs to move. There was no overt reason for the dread threatening to send her spiraling into despair. It wasn't a search like any other, but she'd been on the trail of monsters in the past. She and Saul had found victims of serial killers, abusive spouses, and—the ones that kept her up at night—child predators. There was nothing this killer could have done that she hadn't seen before.

That was the problem, though. She *had* seen it before.

She stumbled to a stop, silently cursed herself, and pushed forward again. *You are stronger than this. You have to be.*

"Lei." Dante's voice stopped her.

She started to snap that she was fine, but he wasn't an idiot, and she was about as far from fine as a person could get. "Yeah?"

"We'll get him. One way or another, we'll get him."

It should have felt like a false promise, but when Dante spoke with such quiet confidence, she almost believed him. Ultimately, it didn't make a damn bit of difference. They'd gotten Travis, and that hadn't stopped the nightmare. It had only postponed it. The only way to truly end it was to follow through on her promise to Emma and end the threat once and for all.

But murder was still murder, and neither Dante nor the rest of the cops would be willing to look the other way if she cold-bloodedly cut down their suspect.

Shelve it. Breathe. In . . . one, two, three . . . out . . . one, two, three.

She focused on her deep inhales and exhales as she followed Saul through a gap in two trees and stopped cold. "Saul, hold." Instantly, he lay down. He looked at her expectantly, but she could only stare at the scene in front of them.

They were in a small clearing—possibly the same clearing in the picture the Feds had retrieved from Travis—and before them lay two girls. They were on their backs, their hands demurely folded over their stomachs, their eyes closed.

They could have been sleeping if not for the ragged gashes to their throats.

That was bad, but it wasn't enough to have her stomach trying to force its way out of her mouth. No, it was the fact that looking at those two dead girls was like looking into the past. The blonde wore a cheerleader uniform from the University of Washington, just like Emma had back when they were in college. The Chinese girl wore a yellow sundress that could have come from Lei's closet when she was eighteen. Bright and pretty and completely out of place in this clearing.

Dante stopped next to her. He didn't touch her, didn't do anything but offer support with his proximity. "I'm sorry."

"Me, too." She swallowed past her dry throat. "I have to reward Saul."

"Don't go far."

"I won't." She could feel eyes on her, and it made her skin crawl. The problem was that Lei couldn't tell if it was someone standing in the trees and watching her or the cops now looking at her like she was some kind of plague carrier. Even Isaac didn't approach as he moved to the bodies to examine them.

Lei dug the bright-red ball out of her backpack and threw it for Saul, her mind a million miles away. The first trio of murders had re-created the originals, but these two were specifically geared toward Emma and Lei. Everything from the search to the victims themselves . . . It was a lot.

How the hell did he find two doppelgängers in the same sorority in Seattle, of all places?

The coincidence seemed astronomical, no matter how much planning went into it. Saul bounded back with the ball, and she threw it again, making sure to keep him in sight. The rules of the game kept changing, and she couldn't take anything for granted—not even her dog's safety.

She pulled out her phone and cursed at the lack of service. *Emma is fine. I'm sure Emma is fine. She's most definitely fine.* Wouldn't it be a stroke of genius to draw them out here and then attack while they were too far away to help and Emma couldn't call out for reinforcements? Lei held her phone up, but the bars remained stubbornly empty.

"Emma is fine."

She jumped. "Isaac, I didn't hear you come up."

"Yeah, I noticed." He smiled, but not like he was particularly happy about something. "I know she doesn't think much of me, but I put two people on the house to keep her safe. Whoever this sick fuck is, he won't touch her."

If there was anything positive resulting from Isaac's crush on Emma, it was that he felt invested in her safety. His people weren't exactly elite soldiers, but maybe an obvious police presence would be enough to deter the killer from trying anything.

She hoped.

Lei pressed her lips together. "I'll feel better when we get off this mountain."

"Me, too." He searched the trees as if expecting an attack at any moment. "I've run through these parks since I was old enough to be unsupervised. I've never worried too much about anything worse than a fall happening—until now." He dragged his hat off his head and smacked it against his thigh. "Screw this bastard for taking away that feeling."

She almost pointed out that the dead girls behind them were more important than his feeling safe, but Lei managed to keep her mouth shut. Isaac wasn't a bad guy, but he didn't have much in the way of empathy. Everything came down to how it affected him and the people he cared about. He might not be ready to launch a vendetta because of the two strangers who had died, but this killer had threatened Emma and made Isaac feel unsafe, and *that* would provoke a response.

Lei didn't care about why he helped them, as long as he did.

Saul trotted up and dropped the ball at her feet with a happy doggy grin. She knelt and dug through her backpack to get the bowl and a bottle of water for him. "You did good, boy." Once he was happily lapping it up, she sat back and watched the cops process the scene. Despite never having worked together, to her knowledge, the Feds and detectives moved as a cohesive unit. One of the detectives peeled off and headed back for the car—presumably to call out for backup and all the personnel required to process the scene and haul the bodies out of there.

She felt Isaac looking at her, as if waiting for her to break down into hysterics. "You don't have to babysit me. This isn't the first crime scene Saul has found."

"It's different."

Yes, it was. These girls were dead because of *her*, even if it wasn't her hand that had held the blade. It didn't matter that the killer was the one playing games. She was more than willing to play. She wanted to scream for him to target *her*, because at least she knew the attack was coming. If he killed her, maybe it would end. If she was the one who pulled the trigger, then it would *definitely* end.

You know better. It doesn't end until Travis is dead.

It would be a long time coming. California hadn't executed a prisoner in roughly ten years. Lei wasn't exactly an advocate for the death penalty in general—there were too many human errors possible in trials to kill someone over, and reversing a death-penalty sentence was nearly impossible—but she knew for a fact that Travis Berkley was guilty and deserved to die.

He was only thirty-five. He could live for another forty years—longer, even. Hoping he was shanked in the shower was all well and good, but if it hadn't happened in twelve years, it probably wasn't going to. Travis was too smart to get into direct confrontations he didn't know he could win.

She frowned. *Wait, that doesn't make sense.* Lei pushed to her feet and paced a few steps. Travis didn't do direct confrontation. He was sly and too smart for anyone's health, but he was the bogeyman in the closet—he waited until he knew he'd have the upper hand and he'd ambush. This—the mind games and the task of tracking these girls—didn't fit. It was too in-your-face and showy. The first recent murders weren't, but everything that came after didn't fit the profile.

"Lei?" Dante walked up, watching her closely. "Is everything okay?"

Isaac took that as his cue to head to Clarke and offer to help take pictures of the scene and area. Lei was thankful for the slightest bit of privacy. "This doesn't fit the profile."

Something like respect filtered into his dark eyes, and it was like the clouds parted and the sun kissed her face. Lei rocked back on her heels, trying to get control of her response. Dante was gorgeous, no doubt about that, but she had more important things to focus on than the strange feeling in her stomach that roiled whenever he got close.

Dante nodded. "You're right. We haven't had the time to sit down and work one up, and because we were working with a copycat, some of it would mirror Berkley's original profile. But this doesn't fit. It's more than transferring them from the sorority house. He brought them out here solely to play games with you. This is a hoop for you to jump through." He motioned to the dead girls. "Berkley is smart enough to pull this off, but—"

"He's more likely to slip through my window in the middle of the night, murder me, and slip out again without being caught. Everyone would suspect it was him, and he'd get off on the fact that they might suspect it but couldn't really prove anything. That was what did it for him—being the smartest motherfucker in the room. But he doesn't need anyone else to tell him that he is. This guy does."

"You're right. It changes the rules." His shoulder brushed hers, the tiny contact grounding her. She had no right to that comfort, and he probably didn't even realize he'd done it, but she didn't care. Lei didn't have the ability to lean on anyone, and she wasn't going to start now, but for the first time in more than a decade, she didn't have to be the strongest person in the room.

She crossed her arms over her chest and forced herself to move a few extra inches away. "How long until they can move the bodies out?" She'd done her job. She'd jumped through the hoops the killer set. She wanted the comfort of her home's four walls and locks between her and the rest of the world.

Stop that. That works for Emma. If you cower now, you'll never stop.

Right then, looking down at a dead version of herself, she could see how cowering would be a legit option. Lei took a breath and then another. *No.* She glanced over to find Dante watching her with an unreadable look on his face. "I'm sorry, did you say something?"

"A couple hours until the medical examiner gets here and we're able to retrieve the bodies." He shifted closer, eating up the distance she'd put between them. "I can send Clarke back to the house with you if you need to go. Or Isaac, since you know him a bit better."

She almost said yes. She wanted time and space to get her head on straight and take the necessary step back to be able to look at this as if it were a case she wasn't directly affected by.

No, not affected—targeted.

But that was the exact reason she couldn't afford to fold. This wasn't the end. She had every suspicion that the killer somehow was watching. Even if he wasn't, the cops *were*. Lei squared her shoulders. "We'll stay."

CHAPTER ELEVEN

Dante could tell that Lei wasn't really okay. It was there in her too-wide eyes and the way she held herself perfectly still to avoid shaking. Even her dog seemed to know something was wrong because he kept shooting her worried looks even as he panted happily.

That said, she wasn't in danger of falling apart at that moment, and the crime scene was as fresh as it was ever going to be. "If you need something, I'm here."

She opened her mouth like she'd shoot him down but finally gave a jerky nod. "Thanks."

There was nothing else to say. Hovering over her might piss her off and distract her, but it wouldn't help these two girls find justice. He kept one eye on Lei and walked back to where Clarke and Sheriff Bamford stood looking down at the bodies. "Interesting posing."

Clarke nodded, her blue eyes narrowed. "This guy is supposed to be a sexual sadist, and he posed them like they're innocents."

"They *are* innocents," Sheriff Bamford growled.

"Yeah, no shit." She waved that away. "I don't mean in reality—I mean his perception of reality. Berkley is a textbook sociopath. He sees everyone around him as a means to an end, and he saw his victims as subhuman. He got it up enough to rape them before he killed them, but that was less to do with sex than it was to do with power. He debased them and made them suffer before he took their lives."

Dante studied the women on the ground. "We'll have to wait for the ME, but their poses are night and day from the others." He'd seen pictures of how the other three victims were found. Those girls would have passed for Berkley's victims. These wouldn't. "Either he's slipped his leash, or he's so hyperfocused on Lei and Emma that he's raised them to worship status." Neither option was a good one. With the unsub acting as a copycat, they could at least partially anticipate his moves. If he was off the rails for some reason, he could strike anywhere, in any way.

The thought had Dante checking to make sure Lei was in sight. She sat against a tree, Saul curled up against her leg, both woman and dog watching the proceedings with wary gazes. Clarke shifted, bringing his attention back to her. He pulled out a pair of gloves. "We have to go over this scene before something else happens to contaminate it. If we can get a good layout set up for the techs, that will make everyone's life easier." Not to mention get them all off this mountain sooner rather than later.

Detective Smith returned from the cars. "They'll be here in"—he glanced at his watch—"a little over an hour."

"Plenty of time to get started." They'd taped off the part of the clearing where Saul had led them through—which meant the unsub had most likely hiked in that direction. He knelt next to the tape, careful to keep himself off the trampled weeds. Dante wasn't much of an outdoorsman, but he'd spent enough time around outdoor crime scenes to know what to look for.

"Clarke, come here."

"What's up?" She joined him on the ground.

"This looks like two sets of prints, doesn't it?" He pointed to the indentations where someone's heel had pressed into the ground as they strode forward. About a foot to the right of it was a second set of much smaller footprints. But only one. Dante whipped around. "There's blood under the girls." It had turned the ground a dull red, though their bodies covered most of it.

"And?"

"And Saul didn't need their clothes to track them up here. He tracked a corpse." He met his partner's gaze. "If one or both of them were bleeding, they'd have left a trail that even you or I could have followed—*and* they would have run dry long before they got here." He'd need the ME to confirm, but Dante knew he was right. He felt it in his gut. Though he didn't believe in the woo-woo the same way some cops did, enough experience honed a person's instincts. Murder was his job—in a lot of ways, it was also his life. "One of those girls walked up here, and he killed her here." The question was *why*.

Actually, no, that wasn't the question at all. Easier to carry one dead body than to carry two. Equally easier to subdue one terrified woman than to subdue two. *Smart of him.* But if he was weighed down with a body, the other girl could have . . . Dante leaned forward, noting the depth of the footprints. Those girls weren't particularly large—they were actually on the lean side. Unless one of them had disproportionately large feet, there wasn't a damn reason the smaller set of prints should be deeper than the larger.

Unless she was carrying the dead body.

Goose bumps rose in a wave down his arms, and he fought down a shudder. What the unsub had done to the other three girls was horrific. But forcing a girl to carry her dead sorority sister up several hundred yards into the woods and then killing her . . . There weren't words to describe how monstrous that was. "Mark the prints."

"Sir, yes, sir." But there was no bite to Clarke's voice. She must have realized the same thing he had, because her blue eyes took on a haunted look. "We'll find him, Dante."

"I know." Even as he said the words, memories rose. They didn't close every case. There were always ones that drew out too long and went cold. Sometimes a new killing would revive it years later, but in some the unsub never revisited that MO. There was no closure for the families and no peace for the victims.

This would be different. He wouldn't allow Lei and Emma to live the rest of their lives looking over their shoulders for the predator who seemed focused on them.

They moved around the clearing in ever-widening circles, but aside from the prints, there was no convenient note left detailing the unsub's plans or a knife with his prints and the victim's blood on it. The bodies themselves were the biggest clue, and they didn't want to shift them until the ME arrived.

Dante checked his watch and then looked at Lei. Her adrenaline rush couldn't last forever, and if he let her crash here, he'd have to convince her to let him carry her out of here. It wouldn't do a damn thing to help her feel more in control—but getting her home would help. "Why don't you take Lei back?"

"Me?" Clarke shook her head. "No way. I don't do the babying—that's your department." She hesitated, her blue eyes losing some of their edge. "Hell, Dante, why don't you just talk to her? She looks like she needs it."

He couldn't argue that, but it felt like the height of selfishness to take even the smallest moment away from the case, especially with the two dead girls lying there in witness. "You have this handled."

"That's not a question, so I'm not going to treat it like one. No shit, I have it handled. I could process a crime scene in my sleep, and even these three guys aren't enough to irritate me more than normal."

"Be careful. We don't know where he went. He could still be around."

She raised her eyebrows. "I could say the same to you. It's not *me* he's fixated on. It's her."

With that comforting statement, she turned back to speak in low tones with Sheriff Bamford.

Dante walked to Lei, letting Saul see him coming. The dog hadn't left her side once she'd stopped throwing that ball, and he must have picked up on everyone's tension, because his big body shook with a silent growl when Dante got too close. He raised his voice slightly. "Lei."

Her eyes flashed open. "What's wrong?"

"Nothing's wrong." Aside from the obvious. He held out a hand. "Let's go."

"They haven't finished processing the scene yet."

From the stubborn set of her shoulders, she was as likely to bite his hand off as take it if he offered to help her up. Too damn bad. Dante leaned forward, blocking out her vision of the bodies. "Emma is probably worried sick, and your dog is hyped up from how rattled you are. You can't do anything more for these girls here. Let's go back to your place. We'll call Britton, talk, and figure out a plan of attack."

Her gaze sharpened on him. "A plan of attack."

Knew those would be the magic words. Lei didn't do well with inaction, and if she wouldn't accept traditional comfort, he'd give her something else to focus on. "Yes. We're not going to sit here and wait for him to strike again. He's not a ghost. He's a man, and men make mistakes. We'll find it, and we'll exploit it to find *him.*" He held out his hand again. "What do you say?"

"I say that sounds like a plan." She carefully placed her hand in his and let him pull her to her feet. "Saul, come."

They turned and walked back the way they'd come. Dante watched everything and nothing, trying to follow any sudden movements between the trees. If the unsub had been there to see them find the bodies, he doubted he'd stuck around. The man was too smart to be caught so easily, but stranger things had happened.

"He'll have wanted to watch."

Surprise flared at her mirroring his thoughts, and then he kicked himself for feeling surprise. Lei's need to face down everything she feared would have resulted in her doing plenty of research on the kind of monster Berkley was. Her job would only further that requirement for knowledge. "You're good at this."

"I have to be." She shrugged and stepped over a fallen log. "I didn't know. I was dating Travis for months, and I had no idea that he was capable of what he did. I've done everything I can to make sure I never make the same mistake."

He understood it, even if she was wrong. He'd bungled trying to explain that last time they talked, so he chose his words with care. "There are degrees of predators. From Gein to Dahmer to Bundy. Some of them you might not look twice at, but if you have a conversation with them, red flags will start flying. And some of them can fool people who train most of their lives to hunt killers."

"Travis is no Bundy," she said flatly, her voice stripped of all emotion.

He wasn't so sure. Berkley's spree killing was too over-the-top to be compared to Bundy's long years of murder, but they shared key similarities when it came to personality. "Knowing what I do about his family, he was taught to lie from birth. That kind of social conditioning makes it easier to fool people who aren't expecting it. You didn't know to watch for it before—you do now." Dante should stop there, but something about this woman disconnected the brakes between his brain and his mouth. "Do you trust anyone besides Emma?"

"I trust Britton."

He smiled despite himself. "He does inspire trust, doesn't he?" Britton was larger-than-life. Every single person on his team admired him, even if they didn't always agree with him. Some of them downright worshipped him. He'd played the role of savior to countless victims over the years, though usually in cases not as extreme as Lei's and Emma's.

Just a little normal murder. Right. I'll make sure to bring that up in conversation next Christmas—further proof of just how far I've walked into the shadows.

Lei ducked under a branch. "Britton was the first one who looked at me without any doubt that I was telling the truth. That kind of thing makes an impression." She breathed out what might have been a sigh of relief as they reached the access point where they'd parked the cars. "We made it." Dark humor lit up her eyes. "I don't suppose the killer will decide to try his luck and ambush us so we can put an end to all this bullshit here and now?"

Dante made a show of looking around. "It doesn't seem like it."

"Pity. I have a lot of aggression to work through."

Lei drove. Once they hit the main highway, she knew these roads better than Dante did, and she had too much nervous energy to just sit in the passenger seat and hold still. Through it all, she kept shooting looks at the man beside her. She hadn't misread his dry humor before. When they'd first met, she'd had him pegged as a by-the-book kind of guy, and nothing she'd seen since then had disabused her of the notion. It wasn't that he had a stick up his ass, exactly, but he held himself a little too tightly. This wasn't a guy who relaxed with a beer after work and kicked up his boots on the coffee table to watch whatever sports game was on.

No, she'd bet her last dollar that Dante spent his free time going over cold cases or doing further work on whatever active case he had.

She . . . liked that about him. She liked that he took the job seriously, that he'd been doing it long enough to be good at it, but not long enough for bitterness to take hold and sour him to the world. He still cared. He might have created a careful shell around himself to keep the darkness at bay, but in the center of it, he was still a good man.

It drew her like a moth to a flame. No, that wasn't right. Her attraction to Dante wasn't dangerous, exactly. It was more the feeling of coming home to find a single light left on and knowing with utter certainty that she wasn't alone in the world.

But then he looked at her, and the carefully banked heat in his dark eyes gave the lie to all her thoughts of comfort and safety. Dante might not burn her to ashes . . . but he might light the match so they could burn together.

How selfish can you be, Lei? You just drove away from two dead girls who were only in that place because of you. *Ogling the beautiful FBI agent and thinking about how you'd like to burn for him . . . No. Just no. He's not for you. No one is.*

The voice in her head sounded a whole lot like Travis.

To distract herself—distract both of them—she checked on Saul in the backseat—asleep and twitching with doggy dreams—and said, "How does a rich kid end up in the BAU?"

Dante huffed out a soft laugh. "You sure you didn't get some training from Britton on the side?"

"Nope." Though Britton had offered to give her a tour of BAU offices if she ever made it to the East Coast. She knew what he was trying to do, and she wasn't exactly opposed to the idea of being a federal agent . . . but she had Emma and Saul and their business in Washington. She couldn't leave all that behind to run off to chase serial killers, and the BAU didn't have a canine division. Her skill set wouldn't fit, and she'd be starting from the ground up.

She still thought about it sometimes, though.

"How did you know?" When she hesitated, he shifted in his seat to face her. He'd managed to control the heat she'd seen earlier, and he was every inch the professional Fed again. It made her want to ruffle his feathers. Dante gave a slow smile. "Walk me through it and I'll answer whatever questions you have."

He *had* to know how tempting that was. She had a lot of questions. "No circling. No changing the subject."

"Deal."

Like shooting fish in a barrel. "Your suit is a little too big, but it's a much higher quality than your partner's. Your grammar is damn near perfect, and the way you carry yourself is as if you're used to being listened to and watched. It's easy to fake having money, but you downplay all these things, which makes me think your parents aren't too thrilled that their son joined the FBI instead of following in his daddy's footsteps to be a"—she considered—"doctor?"

Dante grinned, his teeth a white flash against his dark skin. "Brain surgeon."

"Of course." She'd bet Dante was just as meticulous as his father had to be in order to excel at a profession like that. He'd no doubt done his research on her, but she felt compelled to offer, "My father is a professor of psychology at UCLA, and my mother is a licensed therapist."

His eyebrows rose, though there was no surprise on his face. "Makes for living your childhood in a fishbowl."

"That's what it felt like sometimes." Perfect Lei Zhang, daughter of two equally perfect parents, in their devastatingly perfect life. Except when it wasn't perfect. They might have saved their fights for behind closed doors, but there were still fights. Not that they'd allow anything so imperfect for their only daughter. There was no room growing up for messy emotions, because her mother would force her to sit down and talk through it until she wanted to rip out her hair. Some things needed to just be felt without being analyzed to death, but that wasn't a luxury she was allowed. *Poor little rich girl.*

Dante settled back into his seat. "People come to the FBI from all walks of life, so coming from money isn't exactly a point against me, but we also deal with a large variety of law enforcement agencies. I don't try to hide it, exactly, but there are enough things about me to get people's hackles up without throwing money into it."

Because he was a black man. She opened her mouth, paused, and shook her head. *Keep it light—as light as it can be, considering the current circumstances.* "Let's be honest—no one likes the Feds."

He laughed. "That's true enough. Okay, you have questions—let's get to them."

She checked the time. They had barely fifteen minutes of driving left. No chance to circle around what she really needed to know, so she didn't bother. "You met with Travis."

Instantly, Dante was gone, and the FBI-agent mask replaced his warm smile. "Yes. We found the photo in his cell."

She didn't want to ask, but she made herself do it anyway. "I need to know how that conversation went." *I need to know when he's coming for me.*

"Are you sure?"

Not in the least. "I wouldn't ask if I wasn't."

He sighed. "It would have been a more pleasant conversation if you asked my favorite color or what my favorite subject in school was."

"We don't have the luxury of pleasant conversation." But she found herself wanting to know, despite that. *Selfish.* "What is your favorite color, Dante? What was your favorite subject in school?"

Another flash of those perfect teeth. "Green and history. Yours?"

"Gray. Chemistry." Once upon a time, her favorite color was pink, but there was no room for pink in her current life. She pressed her lips together, letting herself have a full ten seconds of peace over what passed as a normal conversation. *This is what it could have been like if we'd met under different circumstances. Just a guy and a girl and a perfectly normal first date.*

Except for the fact that he's an FBI agent, I train cadaver dogs, and my ex is a mass murderer.

She focused on the road in front of them, pocketing the warmth in her chest to hold close later, when things invariably got worse—because they would before this guy was caught. "Travis?"

For a moment, it seemed like he might not answer, but he finally said, "Berkley wants us to think he has control of the situation. Whether he actually does or not is up for debate, but he has some kind of connection to the unsub because he had possession of that picture with the coordinates on it."

"There's more." She could see it written all over his face.

Dante nodded. "He expressed interest in you, asking after you, and there were a couple books in his cell that make me think he's been following your career."

Something cold and painful lodged in her chest. She gripped the steering wheel, staring straight ahead. It was one thing to suspect that Travis had sicced his animal on her. It was something else entirely to consider that he'd kept such a close watch on her for the last decade. Oh, she hadn't been in hiding—all it would take was a couple of Google searches to find out her job—but it still felt as if she'd been dunked in filth. It tainted everything she'd done to date to imagine him reading through the articles, that smug look on his fucking face.

Breathe. He's still in prison. You are still alive. You won.

It didn't feel much like winning. It felt like she'd just bought herself a little time, and now she'd have to pay the piper.

No.

Travis thought he owned her. He'd always thought that, though she hadn't recognized it until much later. She was a pretty toy that he'd played with until he became bored, and then he used her to play a different kind of game. Now he wanted to do it again.

Breathing slowly did nothing to stem the panic building with each heartbeat. "I need to pull over." Her words came out calm and almost detached. A small mercy, that. She turned onto an old logging road and put the car in park. It wasn't enough. The metal and plastic and leather comprising the car felt like it was being crushed down around her, cutting off the air in the cab. "I just . . . I need a few minutes." She jumped out of the car and slammed the door.

Lei was distantly aware of Dante following her out onto the dirt road, but she couldn't focus on him when she was so close to coming apart. Twelve years. *Twelve years* . . . and Travis was still fucking up her life. She ran her hands over her face and up into her hair, yanking out her ponytail holder. It shouldn't make a difference that he was checking up on her, but with two dead girls in the forest who could have been her and Emma's sisters, there was no avoiding feeling hunted. It didn't matter if Travis's hand held the knife or if he'd worked with someone else to do it—his fingerprints were all over this.

He couldn't let this go. He couldn't leave the job half-finished.

She spun on her heel and almost ran into Dante. He stood there, steady as the mountain at her back, his calm rolling over her in waves. Lei shuddered, her pieces rattling together in a sound she could almost hear, for all that it wasn't physical. She needed the steadiness he represented. Her own failed to keep her on her feet. It took everything Lei had to keep her voice contained, even if her words were their own form of weakness. "I have one more question."

"Ask."

This was her chance to back off, to regain some semblance of strength. Of independence. To not let fear win.

She couldn't do it. Not with Dante standing so close, offering her something she desperately needed even though he didn't put into words. She had the sudden feeling that she could have asked him damn near anything, and if it was within his power, he would have given it to her. No questions asked.

She didn't need the world. She didn't need anything extravagant. She didn't even need to be saved, not really.

All she needed was to lean on someone else, just for a minute or two, until she could pull herself together again and charge forward like she always had. She swallowed hard. "Hold me? Just for a few seconds?" The comfort ultimately didn't change a single damn thing about their current circumstances. She was still on a crash course with the past she'd fought so hard to escape.

It didn't matter. Not in that moment as he held out his arms. He kept still and didn't move toward her, giving her plenty of opportunity to reconsider. As if he knew exactly how skittish this whole situation made her—in a way that had nothing to do with the murders or her ex or the uncertainty of the future. She had no business trusting this man, or letting him hold her in an effort to soak up some of the calm he carried around him like a cloak.

Lei stepped carefully into his arms, forcing herself to go slow. She clung to his steadiness, letting him ground her with his solid body. He was so much larger than she was, his broad shoulders dwarfing hers and his arms coming easily around to hold her tight. *Safe.* His earthy scent reminded her of the national park they stood in, soothing her a little more with each inhale the same way his wide hands on her back seemed to draw out her exhales, deeper and deeper with each breath. There, in the circle of Dante's arms, her thoughts finally kicked out of their frantic circling and became linear again.

This was bigger than Lei. Bigger than Travis. There was so much more at stake than her sanity.

Whoever the killer was, he would save Lei and Emma for last. He hadn't worked up to attacking them yet, but he'd target other victims to taunt them with in the meantime. She closed her eyes and leaned her forehead against Dante's shoulder.

His big hand shifted up between her shoulder blades, grounding her further. The heat of his palm seared through her T-shirt, branding her. It should have scared the shit out of her. She'd had a man scare the shit out of her before, albeit in very different circumstances.

Dante was not Travis.

Dante wasn't even in the same stratosphere as Travis.

He stroked her back several more times, seeming to know that physical comfort was the only thing she'd be able to handle in that moment. He didn't tell her that it would be okay, or dole out meaningless words. He just held her until she took a breath and stepped back. His mouth was tight, as if holding back things he wanted to say, but Dante nodded and moved to the car.

Lei slid into the driver's seat and took a few moments to scratch Saul behind the ears. "Thank you."

"You keep thanking me." He huffed out a strained laugh. "Trust me, Lei. Having you in my arms is anything but a hardship."

She didn't know how to process that, so she turned the car on and pulled back onto the road. "I'm fine. It's okay."

Lies upon lies.

CHAPTER TWELVE

Emma stared at the message on her screen. It had dinged five minutes ago, and she hadn't been able to move since. At her feet, Prince whined and rubbed against her leg, responding to her spike of fear. She'd spent hours in front of her computer today, digging through the police records from the first set of murders, following a hunch she wasn't ready to tell even Lei about.

There was nothing to support her theory, nothing but a faint memory she'd done her damnedest to forget. A soft voice in the hallway, the tread of boots on the hardwood floor. Less than nothing to a terrified twenty-year-old. She'd probably imagined the whole thing while she lay curled up between the couch and the wall, waiting for Travis to find her and finish what he'd started with the rest of her sorority sisters.

He hadn't found her.

She shoved to her feet and paced around the room, pausing in front of the monitors showing the area around the house. Nothing. Less than nothing. It would have given her solace, but that was before the killer had managed to use the motion-sensor cameras against her. She stopped in front of the monitor showing the feed from when he'd planted the purse—because the figure with its hood pulled up and face turned from the camera was definitely a *he*.

A *he* who'd known exactly where her camera was and avoided it easily.

Maybe if she could convince herself it was *only* the motion sensors at fault, she would feel safe again . . . but Emma never really felt safe, so it was a lost cause. She stared harder at the monitors, waiting for some motion or something to reveal itself. She usually had them flipping through on a rotating basis so she could leave a blank one in case the motion sensors were triggered, but she couldn't shake the feeling that he was closing in, and if she couldn't see *every single* inch of the house, he would find a way inside. To come for her.

Crazy Emma.

Paranoid Emma.

It was nothing less than the truth, but at least she'd been able to comfort herself with the truth that her crazy was part of what kept them safe. Lei had her own way of dealing with the trauma they'd gone through, but Emma wasn't strong like her friend. She'd seen the worst the world had to offer, and she wasn't interested in giving it another shot. The veil had been torn away, and there was nothing but ugliness underneath. Even the nicest people had ulterior motives.

Isaac Bamford showed every sign of being a good man. He had a long history in Stillwater, no criminal record to speak of, and he even went to church most Sundays. Even his freaking credit score was as close to perfect as humanly possible. But he looked at her and saw a fragile creature he wanted to protect. He saw a woman who was damaged, and every bit of evidence showed that he believed she only needed the love of a good man to drag her out of the darkness. It didn't hurt that she was beautiful and he wanted to fuck her, too.

All that boiled down to Isaac wanting her to play damsel in distress to his hero. It would make him feel like a bigger man if he saved her—tamed her fears. He didn't seem the least bit interested in the truth—Emma didn't want her fears tamed.

Fear kept her sharp.

Fear kept her and Lei as safe as they were ever going to be.

She walked back to the computer and studied the e-mail that had arrived and set this whole spiral in process. She'd already tried to track its source, but it was pinged through too many servers. Even if she jumped through those hoops—and she would—she suspected it would lead back to a dummy account with a fake IP address.

The message stared at her, terrifying in its simplicity.

I'm coming, Emma.

If the killer was capable of dodging her tracking where this e-mail came from, he was capable of circumventing her cameras. She charged back to the monitors in time to see a flash of movement in the corner of the kitchen camera. *What the hell?* Emma leaned forward, but it didn't repeat itself. She moved to the next camera, the one showing down the hall, in time to see another flash of black as a figure rounded the corner.

Prince whined again, but the sound wasn't his normal plaintive cry for attention. She turned and found him staring at the door to her office, every muscle in his body tense. As if he saw something she couldn't, knew something she didn't.

Emma burst into motion. She made it to the office door in three steps and slammed it shut, not caring that she was giving herself away. If she was Lei, she would grab a gun and rush to defend her house. But Emma wasn't Lei. She was just herself, and the thought of facing down the man who'd killed five girls . . . Her breath hitched as she threw the dead bolt home and dropped the big metal bar into the brackets on either side of the door, barring herself in. It would take a SWAT team to get through that. She hoped. She slumped against the door. No other way in or out of the room, which meant she was trapped, but she had enough bottled water and food to last her and Prince for a week without rationing. There was even a small bathroom.

She was safe.

They were both safe.

Tap. Tap. Tap.

Emma launched herself away from the door and scrambled to press against the wall farthest from it. She held her breath, listening with every fiber of her body.

Tap. Tap. Tap. Tap.

He's tapping on the door the same way he must have tapped on the window so Lei would let him in.

It's not Travis.

But it *felt* like Travis.

"Prince." Her voice came out so hoarse, it was barely above a whisper, but Prince heard her. He raced over and pressed against her side, his gaze trained on the door, his hackles raised.

The killer is in the house.

If she could breathe past the terror turning her lungs to concrete, she might laugh at the absurdity of the thought. Emma stared at the door, half sure that he'd burst through despite the precautions they'd taken.

Lei.

Lei wasn't home, but she would be coming back. She'd walk into the house without realizing that there was danger.

Move.

Emma gave Prince one last squeeze and crawled to her desk. She pulled down the landline, her heart still trying to beat itself out of her chest. Two. Zero.

Tap. Tap.

She jumped, and her finger slid over the numbers. Emma gritted her teeth and started again. Two. Zero. Six.

Taptaptaptap.

She dropped the phone and shoved her fist against her mouth to contain a sob. He was *right there.* She pressed as hard against the wall as she could, her mind terrifyingly blank.

If you curl into a ball and wait for it to end like you did last time, Lei will be hurt. She could be killed.

She dragged in a breath. There was no other option than to pick up the phone and call the only person in this world who mattered to her. She'd hidden instead of fought before, and she was doing it again right now. She couldn't let Lei walk into an attack.

She picked up the phone, and this time she managed to dial Lei. Last Emma had heard, they were going into a part of the Cascades that didn't have good cell service, so when Lei answered, Emma just froze for several long seconds.

"Emma? Emma, talk to me. What's wrong?"

Dots danced across her vision and her lungs shriveled up. "He's in the house," Emma gasped.

Then the room went dark.

Lei punched the speakerphone button and tossed her cell to Dante. "I'm here, Emma. I'm coming." She floored it. "We're fifteen minutes away."

Dante looked like he wanted to rip something apart, but she didn't have time to tell him to focus on what mattered. That bastard was *in the house* with Emma. "Are you in the office or the safe room upstairs?"

"The office." Emma's voice was barely above a whisper.

This was her worst nightmare come to pass. Her fortress of a house had become a trap, and it'd been breached by that sick son of a bitch. They'd deal with *how* he got into the house once they knew she was safe. "We're coming, Emma. Is Prince with you?" Her friend would lose it if something happened to her dog.

"He's here."

She saw their turn coming up and nearly sobbed in relief. *Almost there.* "We're coming up the street. Five minutes." Dante caught her eye, holding up his phone. "Dante is going to call reinforcements."

"Don't hang up."

"I won't." She tore around the corner toward their driveway, nearly taking it on two wheels. *Slow down. If you crash the car, you can't help Emma.* It didn't matter what logic said. Her best friend was in immediate danger, and she was *too fucking far away*. "Emma, talk to me."

"He stopped tapping." A rustling, then her voice came through stronger. "Maybe he's gone."

"Don't you dare open that door. We are two minutes away." She picked up speed, sending gravel flying. In the backseat, Saul yipped in distress, but she couldn't pause to reassure him. If Emma opened that door and he was there . . . "Emma!"

"I'm here."

They came around the last corner, and the house was in sight. "We're here. Stay in the room until I call you. Don't open it for anyone but me or Dante."

"Dante?" Something like amusement curled into her friend's voice.

"Yes, Dante." She didn't look at him as she threw the car into park. "He's been with me for most of the day, so he's obviously not the killer." She grabbed the phone out of his hand and jumped out of the car. Saul tried to follow her, but she held up a hand. "Saul, hold."

He whined, looking at her with those doggy eyes, but she couldn't guarantee his safety in the house. "We'll be a few minutes, boy. You're safest in the car." He was a tracking dog. They'd practiced takedowns a little, but ultimately, Saul's nature wasn't to attack, even on command. He could do it in a pinch, but a gun worked so much better than putting her dog at risk. She paused to roll the windows down and lock the doors. *Better safe than sorry.*

Dante was already at the door, his gun out. The door itself stood open, revealing a line of sight down the hallway and into the sitting room. There was no way in hell Emma would leave it open on her own, which meant the killer had walked through their goddamn front door. She drew her gun, trying to release the tension from her body. If she shot someone, she wanted it to be on purpose, not because she was so spooked she forgot all her training.

Dante hesitated like he wanted to tell her to stay in the car, but he finally nodded as she took up a position on the other side of the opening. He held up three fingers and dropped them one at a time. *Three. Two. One.* Dante moved, stepping into the house and keeping his back to the wall closest to him. "Clear." He spoke softly, the word falling between them in the stillness of the afternoon.

Lei followed him into the house. She'd cleared it more times than she could count, first to practice and occasionally when either she or Emma got spooked. It was different this time. The threat wasn't theoretical or imagined. There was really someone in their house who meant them harm.

"We'll clear the house and then get Emma from the room. She's safe there, for the time being." Dante waited for her to nod and then closed and locked the door. "Stay behind me and stay close."

There wasn't time to argue. She shadowed his path through one room after the other. Sitting room. Bathroom. Kitchen and pantry. All empty. The back door didn't appear tampered with, but they threw the dead bolt on it as well and climbed the stairs.

Dante moved with a calm purpose that she respected even as she worked to mimic it. With him next to her, she had no doubt that if they found the killer, they would deal with him accordingly. *He made a mistake in coming here.*

The upstairs went faster. Her room. Bathroom. Emma's room and bathroom. The spare room that was mostly used for storage because none of their parents were interested in coming to visit their damaged daughters. He looked into the closet stacked high with clear plastic totes. "You said there was a secondary safe room?"

"Yes. It's connected to our closets."

"We'll check there and then head back downstairs." His mouth twisted. "I think he got out before we made it back."

She opened her mouth to reply, but frantic barking stopped her short. *If the killer isn't in the house . . .* She'd left Saul in the car. Defenseless. Lei burst into motion. She sprinted past Dante, ignoring him calling her name, and hauled ass down the stairs. It took her two tries to get the dead bolt slid back, and then she was on the porch. She flew to the car. "Saul!"

He threw himself against the partially rolled-down window, making the door rattle. She managed to unlock it, and he nearly took her to the ground trying to get out of the car. Even though he was obviously alive, she took precious moments to run her hands over his body to ensure there were no hidden injuries. *He's okay. He's fine.*

Dante slid to a stop next to her, his attention on the tree line. She turned to demand they go after the bastard—there had to be a way to track him—when the sound of a four-wheeler tore through the air. Lei shot to her feet, but it was already fading to silence as he sped away from them.

They didn't even catch sight of him.

"Fuck." Her knees went out, and she slid back to the ground, her strength disappearing like air out of a deflated balloon. She wrapped her arms around Saul, trying to comfort them both. *All for nothing. He broke into our home just to prove he could—to prove that we're not safe anywhere.*

Dante's big hand settled on her shoulder, and she didn't shrug it off. She needed the steadying from him as much as from Saul. *So incredibly weak.* Yes, she was. She'd get up in a moment and put her game face on, but right then she couldn't think past the fear clogging her throat and making every breath a battle.

"Emma? Yes, we're here. We've cleared the house. We'll be in shortly. Yes, everything will be fine."

Not fine. Never that. Right now, the false comfort was better than no comfort at all. She gave Saul one last squeeze and stood. The killer hadn't come there just for shits and giggles. He'd had a purpose. Maybe it was to hurt Emma, but since that hadn't worked out, she had no doubt that he'd left them a message of some kind. "Come on."

"Lei." Dante stepped in front of her, his hands once again on her shoulders. "You need to pack. We're putting you up in a hotel."

"No."

His brows slammed down, the first sign of temper he'd shown since she met him. Strangely, it made her like him more. He wasn't perfect—he was capable of the negative emotions to counteract his seemingly unending steadiness. "He's just proven that he can get to you where you feel most safe. Which means it's *not* safe anymore. I'm not going to let you offer yourself up as bait. We'll find another way."

It wasn't about bait. Not really. It was that she'd been made to feel unsafe in the one place in the world where she'd been guaranteed safety. That bastard had taken that from her—from Emma—and she'd be damned before she let him win. It was *their* home. She had to fight to keep from snapping back. It wasn't Dante's fault that she had a point to prove, even if it was only to herself. She wanted him to understand, but one look at his tight jaw and tense shoulders and she knew he wouldn't. For him, the only thing that mattered was ensuring her and Emma's safety. He didn't care that this place represented the life they'd built for themselves. The *future* they'd built for themselves.

She didn't say any of it. "We need to let Emma know she's safe." His jaw tightened, but she kept going. "Then we'll call Britton and figure out a game plan."

Dante couldn't argue with that, and he obviously knew it. She didn't know if he was giving Britton regular updates, but Lei had no problems going over Dante's head to get what she wanted. She might regret the distance it would create between them, but some things were more important than her fledging attraction to this man. Britton would understand why they couldn't leave the house.

And if he didn't?

Well, she trusted Britton. If hell froze over and he disagreed with her, then she'd put serious consideration into following orders and abandoning their home. She might trust Dante, too, but Dante was as emotionally compromised as she was at this point. He wasn't thinking clearly. Neither was she, to be perfectly honest. Britton, however, never ceased to think clearly, and she didn't expect this situation to be the exception to that rule.

"Let's get Emma," she repeated.

Dante finally nodded. "This conversation isn't over."

"I know." She strode back into the house, Saul at her heels and Dante behind. Lei pulled out her phone as she walked and called Emma. "We're here. You're safe. You can open the door now."

A scraping sound came from inside Emma's office, followed by a thump as she dropped the bar from across the doorway. Two locks turned, and then the door was thrown open and Emma was in Lei's arms. "Lei, I swear to God, I thought he would find a way in."

"It's okay. I'm here now." She held her friend close, turning so she could meet Dante's gaze over the top of Emma's head. "Would you mind putting the teakettle on? I think we all could use a cup."

He nodded and headed down the hallway to the kitchen. Lei squeezed Emma. "Is there anything I need to know?"

"He got through my security. He hacked our system, which should have been impossible. The security system is on a closed circuit, and my computer isn't connected to it, so even if he managed to hack me—which he shouldn't have been able to, but it's possible—he couldn't gain access to the cameras without actually being in the house." As she spoke, her shakes slowed and stopped. Tech talk had always helped center Emma before, and it would this time, too.

"We'll find out how he got in." Lei did some quick math in her head. He must have come directly from the bodies, here. There went the theory that he'd stuck around to watch them discover the dead girls. "We have to talk, Emma. I have bad news."

"Emma. Lei." Dante's voice came from the kitchen. "Get in here."

She exchanged a look with Emma, wondering if he'd heard. But she hadn't said anything damning. She kept her arm around Emma, and they walked down the hallway, Prince and Saul trailing behind. Dante stood in the kitchen staring down the dogs' food bowls. "Look at this."

Two giant steaks lay there. The dogs instantly went on alert, but Lei snapped her fingers at them, and they sank onto their haunches. "Don't even think about it." She strode over and crouched next to the meat. Neither she nor Emma would ever give the dogs a freaking steak, so it had to be from the killer. She looked up as Dante handed her a pair of gloves. Once she had them shielding her skin, she dragged a finger over the surface of the meat. It felt grainy, which confirmed what she'd suspected. "It's been poisoned."

CHAPTER THIRTEEN

Dante sealed the poisoned meat and stored it in the fridge they had set up in the garage. The women obviously needed some time alone, so he gave them as much space as he dared and made his calls from the front porch. Far enough away that he wasn't invading their home, but close enough to hear if they needed him.

This case was fucked.

He'd hunted unsubs who made a game of it, who taunted the cops, who skirted the edge of being caught because it made them feel alive to pit themselves against the FBI and come out on top. Those cases were mind trips, and when paranoia set in for the investigators, it could get ugly.

This was different. This unsub didn't give two fucks about the cops. They were a means to an end in order to get to Lei and Emma. He sank onto the top stair and frowned at his phone. Lei and Emma. Emma and Lei. They treated each other like a package deal, so he'd been treating them as the same—at least as far as this case was concerned. There was no telling if the unsub felt the same way.

There was no telling a lot of things when it came to this case.

He called Detective Smith first. Smith answered the phone, breathing hard. "Now's not a good time."

Not a good time for anyone these days. "The unsub broke into Emma Nilsson and Lei Zhang's house and tried to poison their dogs."

Smith cursed long and hard. "That fucking guy. Those dogs didn't do a damn thing and he's poisoning them? That's crossing the line, even for a serial killer."

Dante raised his eyebrows. He hadn't taken Smith for being a dog lover. "We'll need someone out here to collect the evidence."

"Get in line." He paused and seemed to gather himself. "My only available lab rats are out in the woods collecting those two girls you found. It will be hours yet before they're back and have *that* evidence processed. We had a triple murder-suicide this morning, and all my available people are on that. Stay there and keep the scene secure."

There was nothing *in* the scene to secure. Other than the meat left for the dogs, the women hadn't found anything out of place. They were currently holed up in Emma's office trying to figure out how the unsub had gotten around their security, but they'd combed the house first. Everything was accounted for. Nothing was even moved.

As much as he wanted to hover and be sure Lei was okay, the investigation wouldn't pause while Detective Smith got his shit figured out. "With all due respect, Detective, it would be better if you sent a uniform out here to stay with the women so I can be available for the autopsy."

"I'm more than capable of sitting in on an autopsy and writing up a report. You're already there, and Zhang shows all evidence of trusting you. The other one will follow her lead. Besides, even if I wanted to send a uniform, Stillwater is well out of our jurisdiction. You'll have to take it up with Sheriff Bamford." Noises sounded in the background. "I have to go. They're bringing the bodies in." He hung up.

Dante cursed under his breath. That bastard didn't give a fuck about the women being protected. He'd seen a chance to get Dante out of his hair, and he'd jumped at it. There was no fighting the order, either. The FBI was there solely on the invitation of the Seattle Police Department. If Detective Smith decided to play hardball and cut them out, there wasn't much they could do about it. While they could theoretically push Sheriff Bamford to issue his own request for help, that sort of maneuvering was generally frowned upon.

With a sigh, he dialed Britton. As usual, the head of the BAU didn't make him wait long before answering. "Dante. I'm surprised I hadn't heard from you before now."

A gentle rebuke as such things went, but Dante felt the sting regardless. "Apologies."

"No need to apologize. Clarke's kept me abreast of the broad strokes." Britton laughed softly. "She's certainly fond of texting."

Dante closed his eyes and counted to ten. It was that or he might march into the forest, find Clarke, and strangle her himself. She'd *promised* she wouldn't text Britton anymore. As the usual recipient, Dante knew for a fact that what few filters she had in person disappeared when she was texting. "I'll talk to her."

"No need. I knew who Clarke was when I brought her into the BAU." Another pause, and this time Dante could actually feel Britton focusing all his considerable personality on *him*. "I'd like an update."

Dante took him through it step by step. It felt good to lay it out. He hadn't had a chance to do more than react since they were brought in on the case. Britton listened without comment until he finished detailing his conversation with Detective Smith. "What are your thoughts?"

That was the question, wasn't it? Dante had a whole lot of thoughts and suspicions but nothing concrete. He didn't like putting gut feelings out there, but Britton valued that element as much as physical evidence when it came to his agents. "It feels wrong. We've dealt with copycats before, and while they usually deviate at some point, it usually takes more than one scene to escalate to that point. Even the ones that work with the original killer . . ." Dante went still. "You worked the original Berkley case."

"Yes."

Was he imagining it, or was there something guarded in Britton's voice now? Dante shook his head. "You remember that old theory of yours? The one about a possible partner? You might have been closer to the truth than anyone could have dreamed." *Maybe someone named Trevor.*

The Seattle detectives were still combing through Berkley's mail, but so far there was nothing that even looked like it was written in code, let alone something more obvious. The photo had gotten through because it seemed innocent enough—if strange. But that appeared to be the only interaction between the unsub and Berkley. What was more, the unsub had ensured that Lei got the information with the coordinates separate from the police—a way to make sure she stayed involved in the investigation. It was a dare, a challenge, and it reeked of unfinished business.

Britton was silent for a long time. Too long. "We've never been able to prove anything. Berkley took full credit, and Lei and Emma only ever saw and interacted with him. There was no evidence that another person was involved."

That would be important to Britton—the evidence—but Dante heard what he wasn't saying. "But you were sure."

He exhaled. From Britton, that might as well have been a string of cursing to make even a sailor blush. The head of the BAU didn't let a little thing like emotion get in the way of his doing his job—and part of his job was interacting with his agents and helping as necessary. "Berkley fit the profile, but there was something missing. The differing style of the murders isn't unheard of, but every single one of the victims who was strangled was raped, and the stabbing victims weren't."

"I didn't know that. It's not in the file."

"It is, but I didn't categorize them. Several of the victims were both stabbed and strangled, which blurred the lines and seemed to support that Berkley was the sole perpetrator."

Dante thought back over the timeline listed for that night. It was possible that Berkley had beaten Lei, left her in her room, and let someone else into the house. The only person Emma saw in the room where he gathered the girls was Berkley, but that didn't mean there wasn't a partner waiting in the wings. "If they were partners, and Berkley isn't the one orchestrating this, then that would suggest he wasn't the dominant partner."

"Careful of making assumptions. Twelve years is a long time. If there was a partner—and at this point, that's a rather large *if*—there are any number of factors that could go into them finding their independence and functioning separately of Berkley."

They couldn't take anything for granted . . . but that didn't feel right to Dante. The unsub hadn't seen any actual consequences from the Sorority Row Murders. Berkley had gone to jail, so it made sense that *he* would hyperfocus on the women who got away. His partner had no reason to go back to re-create the crimes and hunt down the two escaped victims. Berkley was the one who'd picked Lei specifically to target . . . unless someone else had guided him in that direction.

The thought of Berkley and a partner considering the sorority members to find a woman for their purposes made Dante sick to his stomach. The fact that it was *Lei* was so much worse.

He sighed. "What it comes down to is that we have jack shit—sorry about the language. I haven't had a chance to draw up a profile, but this guy is a lot different than Berkley. He's making bolder moves, and he's on some kind of compressed timeline. It makes sense that he'll either strike at the women or do something to try to draw them out, and he's got enough tech knowledge that he can get around the security they set up."

"Some of the security." In the background, a door opened, and Britton cleared his throat. "I have to go. I think it's best you stay where you are. Have Clarke come to you once she's finished with the autopsy. You have two women who have more knowledge about this case than anyone else, excepting perhaps myself. There are differences between the original murders and the new ones—mark my word. Find what those are and you'll have the first string to tug on in order to find your unsub. Good luck."

"Thanks." Dante hung up, frustration threatening to boil over. He clenched the phone in his hand and glared at it. For the first time since he'd joined the BAU, Britton hadn't had some helpful tidbit of information to share that would put him on the right path. The man had a reputation for being damn near psychic when it came to crime—he knew things he shouldn't be able to. Dante hadn't realized how much he'd taken that knowledge for granted until he no longer had access to it.

"He makes me crazy sometimes, too." Lei stepped out of the screen door and sat next to him on the top stair, a careful six inches between them. "I take it he didn't have any magical advice to dole out?"

He huffed a laugh. "No. I have more questions than answers at this point, and that imbalance only seems to get more pronounced the longer I'm on this case." He almost didn't tell her what he knew, but Lei was as deep into this mess as he was. As a trainer to a cadaver dog, she had more interaction with cops than most people, and all that interaction was official business.

More than that, he wanted to hear her thoughts, to get her perception of the new angle.

"It's still early, but it doesn't look like Berkley and the unsub wrote to each other."

"There are other ways to communicate in prison." She had her emotions locked down tight, but her hands shook where she gripped her knees.

"There are," he conceded. Dante itched to cover her hands with his own, to tell her that it would all work out and they'd find the unsub without another person dying. It wasn't the truth, though—and she wouldn't thank him for the lie. "But for the crime to so perfectly replicate the original, there had to be some significant information exchanged. Some of that was public knowledge, but a good portion the police and courts kept locked down."

"Hard to keep that information completely secret with so many people affected. The college still tried. Serial killers are bad for business." She considered. "Well, we have a serial killer now. I think Travis is technically a spree killer."

"He is, though that term didn't exist until relatively recently, but the nature of the crime edges him more into serial-killer territory. Spree killers tend to use guns—or even knives occasionally. Berkley was . . . something else." He realized he'd been talking to her as if she were another detective and coughed. "Shit, I'm sorry. I didn't think—"

"Don't be sorry." She gave him a humorless smile. "I'm not made of glass. It's been twelve years, and I might be scared out of my mind right now, but it helps to talk it through. Just treat me the same way you treat Clarke and you'll be all set."

"You're not Clarke."

She shut down, the little openness he'd earned up to this point disappearing as if it'd been a figment of his imagination all along. "I can handle it."

It seemed like every time he was around this woman, he stuck his foot in his mouth. Dante dragged a hand over his face. "I'm not saying this right."

"You don't have to explain anything to me." She started to stand.

He reacted without thinking—reaching out and snagging her wrist. It was a light hold, the barest amount of contact to get her attention, but she froze like he'd tased her. *Damn it, there goes my intentions of not touching her first.* Dante spoke quietly, not wanting his words to carry.

"I can't treat you like Clarke because I don't want to kiss Clarke. She's like a sister to me. You are *not* my sister."

Lei opened her mouth, shut it, and opened it again. "Oh."

She didn't pull away, and he permitted himself to stroke his thumb over her wrist. It was so easy to see her as larger-than-life, but when he touched her, there was no escaping the fact that she was a small woman. The skin on her arm broke out in goose bumps, and satisfaction surged. She wasn't any more unaffected than he was. "It's not appropriate or convenient, but I'm attracted to you, and it makes me occasionally say stupid things. Like I said—I apologize."

Another pause, longer this time. She finally sat back down. "You don't have to apologize. Though I don't know that my being attracted to you is a mark in your favor. I have outstandingly horrible taste in men."

She wanted him, too.

He gave himself several seconds to revel in that knowledge, in the shared attraction that could bloom into something truly breathtaking if given half a chance. There was no telling if they had a chance at anything resembling a future, but he wanted to know her. To talk to her about things that didn't directly link back to the most traumatic night of her life or the nightmare they were currently embroiled in. Dante wanted to know her favorite food, to talk about his childhood, to know her dreams for the future. And, yes, he wanted *her*.

Pack it away.

He couldn't protect Lei if he was sleeping with her—if that was even on the table at this point, which he highly doubted—and neither of them would be at their best if they were indulging in their mutual attraction. He should explain that to her, but Lei swayed toward him, a reed bending in a strong wind, and he found himself drawn to her despite all the reasons he should retreat, a magnet to her lodestone.

His lips found hers as if they'd done so a thousand times before—soft and sweet and completely at odds with the tempest raging in his chest. He wanted to deepen the kiss, to stroke his tongue along hers, to memorize her taste. He wanted all of her pressed against all of him, no clothing acting as barriers, several soundproofed walls between them and the rest of the world and hours to spend exploring her body and learning what she liked.

Lei made a sound that was almost a whimper, and then she was in his lap, straddling him as she cupped his face in her hands and took the kiss deeper. Her tongue flicked the seam of his lips, and he took that for the invitation it was. Dante ran a hand up her spine and pressed her more firmly against him and nipped her bottom lip. The move made her squirm, and he had to bite back a groan at the feeling of her pressed against him with only their pants keeping them from . . . *Fuck, get ahold of yourself.*

But there was no stopping this.

It was like the last few days had been building to this moment, a screaming crescendo of need that drowned out everything else. There was no common sense, no brakes, nothing to stop them.

A throat cleared behind them, and Lei shoved away from him. It was only his quick reflexes that grabbed her around the waist before she tumbled down the stairs. He set her on the step and moved back, turning to face Emma where she stood in the doorway, a strange look on her face. She held up her phone. "Clarke is on the line."

"Why didn't she call me?"

She raised blonde brows. "She did. Apparently you were distracted."

He dug his phone out of his pocket, and, sure enough, there were two missed calls from Clarke. *Damn.* For all his talk of keeping his head in the game, the first time Lei looked at him sideways, he was on her like some kind of savage. He glanced at her, finding her dark eyes a little glazed, her lips plumped from his mouth on hers. Sheer satisfaction derailed his guilt. She looked like that because of *him.*

She glanced at him and gave a self-conscious smile. "Busted."

"Phone." Emma's voice took on a shrill quality that pushed Dante into motion. No matter what had just happened with him and Lei,

Emma had been through a terrifying ordeal today. This was just one more shock in a string of shocks. It stood to reason she wouldn't react well to it.

He took the phone from her hand. "Clarke."

"You were kissing the gorgeous Chinese chick, weren't you? You dirty dog!"

She must have heard Emma speaking and deducted it from there—either that or she was taking a shot in the dark. It didn't matter. He wasn't going to confirm or deny. "You have information?"

"Jeez, Dante, take away all my fun. You got to take off and almost had a run-in with the unsub. I've been dealing with the local flavor and watching the mouthy medical examiner cut up bodies. Cut a girl some slack, yeah?"

He held his breath and counted to five. Slowly. "Clarke."

"Yeah, yeah. We are federal agents of the United States, and we should act like it. I've already gotten the lecture more times than I care to count, and it didn't make any impact before now, so you might as well give it up for a lost cause." A door slammed, and the background noise became muted. "I rented a second car and I'm on my way to you."

He watched Lei and Emma walk back into the house. "You know how Britton has that theory about Berkley having a partner?"

"Hmm. Hold on while it switches to Bluetooth." A few seconds later, Clarke was back, her voice tinny. "Okay, I'm here and catching up. Berkley's theoretical partner. The cops on that case already had Berkley in hand, so it didn't make sense to look too closely at the theory that there might be more than one person there. His lawyer could have used that as leverage to create reasonable doubt. Since they *knew* he was responsible for at least half the murders, if not more, they went with the perp they had."

"There should have been *some* kind of evidence of the partner beyond the MO. There was evidence of Berkley all over that place, from DNA to his fingerprints. I'm not doubting Britton—I'm more than convinced he's right at this point—but with as messy as those murders were, something else should have supported his theory beyond the profile he created."

She snorted. "You didn't read the report closely enough. There were well over a dozen unidentified prints in that house. There was some kind of party or get-together or whatever the hell sororities do the week before the murders, and those girls didn't clean worth a damn. The cops didn't look too closely because Berkley's prints *were* there."

Dante pinched the bridge of his nose. "We'll get this bastard. He can't stay away from Lei and Emma, so it's only a matter of time." It wasn't even an issue of offering them up as bait any longer. Lei was right. They would be hunted no matter where they were. At least in the house, the comings and goings of strangers would be noted. In a hotel, all bets were off.

"Listen, I was going to tell you . . ." She cursed. "What the fuck?"

The small hairs on the back of his neck stood up. "Clarke?"

"Oh, *shit*!" she yelled. Then the phone line cut out.

Dante hung up and redialed immediately. It went to voice mail. The feeling of dread only got worse. He ran into the house, nearly trampling Lei in the process. She took one look at his face and her expression fell into familiar professional lines. "What's wrong?"

"Clarke is in trouble."

CHAPTER FOURTEEN

Lei didn't spend her life conflicted. She saw her course of action and went for it. Doubts were for the past and the dark of night where there was no one to stand witness. As she stood in the middle of her living room and watched Dante frantically calling the Seattle PD and then looked at Emma curled up in a ball on the couch . . .

Conflicted.

She couldn't leave Emma. Her friend had just been scared out of her mind. Their sanctuary breached. Their assured safety ripped away. All the measures they'd comforted themselves by taking over the years . . . none of it actually made a difference when push came to shove.

Now Clarke was in trouble, potentially hurt—or worse.

She paced from one wall to the other, glancing from her friend to Dante and back again. He'd leave. He wouldn't have a choice. Even if the PD was on top of things, he would have to go to his partner. They didn't have her exact location, but that didn't mean anything. They could track her phone.

Emma could track her phone.

Lei stopped short. "Emma."

"Yeah?" Emma sounded like a ghost of her former self. She managed to stir to look at Lei, her blue eyes washed-out and tired. What she *needed* was a sleeping pill and eight hours of rest, but they didn't have that luxury right now.

"Can you track her phone? If it's not turned off?" It was going straight to voice mail, but that could mean a number of things.

Emma snorted, the first *her* thing she'd done since they got there. "I can track it even if it's turned off." She shot a look at Dante and lowered her voice. "If she ditched it, that's another story, but even turned off, there's still a way."

"Do it."

Emma hesitated, then climbed to her feet. "Prince, come." The Golden Retriever shot to his feet and trotted after her, tongue lolling.

Lei shifted so she had a line of sight down the hallway and watched Emma duck into her office. She'd find Clarke faster than the cops would, and hopefully in the hustle, no one would look too closely at *how* she found the agent. Dante hung up and cursed. "She left almost an hour ago. She could be anywhere between Seattle and here. Goddamn it, Clarke." He gripped his phone so tightly, she half expected it to shatter.

"We'll find her." Lei moved closer and extracted the phone from his hand—just in case. Then, because she couldn't resist, she took his hand and squeezed it. She wasn't good at reassurances—she'd lost that skill along with so many other parts of herself after Travis—but Dante looked so lost and furious and worried, she couldn't help but reach out. "Did Detective Smith have anything useful to add?"

"They're doing a briefing in the morning updating the new task force with the information they have from the second site." He raked his free hand over his close-cropped hair. "He'd like you to be there for it. Emma, too, though I told him that wasn't possible."

Nothing short of Armageddon would pry Emma from this house, and even then she might decide to try to wait it out. She'd do the same with their current situation. Lei glanced at the hallway. No sign of her yet. "I can't leave Emma."

"I understand. I hope *you* understand that I'm contacting Sheriff Bamford to put a deputy on the house." Dante crossed his arms over his chest. "If he doesn't have the manpower, I'll request it from Britton."

Surprise derailed her thoughts. "What? Why? That's not protocol."

"I'm aware." Nothing budged in his expression. "I'm also aware that you're targeted, and the unsub will be back. I know you don't like hearing it, but it's the truth. There's no avoiding a future confrontation with this bastard, and I'll be damned before I leave you unprotected—both of you."

She chewed on that for a moment. Part of her wanted to yell at him, to rail that they'd been just fine before he showed up and they'd take care of themselves in the future, too. But the truth was that the killer had bypassed all their security and come into the one place that was supposed to be safe. "I'll talk to Emma."

"That's all I ask." His gaze dropped where she held his phone. "You'll be safer here if you bar the doors, but I can't leave her out there." His expression flickered, as if trying to fight against a tide of fear.

Lei moved before she thought too hard about it. She stepped into him and wrapped her arms around his waist. "We'll find her, Dante." What condition they found her in was up for debate, but he was worried enough without her stating the obvious and making everything worse. Loup Loup Pass was hardly treacherous this time of year, but when the rain wet the road, it could get slippery. If Clarke was going too fast . . . She could be down the side of an embankment. *Emma will find her.* At least this time of year, she wasn't in danger of freezing to death while they searched.

Emma hurried into the room. She barely paused at the sight of Lei hugging Dante, waving a paper. "I found her."

"What?"

Lei released him and took the paper from her friend. "Emma knows her shit." She glanced at the location—closer than she'd anticipated. "She made it through the pass. It's about twenty minutes from here." *Close enough that it's possible the killer had something to do with this.*

No, that was crazy thinking . . . Wasn't it?

She was jumping at shadows, and she didn't know how to stop. Every time she turned around, this guy was pulling off something she would have thought impossible before he did it. Hauling two young women out into the woods to create a scent trail for her to follow. Managing to get back to her and Emma's home and break in without Emma's early-warning system sounding the alarm. *He might have been here before without our knowing it. The stalking didn't just magically start up with the murders. This has been planned for a long time.*

What was running an FBI agent off the road compared to that?

She couldn't say it to Dante, couldn't reveal just how paranoid she was.

"You should go. Call Isaac and tell him to bring his people and meet you there. Maybe an ambulance, too." There was one that Stillwater shared with neighboring towns, and the paramedics were mostly volunteers—just like the deputies—but it was better than nothing.

Dante hesitated. "I can't leave you here alone."

"Yes, you can." She moved to the door and opened it. "Emma has me now. I'll keep both of us safe." She waited, holding her breath. "Go."

He finally nodded as if coming to a decision. "Lock the doors. Lock the damn windows. You have your gun?"

"Yes." She wasn't going anywhere without it from there on out. She had a license to carry concealed, and if any cop in the investigation had a problem with it, they could shove off. They'd already proved that they couldn't protect Lei and Emma. They didn't get a say. Dante was different, but his loyalties were split—and rightfully so. That didn't change the fact that the only person she could rely on was Emma.

"I'll call as soon as I know something." He brushed a finger along her jawline, the touch so soft, she was half sure she'd imagined it. And then he was gone.

Lei stood there until his taillights disappeared into the growing darkness, and then she shut and locked the door. She paused, still touching the dead bolt. "The doors were locked before."

"Yes. Always."

Then how the fuck had the killer gotten inside? The security cameras being overridden was scary, but ultimately technology was corruptible—Emma's skill set was more than proof of that. Her custom-locked doors should *not* be. Emma had petitioned for some fancy locks that could be coded to them, but Lei didn't trust technology as much as her friend did. When they were installed, there were only two copies of the key made. Lei had one. Emma had the other. Hers never left her pocket when she was outside the house, and the house was *locked* when she was inside. Emma never left the house, period. There should have been no damn way for the killer to get past their locked doors and leave the front one open for Lei to find.

She turned and leaned against the door. "Where is your key?"

"My key?" Emma frowned and pulled at the chain she always wore around her neck. It held a single key and a zip drive. Lei had never asked what was on the zip drive, but Emma had carried it on her person for years. It was one of the few secrets they had from each other. Emma touched the key. "Why?" Her expression cleared. "You think he somehow got a copy of the key? But that doesn't make sense. We both carry ours on us, and there aren't others."

They'd gone so far as to hire an out-of-state guy to do the windows and doors, and Emma had done an extensive background check on him before they contacted him. There was no way *he* was connected to this.

But they couldn't afford to assume anything at this point.

Lei took a deep breath. "Dante and I cleared the house, but we need to go through it again. While we do, talk me through what happened."

Emma had given Dante a rundown, but Lei knew her friend—and she was holding something back.

They started with the sitting room. Lei checked each window's lock and tried to muscle them open to make sure it held. It only took a minute to check them all, and then she headed into the living room. "Emma. Talk."

"I did all the checks after you left. Both doors. All the ground-floor windows. Prince and I were set up in my office while I worked through the background checks I put together on the agents."

She shot Emma a sharp look. "Britton vouched for them."

"Britton is human, not the god you think of him as. He's capable of making mistakes."

She opened her mouth to argue and then thought better of it. Another window down. "Did you find anything?"

"No." Emma sighed. "Dante graduated Stanford with honors and probably could have gone into any career he wanted to in his field, but something happened. He was home during that summer after graduation, and then that fall he enrolled in the FBI Academy. That's where Britton found him, and he went straight from the academy to the BAU. He's got a decent rate of cases closed, and there haven't been any complaints filed against him that were legit. He still visits his parents every Christmas, but doesn't seem to go home that often during the course of the year."

It matched up with the tidbits she'd gleaned from his comments. Something tight inside her unraveled a little. There were no warning signs with Dante. Twelve years of hindsight gave her the ability to see that Travis *had* warning signs. She couldn't have known that he was a killer, but he'd been controlling and completely willing to level emotional abuse and manipulation at her if it would suit his purposes. She hadn't cared. She'd been too in love with the idea of him to realize that the glossy exterior covered a rotting heart and a sociopathic brain.

Dante was different.

She hoped.

They moved to the kitchen, and Lei started with the door and then moved to the small window over the sink. "And Clarke?"

"Clarke is . . . different." Emma grabbed two doggy cookies from the jar on the counter and knelt to give them to Saul and Prince. "She grew up in foster care. I'm not really sure what happened to her parents—if there are records of it, they're not electronic—but she bounced from home to home from the time she was five. After she barely graduated high school, she dropped completely off the radar for two years. The next time I found her was when she was enrolled in the academy—with Britton's recommendation."

There was a story there, but it wasn't connected to their current situation. Lei gave a mirthless smile. "Britton sure does love his strays."

"Yes, he does." Emma stood and they walked upstairs. "Both agents are aboveboard. Neither was close to California twelve years ago, and they have no connection to Travis or the Sorority Row Murders. Britton excepting, of course."

"Of course," she murmured. Lei stopped at the top of the stairs and faced Emma. "You were listening to Dante's calls."

"So were you. I was just less obvious about it." Emma shrugged, completely unrepentant. "I don't know if there was someone else there that night, but if the agents think it's possible, then it is. It changes the framework of my search, and I haven't had a chance to implement it."

No one was ever *truly* off the grid, not unless they went to great lengths and stayed out of well-populated areas. If this killer was somehow connected to the original murders, there would be a record of it *somewhere*. The search was too broad, though. Even with Emma's skills, Lei didn't have much faith that they'd somehow stumble across the lead that would crack this whole case wide-open.

They moved through the bedrooms, testing windows. Every single one of them was secure and locked. *What the fuck is going on?* It would have been a whole hell of a lot more comforting if they discovered the killer had climbed in through a window or something that they could *deal* with. As it was, he might have been a ghost, because they had no way to keep him out.

Her stomach tried to twist at the thought, but she took several calming breaths. It didn't work to distract her from the fact that they most definitely weren't safe in this house. *This is what you planned for.*

What I planned for was Travis.

This isn't him.

In a way, that was so much worse. "Let's check the safe room." They'd missed it in the first search with Dante because the killer had obviously fled the house, and getting to Emma was more important.

She had to keep moving, because if she didn't, she might actually panic. If she lost control, there would be nothing to anchor Emma, and Dante would come back to find them locked in the damn safe room, having a collective panic attack.

She strode into her bedroom, taking it in with a single glance. She didn't do clutter, so if anything had been touched, she would have known. Everything was exactly where it should be. Lei headed into her closet and shoved the hangers containing her coats to the side. It took seconds to type in the six-digit key code, and then she muscled the door open and stepped inside.

And stopped cold. "Fuck me."

"What? What's going on?" Emma started to shoulder past her and ended up clinging to Lei instead. "What the hell?"

A blanket lay in the middle of the floor, a human-size indentation on it. Lei stepped farther into the room and twisted to watch the monitors set into the far wall. They showed everything that Emma's downstairs did. All the rooms in the house, though *this* safe room included cameras in both women's bedrooms and closets. "He was here." She spoke through numb lips. He'd *watched* them.

But how?

She crouched and ran a finger over the blanket, coming up with a thick layer of dust. *Several months' worth—maybe even several years.* Lei didn't know if it was a good thing or a bad thing that he hadn't visited the room in a long time. They were never inside it. They did system checks once a month, but they were remote. Emma's office safe room was the one they'd always assumed they'd have to use, because Emma spent most of her time in that space, and Lei did as well when she was home. To get to *this* room, someone would have to bypass all the security measures in place and *walk past one of their beds.*

She shuddered, her skin breaking out in goose bumps. There was no telling how long ago the killer had been there or what he'd seen.

Long enough to figure out their habits and how they operated on a day-to-day basis.

The question was—how did he get in?

CHAPTER FIFTEEN

Dante met Sheriff Bamford at the place Emma traced Clarke's cell phone to. The man had aged ten years in the last twenty-four hours, dark circles developing beneath his hazel eyes, and his skin seeming to almost sag in exhaustion. Dante didn't imagine he looked much better.

Bamford yanked his hat off and raked a hand through his hair. They stood at a little rest stop about twenty minutes outside town. The squat concrete building wasn't much to look at, and the whole site seemed abandoned—not uncommon for the time of day. "She must have stopped here before she called me." *Damn it, Clarke, why didn't you just drive through?*

"Split up and search?"

He nodded. "You have other deputies coming?"

"They've all been on call for three days straight." Bamford shook his head. "We're not equipped to deal with this level of shit. The most crime Stillwater has seen was a B&E last year because Brent and Brandon Gilsbreath got drunk at the bar and decided it'd be a fine time for snacks. They even left the money on the counter to pay for the chips and beer they walked out with."

Typical small-town stuff. Even this close to Seattle, they had a quiet little community that boasted the belief that nothing bad could ever happen to them. Until it did. Dante wasn't there to shit on the other man's stress, but he could give two fucks if Bamford was overwhelmed.

Clarke was missing.

He left the man standing there and stalked around the edge of the rest stop again. Nothing. The highway ran to the south of the stop, cars flying past every few minutes. It created the opportunity for witnesses, but the stop was intentionally positioned a couple of hundred yards off the road. If someone snatched Clarke, all they had to do was drag her around the other side of the building and they'd be out of sight.

With that driving him, he walked until the concrete walls blocked his view. He could still hear cars when they drove past, but it felt muted there, as if the trees bordering the back side of it were closer. A chain-link fence bordered the property, but it was hardly a barrier if someone was determined. *How the hell did he know she was here?*

The unsub had been at Lei's house. He was sure of that. Not only had Emma heard him, but Saul had been in a frenzy, and both Dante and Lei heard the four-wheeler fleeing the scene. There hadn't been nearly enough time for him to drive back to Seattle, find Clarke, and follow her to this rest stop so he could ambush her.

It didn't make sense.

Frustrated, he strode to the fence and moved along it. There was no sign of tampering. Nothing to indicate the unsub had come through there. There were no other cars here, though, which meant the unsub hadn't come in his own car or there would be an abandoned vehicle there . . . He rubbed his temples, gritting his teeth against the headache pounding there.

"Agent Young."

He opened his eyes to find Sheriff Bamford down on one knee and peering at the overgrown bushes on the other side of the parking lot nearest the highway. Dante hurried over as the sheriff picked up a plain black phone. He clicked the home screen, and a picture of a middle finger, nail painted black, appeared.

Clarke.

Dante turned a full circle, but there was nothing else. Nothing to indicate what had happened to her. Slow horror rolled through him. *What if this isn't connected to the unsub?* As a BAU agent, he knew all too well how monstrous the world really was. Clarke was one of the most capable agents he knew, but when push came to shove, she was still a 120-pound woman. If someone surprised her . . .

But that didn't make sense, either. She'd been in her car when she'd called him, probably pulling out on this exact exit to get back onto the road. There was no evidence of an accident.

He must have been in the backseat. Clarke knows better than to leave the doors unlocked, but shit happens sometimes. If he hid back there and surprised her, she wouldn't have had a chance to fight back or do anything.

"You need to put a BOLO on the plates."

Sheriff Bamford sighed. "She's in a rental car. Don't even know what the plates are. I can find out, but I'll probably need a warrant and for you to file a missing-persons report to make it official."

More wasted time. Dante had never chafed under the restraints of the law. The rules were there for a reason, and they might be inconvenient at times, but they served the greater purpose.

There was no purpose in this.

His body burned with the need to sprint down the highway and search for Clarke. To call every person he knew locally and demand they help him. To . . .

He closed his eyes, inhaled deeply, and let the fresh pine scent of the surrounding trees soothe his rattled nerves. Clarke was an FBI agent with more than half a decade of experience under her belt, and she'd been a survivor a long time before she ever enrolled in the academy. If there was a way to make it out of this situation, she would do it. He needed to play this by the book even if it felt like wasting time. "I'll file the missing persons."

"Good." Bamford sounded downright relieved, as if he thought Dante was in danger of losing control and freaking out. Considering how close he'd been to doing exactly that, he didn't blame the man.

Dante headed back to his rental. "I'll follow you back to the station." He climbed into the car and waited for the sheriff to do the same. Then Dante made his calls. He started with Lei.

She answered after a single ring. "Did you find Clarke?"

"No. Her phone is here, but there's no sign of her car or her. Because she's driving a rental and we don't know the plates, I have to file an official missing-persons report to get the ball rolling on a warrant to *get* the plates." *So much wasted time.*

"Shit."

"My thoughts exactly." He stared at Bamford's taillights as they merged onto the highway. They'd have to find an exit to turn around so they could head back to Stillwater. "How are you holding up?"

She laughed, the sound a little hysterical. "Just fine, considering the circumstances."

He'd never heard her sound so freaked out, and she'd been the one to find two bodies earlier that day. *Holy shit, that was today. It feels like a thousand years ago.* "Lei, talk to me." If something had happened to rattle her, he needed to know. Too many balls in the air. Too many distractions. The danger hadn't passed for Lei just because Clarke was now *also* in danger.

"We're safe. I'll fill you in when you get back, but we're not in immediate danger." Something dark entered her tone. "We should have more information by then, too."

Something had most definitely happened. "Lei—"

"If something happened to Clarke, you need to call Britton. I'll text you a little bit later, but we're okay, Dante. I promise."

He believed her that they weren't in any immediate danger—Lei was too smart to lie to him about that—but he didn't like her dodging the question. That said, she was right about calling Britton. He couldn't leave Clarke's missing-persons report unfiled because Lei was upset. His partner's immediate safety was more important than potential emotional trauma. Lei was more than just a victim, but he couldn't afford to let his feelings for her affect his ability to do his job. Dante had to remember that. "I'll call when I know something."

"Okay."

"Stay safe, Lei." He hung up and immediately called Britton.

Despite the fact that it was nearly midnight on the East Coast, Britton answered right away. "I didn't expect to hear from you again today."

"Clarke's missing." He passed along every detail he knew, both about the timeline and the scene, but it was a pathetically small amount. "There was nothing at the rest stop but her phone. No blood. No skid marks on the pavement. No broken glass. She's just . . . gone."

"It's highly improbable that it's the unsub."

"I realize that." He tried to keep his tone even, but fear burrowed deep, turning his insides to ice. He shuddered. Dante had never, ever become emotionally involved in a case before. It was a trait that he shared with his father—the ability to take a step back and think logically no matter what was going on around him. It made his father one of the best brain surgeons on the East Coast.

This case had Dante emotionally compromised on two fronts. Clarke wasn't just his partner, she was his *friend*. And Lei . . . he didn't know what Lei was to him yet, but she was more than a chess piece within the case. "But we can't ignore any possibilities."

"Of course. You're right." Britton was silent for a long moment. "I'll send in Tucker Kendrick. He just finished up a case, so he's free. This situation is escalating at an unprecedented rate." Another pause, longer this time. "You realize this isn't a reflection of my belief in your ability to do your job."

Dante clenched his jaw against the sharp words crowding his throat. He knew Britton didn't think less of him for shit hitting the fan, but he resented feeling like his boss was handling him. "I'm aware." He didn't even mind Tucker, for the most part. The man had a mouth on him, but it was nothing compared to Clarke's.

Clarke.

Ahead of him, the sheriff turned into the police station parking lot. Stillwater's police station was a tiny little building that looked like it'd been added to the equally tiny courthouse as an afterthought. *Clarke's fate is in the hands of a man who's never dealt with a serious case in his entire career.*

It didn't matter. He wasn't about to sit back and let Sheriff Bamford blunder through trying to find her. "I'm here. I have to go. I'll keep you updated."

"I'll be in contact. And, Dante . . . you're not alone in this. We'll find Clarke."

The words comforted him, even though they had no right to. Dante knew too damn well how many people up and disappeared each year in this country alone. Sure, some of them were voluntary—people who got in over their heads or hit a breaking point and walked away from everything they'd known. But a percentage of those missing-person cases were actually murders that might never be solved. *I can't think like that.* "I'll call you when I have something to update. Lei and Emma are at their house, but Sheriff Bamford has assured me he's sending a deputy to monitor the situation."

"Good, though I'll feel better when one of our people is there. There's something off about this case, but I can't put my finger on the issue. Keep your wits about you."

"Will do." Dante hung up. He parked next to the police cruiser and got out before he could think too hard about all the things that could go wrong—and all the things that already had.

It's too much of a coincidence that this is unrelated. The odds are astronomical.

Which meant if they found the unsub, they'd find Clarke.

"I'm so sorry, Ms. Zhang. Your brother had your code and your password. Seeing as how you signed the contract with the safety feature of releasing the pass code in the event you forgot it, we were following protocol."

Lei closed her eyes and rested her forehead against the doorframe. *My brother.* Since she didn't *have* a brother, that was quite the feat. "I understand." She hung up. "How the hell did he get my password? It's just a jumble of numbers, and the only place I had it saved was on the closed-network computer."

Emma flinched. "Shit."

"*Shit* is not a word I want to hear coming out of your mouth right now." She tried and failed to keep accusation out of her tone. *This isn't Emma's fault any more than it's my fault. We're both in over our heads.* Lei took a measured breath and moderated her tone. "What happened?"

"I was clearing out the files and switching the nonsensitive ones to the other system. I dumped a bunch of your stuff into a file with your name on it and moved it." Emma's shoulders bowed. "I didn't realize you kept your *password* in a Word file. Why don't you write it down like a normal person?"

It wouldn't have made a difference if she had. The bastard had been in their house, moving through their things. She'd bet good money that if he wasn't able to find access electronically, he would have come there and done it in person. She shivered. "At least we know how he did it. Is there a way to keep him out of our system?"

"I'm trying, but . . ." Emma lifted her hands and let them drop into her lap. "He's better than I am. I'm good. Really good. But he's outmaneuvered me at every turn. I can't guarantee that I can kick him out indefinitely." She lifted her chin. "He's out now, though."

"That's something, at least." It didn't feel like much. It felt like they'd been played. All this time, she'd been so smug about her impenetrable house, and there had been someone lurking close enough to watch her sleep. "Why didn't he just kill us when he was in the house before? He had the chance." Lei came and went, but Emma was always there. Saul might not have picked up on a new scent, but he'd have sensed an intruder—of *that*, she was sure. Prince mostly stayed with Emma, which meant he stayed downstairs in her office more often than not. Maybe the killer hadn't wanted to risk facing the dogs in the effort to get to the women . . .

She didn't know. There were far too many things she didn't know at this point. All she really had was projection.

Emma's fingers clattered against the keyboard as she shuddered. "Can we please stop talking about home invasion and murder?"

"We have to face this and figure out the extent of the damage. We're not safe here." The killer could come back at any point. *Except it's possible that he's occupied with Clarke right now.* Lei closed her eyes, counted to ten, and then counted to ten a second time. It didn't calm her racing heart, but it helped her take a slow step back to look at the bigger picture.

Dante couldn't be sure the killer had Clarke, but Lei had no doubts. There was no such thing as coincidence, and it would be one hell of a coincidence if some random predator attacked the FBI agent here investigating murders linking back to Travis. No, this was connected. She was sure of it. "We need to find Clarke."

"What? Lei, we need to get someone in here to change the locks, and more bars on the windows wouldn't be amiss. Not to mention we need to change all the codes, but we can't do it online or over the phone, so we'll have to have the company send out someone to do it." Emma spoke so fast that her words almost ran into one another at the end of the sentence. "Clarke is a badass FBI agent. If she can get taken by him . . ." She shook her head. "If she can, then we don't stand a chance."

Panic. Fear. Something akin to hysteria. She actually *looked* at Emma. Her friend's hands shook, and she was too wide around her blue eyes. She wore the same yoga pants and loose shirt she'd had on yesterday, and though her hair was up in a ponytail, it had started to look greasy. *Shit.* She should have known Emma would start to lose it. *She* was starting to lose it, and Lei was usually the more controlled of the two.

"Emma, look at me." Lei bent to catch her friend's gaze. "Take a break."

"I don't need a break."

Lei grabbed the coffee cup before Emma could get to it. "Yes, you do. When's the last time you slept?"

"I *can't* sleep." Emma pulled her knees up and wrapped her arms around them. She very carefully didn't look at Lei. "Every time I close my eyes, I see him. He's wearing that fucking button-down and jeans, and there's this spot on the right cuff. I looked and looked at that spot, and it was only after he left the room with Hilary that I realized it was blood." She raised haunted blue eyes. "And then I see their faces. Not before. After."

After Travis was through with them.

Lei had climbed out the window and fallen to safety, though escaping had almost killed her. Emma had walked out of that sorority house of her own power. They never talked about what that walk had been like. She knew Emma had checked on Hilary and Kristen before she fully understood that all their sisters were dead, but only because it had come out in the trial. Even in therapy, Emma didn't talk about that nightmarish trip—and Lei didn't blame her for wanting to block it out completely. She took her friend's hands, and it struck her that she didn't know which one of them was the source of the shakes causing tremors in their clasped fingers. "Honey, you can't keep going like this."

"I can't sleep, Lei. He got inside the house before. He can do it again."

She pulled her friend to her feet. "Come on." Lei didn't bother to wait for Emma's arguing before she towed her up to the stairs and nudged her into her room. "Take a quick shower. I'll be here." She nodded at the two dogs waiting just outside the bedroom door. They were technically trained not to come in without permission, but both she and Emma slept with Saul or Prince in their rooms more often than not. "We'll all be here."

Emma hesitated, but finally nodded. She left the bathroom door cracked, and a few seconds later, the shower started.

It was only then that Lei sagged. She was close enough to the bed that she landed there instead of the floor, and she bent in half to rest her head in her hands. *Too much. Too many things have happened.* She couldn't process any of it—she didn't have the time or capacity.

The search. The dead girls. The break-in. Clarke missing.

Dante's kiss.

She settled on the last, because it scared the shit out of her slightly less than the others. If she concentrated, she could still feel his big hands on her waist, his strong body against hers, his mouth taking control the second they made contact. She should have moved away instead of forward, shouldn't have climbed into his lap with absolutely no prompting, should have . . .

Lei sighed. It didn't matter what she *should* have done, because she *had* kissed him—or let him kiss her. She wanted to kiss him again. She flat-out wanted him. She wished she could chalk it up to her being emotionally unstable because of the case and the memories that had been gliding ever closer to the surface. It would be a lie. If she'd walked into a room on a normal day with no stakes involved and seen Dante, she would have felt the same uncomfortable fluttering in her stomach, the same sheer desire. She knew that without a shadow of a doubt.

Lei had more or less given up on the opposite sex. She didn't trust people, and getting naked body and soul with another person required at least a modicum of trust. After her handful of disastrous relationships over the last decade, she'd just . . . given up. Resigned herself to a life with Emma and their dogs and their jobs. It might have been enough. It *should* have been enough.

But being around Dante had her thinking thoughts that reminded her of the girl she used to be. Before. The one who was sure she'd find love and have a better relationship than her parents had. The one who had the world at her feet and didn't know what real damage was.

What would Dante have thought of that girl?

What would I have thought of him?

The shower shut off, and she forced herself into movement. She couldn't let Emma know how close she was to breaking down. She was the only thing holding this situation together—there wasn't room for *both* of them to lose it. Emma needed strong support more than Lei did, so Lei would be that strong support. There wasn't another option.

She walked around the bed and patted the mattress. "Up, Prince. Up, Saul."

The dogs scrambled to obey, their shaggy bodies radiating sheer joy to be breaking a rule yet again. Emma slipped out of the bathroom wearing another pair of black leggings and a tank top. She disappeared into the closet and came out with another baggy sweater—this time in a deep blue—and thick socks. Her boots were next, and she sat on the edge of the bed to lace them up. "You should probably shower, Lei. I'll be okay for a few minutes."

She didn't have to say it twice. Lei swore she could actually feel the grit on her skin, and she wanted out of those clothes and into something clean. "I'll be right back." She almost called Saul to her but reconsidered at the last second. It was only a quick shower.

She walked the few short paces down the hall to her room and straight into her bathroom. Lei didn't bother to leave the door open.

There was something about being in a room with the door cracked that set her teeth on edge. Anyone could stand just out of sight—listening, watching. An irrational fear, to be sure, but it didn't feel particularly irrational after today. She locked the door, paused to check the linen closet and ensure there were no murderers hiding behind the shower curtain, and then she turned on the water and stripped.

Stepping beneath the near-scalding spray was a little slice of heaven. She tilted her head back and let the water drench her hair and just . . . existed. Lei gave herself a full thirty seconds, and then she opened her eyes and scrubbed herself down thoroughly. She shampooed her hair twice, mostly to prolong her reason for staying in the shower. But she could only leave Emma waiting for so long, so she braced herself and turned off the water. Lei dried off quickly and wrapped her long hair in a towel on top of her head. She straightened, and froze.

There, in the middle of the mirror, someone had written the words *I miss you, Lei-Lei.*

She staggered away from the mirror. Her back met the wall, bracing her, keeping her on her feet. "He's not here," she whispered, trying to make it the truth. "Travis is in prison." The truth didn't matter. Her body screamed at her to run, run, run until her legs gave out and she was miles away from this place. Until she found a city she could melt into and disappear forever.

Until she escaped Travis once and for all.

Except she never would. Travis had ceased to be a person the second dawn stole over the sky the morning after the massacre. He'd evolved into a dark god she could never escape. Some days, she wasn't sure she *had* escaped. He still took up too much space in her life, and she suspected he always would. She might have walked away from the Omega Delta Lambda house, but the old Lei had died there as surely as her sorority sisters had.

She forced herself to walk to the mirror and dragged her hand over the words. He had to have written this when he'd broken into the house earlier—either before or after he'd gone for Emma. He'd known that eventually she'd come in here to shower, and the steam would reveal the message, so she'd see it when she was at her most vulnerable.

Fuck that.

Lei kicked her dirty clothes to the side and grabbed her gun and holster. She stalked, naked, into her bedroom and then her closet. Anger pulsed in steady waves as she dressed, choosing faded jeans and a long-sleeve T-shirt, wool socks, and her extra boots. She grabbed a jacket, too, just in case. Lei slipped her shoulder holster on and, after checking her gun, added it.

She found Emma sitting on the bed, her back propped against the headboard. She narrowed her eyes at Lei. "What happened?"

"Nothing important." She shut the door and walked to the empty side of the bed. "It's been a long day."

"You can say that again."

Lei sat on the bed, mirroring Emma's position. Saul immediately rearranged himself between her and the side of the bed, and Prince lifted his head from where he'd laid it on Emma's stomach to woof softly. They were as safe as they were going to be. "Try to sleep, Emma. I'm here. I won't let anything happen to you."

Emma slid down to lay her head on her pillow and laced her fingers through Lei's. "I'll just close my eyes for a few minutes."

"Okay." Lei stared at the door. Emma held her left hand, so she could draw her gun with her right, easily. The dogs would give a better early warning than any electronic alarm that could be bypassed. Both she and Emma wore clothes and boots, so if they needed to run, they could without hesitation.

They were as ready as they were going to be.

She squeezed her friend's hand and settled down to wait.

CHAPTER SIXTEEN

Dante managed to catch a few short hours of sleep after filling out the missing-persons report for the sheriff. He'd wanted to start searching immediately, but without some kind of lead—or, at minimum, the rental car make, model, and license plate number—it would be a waste of time and resources. He hated that he could measure things by that standard, but there was no help for it.

He took a quick shower and got ready, exhaustion starting to set in. It was too early in the case to be this tired, but most cases didn't involve this amount of activity. Serial killers tended to have cooling-down periods between kills when they liked to relive the details of the murder in vivid color. As time went on, those fantasies lost their allure, and the killer was driven to murder again. And so on.

There wasn't any of that with this case.

The unsub had the feeling of someone with a plan, an endgame that drove him to keep to some kind of schedule. Whether that endgame was his or Berkley's was still up for debate, but so far there wasn't a damn bit of evidence that Berkley had enough contact with the killer to justify the belief that *he* was behind all this.

It was enough to make him wonder if Britton wasn't right and that there had been another person in that house twelve years ago.

He had to talk to Lei about that possibility, but it'd wait until after the autopsies.

Still . . .

Dante got on the highway heading for Seattle and dialed Lei. He needed to hear her voice, to know she was okay—or at least holding it together. That kiss had been . . . He shook his head. A bad idea. Lei's alibi might be solid enough that she wasn't a potential suspect, but she was still connected intricately to the case. Getting involved with her in any way was a mistake, and unprofessional in the extreme.

He didn't care.

She answered, her voice quiet. "Hey."

"Hey." He cleared his throat. "How are you doing?"

"Oh, you know, scared out of my mind and furious because I'm scared." She paused, sounding almost shocked she'd admitted that aloud. "We're fine. The house is as secure as it's going to be, the dogs are on alert, and Emma and I are safe."

"Good." He would have felt better if she'd let him cart them to a secondary location, but nowhere was really safe until they found the unsub. "I have to go into Seattle for a bit, but I'll be by sometime today. There's a theory I want to go over with you—with both of you."

"We'll be here." She gave a mirthless laugh. "Where else are we going to go?"

"Call me if you need anything." He wanted to keep her on the phone, to draw out this conversation until he could almost feel her presence, but that was selfish reasoning. "Get some sleep, Lei."

"Maybe when the sun's a little higher in the sky." She cursed softly. "Why do I keep doing that? I'm not an oversharer."

"It's okay. I'd rather you shared than kept it all locked up." He wanted to *know* her, and he wanted her to trust him enough to share some part of herself. "Stay safe."

"Yeah, you, too. I'll talk to you later." She hung up.

Dante turned his thoughts to the case as he drove through the pass and down into the greater Seattle area. They had a plethora of information, but nothing about it was helping to narrow the field any. This unsub was undoubtedly a white male somewhere between twenty-five and forty-five—probably leaning to the older end of that spectrum, considering his probable participation in the first set of murders at the sorority house. But that didn't ultimately tell them anything, because most serial killers were white males in that age range.

This unsub was also highly organized, from the way he had set up the two separate kill sites, and he had to have serious knowledge of hacking, because Lei and Emma's security system was top-of-the-line. It *shouldn't* be able to be hacked. Dante's forte didn't lie in that direction, but he was savvy enough to know that nearly everything was hackable given enough time and skill.

Their unsub had both in spades.

He'd planned these events down to the last detail. This series of murders was likely years in the making. Maybe Berkley being caught had scared him—or maybe it had been exhilarating to get away unscathed.

Dante frowned. That was the one problem with this theory—if Berkley had worked with a partner, why hadn't he used that knowledge to leverage either a plea bargain for himself or to create reasonable doubt? He would have had a good shot at the latter, and a better-than-good shot at the former. It didn't make sense . . . unless Berkley was the submissive partner. The thought raised the small hairs on the back of Dante's neck.

They were in trouble. That was for damn sure.

He made it to the morgue before the early-morning commuters were out in force, and then he just sat in his car. Clarke should be there. She should be sitting next to him, bitching about needing coffee this early in the morning, or bouncing ideas off him as she formed her own profile of the unsub.

Instead, she was missing.

And there wasn't a single damn thing he could do about it.

Dante took a couple of minutes to check his e-mail. Britton had forwarded Tucker's flight information—the man would be there around noon. Too early for him to drive back to Stillwater before Dante picked him up. He growled and then forced himself to take several deep breaths. Lei had survived this long without him standing over her. She'd be fine today, too.

He climbed out of his car and headed inside. As he strode down the hallway to the autopsy room, the scent of the building clung to the back of his tongue. Death and chemicals and something like sorrow. It had always seemed strange to him that sorrow had a smell, but he'd spent enough time around murder victims and their families to recognize it.

Detective Smith had arrived before Dante, and he spoke softly into his phone just outside the doors leading to the bodies. He held up a hand to stop Dante and hung up. "Heard about your partner from Sheriff Bamford. We'll do what we can from this end, too."

"Appreciate it."

Smith looked through the narrow windows to where Dr. Franco stood next to the two victims. "This doesn't sit right, you know? This bastard is playing games."

"Yeah, he is." He wasn't in the mood for small talk, but obviously the detective was, so Dante forced himself to smooth away any impatience. The locals wouldn't share information if he antagonized them, and snapping at Smith for no damn reason would do exactly that. "Have there been any developments?"

"There were some fibers found on Luna, but God knows how long it'll take the lab to process." Detective Smith snorted. "Won't matter anyways. Fiber and hair aren't good enough evidence to link a crime to a person. Did you know that shit?"

"I did." New technology had proved that both fiber and hair samples were inconclusive when it came to matching up with their sources. Realizing how many cases had been solved with inconclusive evidence had sent a lot of people into a frenzy. "It still helps to have as much information as possible." Even if they couldn't link the fibers back to a specific vehicle or piece of clothing, they could narrow down a number of other things. It would give them a place to start. *Hopefully.*

Smith huffed. "Guess so. We want this freak caught as quickly as possible. Both the college and the girls' parents are breathing down my neck. The rest of the sororities want a statement saying that *their* girls are safe." He rubbed the back of his hand across his mouth. "I can't make assurances like that. We don't know where he's striking next. We don't know who he is or if he knew the girls. We don't know *shit.*"

"We know that he's connected to Berkley. And to the survivors." He belatedly realized he hadn't updated Smith on the break-in. "We need to talk about that."

"After the autopsy." Detective Smith gave himself a shake and strode through the doors, leaving Dante staring after him.

It couldn't be clearer that Smith wasn't happy about being tied to this case. He was the kind of old-school cop who preferred to find the perpetrator, close the case, and move on to the next. No fuss, no muss. No politics.

Unfortunately, politics were the least of his worries at the moment. With every death the unsub racked up, the public's fear and anger would grow, and it would turn on the cops investigating before too long. These cases were never solved fast enough. It didn't matter that Smith had played things right from the start—calling in the Feds at the first sign that these murders weren't what they seemed was better than most cops did. No one liked to share or admit that they weren't totally capable of doing the job without help. It created a whole hell of a lot of resentment when they had the truth shoved in their face and had to ask for FBI assistance.

It was neither here nor there. He couldn't worry about the future or the past or Clarke. Right now, the victims demanded his full attention, and they deserved better than to have him distracted.

Dante made a conscious effort to let go of all the baggage clinging to him and headed through the doors after Detective Smith. The man had taken up the same position he'd held for the last autopsy—he leaned against the counter with his arms crossed and brows lowered. For his part, Dr. Franco didn't seem bothered by the detective's glower. He nodded at Dante. "I have bad news and worse news."

"Let's get to it." He moved closer so he could look down on the two girls. Even bracing himself for it, the shock of their features still set him back on his heels. At first glance, they were shockingly close to Emma and Lei. It was only when he looked closer that he noticed the blonde's hair was a little too uniform to be natural, and she was a little thinner. The other girl's skin was a shade too dark to be Lei, her face wider and her jaw more defined.

Still . . . too close.

"They were both killed with a slash to the throat, but their deaths were a good six hours apart, give or take." Franco moved to a point between the gurneys and motioned to their throats. "Nearly identical slash from left to right, and judging from the angle and the depth of the cut, I'd say he stood behind them while they knelt. Either that or he's at least six five." He shrugged. "They're not particularly tall for women, but I suspect we don't have a giant on our hands."

They didn't know *what* they had on their hands, so they couldn't afford to rule out the possibility that he was extremely tall, but Dante was inclined to agree with the medical examiner. The unsub would get off on the power of standing over a helpless woman, of being well out of the way so he could enjoy the way the blood arced across the ground in front of him . . .

Dante frowned. "There was a lot of blood on the ground, but there wasn't on either of the front of their clothes."

"I noticed that, too. With the blonde it makes sense, since she was killed earlier, but he had to have stripped the other, killed her, and redressed her. Or she was dressed differently before she died . . . Not my department. That's for you two to figure out." Franco pointed to two sealed bags sitting on the counter. "Their effects." He made a visible effort to brace himself. "Remember how the first murders were weird? These ones are, too. Just . . . different weird." He touched the blonde's hair. "This is freshly dyed. It's possible that our girl decided to do it the day before she died, but judging from her school ID, she's naturally a dark brunette. To get this color blonde takes some serious time, and the lightening products would agitate the skin on her scalp. There's none of that, which makes me think it was done postmortem."

"She died first."

Detective Smith roused himself from the counter. "How the hell do you know so much about hair, Franco?"

The medical examiner gave him a sour look. "My sister went through beauty school a couple years back. Trust me, I know more about hair than any man needs to." He turned back to the other girl. "Which leads me to this one." He held her hair up. "See this? It looks like it was hacked off all at once, the way you see people cut through ponytails. Unless *this* girl up and decided to cut her own damn hair, the killer did it as well."

It was roughly the same length as Lei's. Dante walked to the bags with the girls' effects and dug out their IDs. He held them up. "Close, but not close enough."

"Eh?"

"He wanted these girls to look like the two who survived the Sorority Row Massacre twelve years ago. The other three weren't quite right. These two were, but he needed to make some superficial changes." Now that he thought about it, they'd been wearing clothing that could have come from college-age Lei's and Emma's closets, at least according to the earlier pictures he'd seen of them in the case file. The blonde,

Jennifer, had on a cheerleading outfit, and Luna had worn a bright-yellow sundress. "He was sending a very specific message."

Franco looked down at the girls. "Not the kind of message someone wants to get."

"No. Definitely not." He tamped down on the urge to text Lei to make sure she was still okay. She was fine. If she needed him, she would call. His hovering didn't do a damn thing but drive her nuts. The insane urge rose to call his father and ask how the hell the man's calm never broke during surgery. Surely there were times when the patient looked a little too close to someone he knew, or maybe *was* someone he actually knew.

He already knew the answer.

His father's calm had never faltered. The man's distanced attitude didn't even falter in their home, so why would it at work?

Set it aside.

Dante studied the dead girls, wishing Clarke was there. He needed her acerbic comments to keep him focused on the present and not everything that could go wrong if he made a misstep.

Another misstep.

He'd already made a few. Being around Lei made it hard to focus, and he kept missing things he had no business missing. It wasn't unusual for Clarke and Dante to split up to work different aspects of the cases they were called in to assist with, but . . .

No use to whip himself over it now. He'd made the choices he'd made. There was no changing them. "What else can you tell me?"

"Luna was raped before she was killed, but Jennifer wasn't. He didn't cut them up the way he did the first three, and if this wasn't obviously connected, I wouldn't have any kind of way to confirm they were connected."

Luna was raped. Luna, who'd had her hair hacked off to give her an approximation of Lei. *Bet he waited until after he cut her hair to do it. And he probably killed Jennifer first to keep Luna in line—and to give himself time to dye her hair.*

He'd kept them somewhere. Would he risk bringing them to a place he owned, or would he do something like rent a hotel room? *The hotel room. Easy enough to give the wrong name if you pay cash, and any place that doesn't require ID isn't going to have much in the way of security cameras.* Another lead that wouldn't take them back to the unsub if they tugged on it, but he'd bet if they found the hotel room, they'd find the first murder site.

The unsub also had access to a car—though they'd known that by the distances he seemed to travel with ease, from Seattle to Stillwater to the access road that had led them to the bodies. Hard to say if he'd rented it, but Dante's gut said he'd already owned it—the better to prepare for the plan being enacted now.

He'd raped Luna.

Dante came back to that, to the significance behind it. His gut already knew this unsub was unhealthily focused on Lei, specifically, but this just further confirmed it.

"With one exception."

He focused on the medical examiner. "What exception?"

"Here. Remember how he carved up the other three girls? He didn't do that with these two, but he did leave this." He pulled off the sheets covering the girls so that Dante and Smith could see the jagged wounds carved into their pelvic areas. It took his brain several seconds to register what his eyes were seeing. "That's a *T* and a *B*."

"Yes, it is."

"*B* as in Berkley," Smith muttered. "*T* as in Travis."

Or Trevor. Whoever the hell Trevor was, if he even existed.

Franco grimaced. "He's one hell of a fan."

Or maybe he just doesn't want us to realize he's been part of this from the very first murders twelve years ago.

CHAPTER SEVENTEEN

Make one goddamn mistake and get trussed up like a Thanksgiving turkey.

Time had lost meaning for Clarke. The last thing she remembered was talking to Dante as she pulled out of the rest station, and the next she woke up in someone's basement, her hands and feet bound. *He must have been in the backseat.* Usually, she did a full walk around her vehicle before she got in, just to be safe. There were far too many cases out there of women being assaulted or murdered because they didn't realize they'd locked the predator in the car with them. She hadn't bothered this time because it was a rental and she was at a deserted rest stop in the middle of the mountains.

If I live through this, I'm never going to hear the end of it from Britton and Dante.

She smiled through her dry lips at the thought. It was a nice thought, definitely not at home in this dingy basement. It looked like thousands of basements across the country—concrete floors and walls, broken only by a few beams running from floor to ceiling in an approximation of where walls would be if the owner ever got around to finishing it. She was dry enough, but the whole place gave off a damp vibe that Clarke couldn't shake.

The sole source of light came from a short, rectangular window situated high on the wall. Since Seattle was perpetually cloudy and drowning in rain, it was shit for illumination. Clarke shifted, testing her bindings.

Coarse rope fastened her wrists together, her hands palm to palm. Between the thickness of the rope and the complicated knots, she didn't have a hope in hell of gnawing her way free. The bastard had taken both the knives she kept on her person at all times.

Even if she could get her hands free, the manacles around her ankles were the real problem. *Fucking manacles. Who the hell does this guy think he is?* Her bravado felt brittle, even in her head. The chain bolted to the floor had just enough give that she could theoretically make it to the bucket situated under the window, but going any farther was out of the question. Clarke really, really didn't want to think about the acrobatics involved in *that*, so she focused on how the fuck she was going to get out of this mess.

He had to come back eventually. If the only thing he wanted was to kill her, he could have managed that easily enough while she was unconscious. There was no damn reason to bring her back here and put time and effort into this setup.

Though with whatever he has planned, I might be wishing for death by the end of it.

No. She wouldn't think like that. She *couldn't* think like that. Despair might not kill as quickly as a knife, but it was just as deadly. The minute she gave up was the minute she signed her own death warrant. Dante would be frantic to find her, and Britton would send reinforcements. There was help coming.

But that didn't mean she'd sit here and wait like some goddamn princess in a tower.

Clarke shoved her hair back as best she could and shuffled to her feet. There had to be something in this basement she could use to her advantage. It was just a matter of taking a step back and looking at the situation. She'd faced worse odds before.

She just couldn't remember any specific time off the top of her head.

Damn it, no. I'm not giving up. There's a way. I just have to find it.

She refused to believe anything else.

Saul's barking brought Lei running from the kitchen. She'd finally managed to convince Emma to eat something, and now it looked like they had company. She opened the door and watched as Isaac's cruiser crawled to a stop in their driveway. "We're going to have to hold off on breakfast," she called. "We have a visitor."

Emma appeared in the doorway leading into the kitchen with a butcher's knife in her hand. Lei stared. *God, we are so broken.* She forced a smile. "Honey, I know you're not keen on Isaac, but maybe let's not threaten a police officer with a deadly weapon before ten in the morning?"

She looked down at the knife as if seeing it for the first time. "Shit. I'm sorry. I didn't even realize I grabbed it."

Oh, Emma. Lei didn't know how to fix this. She couldn't even fix herself, let alone her friend. Some things a person just had to live with. What they'd gone through was one of them. She didn't bother to try for a smile. "Why don't you put that away before he sees?" As Emma disappeared back into the kitchen, Lei turned to face Isaac.

He walked up the steps as if there were twenty-pound weights attached to his feet. Isaac swept his hat off his head as he walked onto the porch. "Lei."

"Isaac." She didn't want him there, didn't want *anyone* in their house. Dante was one thing, because his presence didn't . . . ruffle things. It was too early to really trust him, but something inside her relaxed when he was around in a way she wasn't able to quantify. She felt like she *could* trust him, which was a revelation in and of itself. The only other person who'd made her feel like that was Emma, and only because some days it felt like they were two halves of a sick mess she had no name for.

Isaac wasn't like that. She didn't have a lot of faith in his ability to do his job in the current situation. He was more than able to handle the various petty crimes that came from living in Stillwater, but they'd bypassed normal four murders ago. Her stomach lurched at the thought, but she kept her unease off her face. "What can I do for you?"

"Nothing to worry about—just a shift change. I sent Rick home to catch a bit of sleep, so I'm taking over." He seemed to notice her tension. "Is everything okay?"

The temptation rose to spill everything, to tell *someone* that not only had the killer broken into their house and threatened Emma, but he'd been there all along, poisoning their safe space so thoroughly, she didn't know how it would recover.

She couldn't do it. She couldn't expose the throbbing nerve of her fear to Isaac. Eventually, she had to tell *someone*, but it would be Dante when he finally showed back up again. He, at least, knew the full story to date and had the knowledge to help predict the killer's movements.

And if Isaac knew how scared they were, he'd set himself up in their parlor or on their porch and never leave. It was the kind of man he was. He saw a need and he filled it, regardless of whether his brand of help might hurt more than fix things.

Lei felt Emma's presence at her back, bolstering her. It gave her the strength to smile and push off the doorframe. "We're as good as can be expected."

"Yeah, it's bad business." He was mangling his hat in his shifting hands, his nerves getting the best of his usual good nature. And why not? Serial killers were supposed to be the stuff of titillating fiction. They weren't supposed to crop up in small towns in Washington State where Sheriff Bamford made his home.

She stepped back. "You want to come in for coffee or something? We have a lot of work to do today, but we can spare a little time."

"No, no, that's okay. I just wanted to let you know I'd be out here so you weren't startled by Rick's being gone." He stepped back, and his gaze went over Lei's shoulder. His smile lost its strain. "Morning, Emma."

"Isaac." She came to stand next to Lei, their shoulders brushing. Presenting a unified front. Lei was just relieved that the butcher's knife had disappeared. Emma turned to her. "I have a lot of work to do. Meet me in the office when you're done?"

"Sure."

Isaac's face fell as soon as she disappeared from view. "That woman makes me crazy." He shook his head. "I don't understand her. I think we'd suit, but she won't give me the time of day to convince her of it."

I think we'd suit, Lei repeated silently. It really was another world up here, and Isaac was a throwback to a different time. It wasn't necessarily a *better* time, but different. It wasn't her business, and Emma wouldn't thank her for interfering, but her self-control had been whittled down to a little nub from all the bullshit going on lately. She stepped onto the porch and shut the door behind her. "Isaac, have you ever thought that she just might not be interested?"

"Why wouldn't she be?" There was no arrogance in the question, just sheer curiosity.

Far be it from Lei to give relationship advice, but she had taken the first step, and now she was committed. "You know what happened to Emma twelve years ago—to both of us. That is the kind of thing that leaves its mark. It's not something the love of a good man can 'will away.' Emma is who she is. I don't know what she does or doesn't feel for you, but I'd say her signals have been pretty damn consistent." *Not to mention you look like you'd be right at home in the middle of those god-damn Christmas cards she gets from her bitch of a mother, and even if you were a perfect match in every other way,* that *would be enough to make*

Emma push you away. She braced herself, waiting for his anger, his hurt, maybe even ugly words.

But Isaac just deflated a little. "That's fair." His response made her like him, just a little. He wasn't a bad guy, but he also wasn't the right one.

Lei wasn't sure if there *was* a right one.

He gave himself a shake. "You ladies leaving the house today?"

"Not planning on it, but if something comes up, I'll let you know." Emma, of course, wouldn't be leaving, but Lei could already feel restlessness building inside her. She didn't like being locked in, even if it was in her home. She needed the freedom of movement without those four walls closing in on her. That wasn't something she was about to admit to Isaac, though. Lei hesitated. "Have you found out anything about Clarke?"

He shook his head. "She up and vanished. We have a search going for her rental, but there's been no news so far."

"Damn." She liked Clarke. Worse, Lei couldn't help feeling that if the agent hadn't been assigned to this case, she wouldn't have been taken. Maybe that was crazy talk, but the belief burrowed down deep and took root inside her. She hadn't done anything but survive something that should have killed her twelve years ago. It wasn't her fault that any of this was happening . . . but she couldn't help the guilt that wrapped around her throat in a stranglehold. "Let me know if you find something?"

"Will do." He backed down the stairs and slung his hat back onto his head. "I'll be just down the way. Holler if you need something."

"Sure." She waited for him to climb back into his cruiser before she walked back into the house and shut and locked the door. Lei leaned against the steady wood and closed her eyes. Too close. Too confining. The sheer helplessness of the situation threatened to send her to her knees. She couldn't let fear rule her. If she faltered now, she'd never get back up again.

The only reason things felt so out of control now was because the killer could be anyone. She opened her eyes. No, not anyone. She knew it wasn't her. She knew it wasn't Emma. And it couldn't be Dante, because he'd been with her when their house was broken into. Three people in a case involving . . . a lot. Lei pushed off the door and headed deeper into the house. "Saul," she called softly.

His dog tags clicked as he trotted to follow her into Emma's office. He raced around the room, not touching anything, but sprinting circles. *I'm not the only one getting stir-crazy.* Her phone buzzed, and relief made her a little giddy when she saw Dante's name pop up. "Hey."

"How are you holding up?" His warm tone steadied her. She hadn't known him long enough to let herself lean on him. She shouldn't let herself lean on *anyone*. But that didn't stop her from feeling like she was a little safer just from talking to him.

She walked to the wall of monitors and watched Isaac park his cruiser about a hundred yards away from the house—right at the first bend in their driveway. "We made it through the night. How are you? Did you manage any sleep?"

"A little." He cleared his throat. "Britton sent a secondary agent here, and we'll be heading your way later this evening. We just have a couple interviews that can't wait."

No reason to feel disappointment that there were several long hours stretching out between now and when she'd see him next. She nodded and forced a smile.

"I don't know if anything will come of it, but we can't afford to cut any corners here. This unsub might have stalked the girls through tech alone, but there's a chance he met at least one of them in person, so we have to cross all our t's and dot all our i's."

He might have met one of them the same way he met me. The thought left a sour feeling in her stomach. If it was a matter of repeating history, it should have ended there in the sorority house. It shouldn't have involved a trek in the woods and games played with Lei and Emma.

Except we don't really know what would have happened if Travis had gotten away that night . . .

Unless this *is what would have happened.*

She pressed her hand to her chest, wishing she could calm her racing heart. "It's okay, Dante. We have plenty to keep us busy."

"We didn't get a chance to talk earlier. You said you had something to tell me?"

Telling Dante now ran the risk of him dropping everything and coming to her, but holding back important information right now was the height of stupidity. "The killer managed to circumvent our safe room. He had codes. There was a blanket there, and judging from the amount of dust on it, it had been there awhile." She took a careful breath, thankful that he didn't interrupt her. "He's been watching us a long time—years, maybe."

"Sheriff Bamford is there."

It wasn't a question, but she confirmed it anyway. "Yeah, I'm watching him sitting in his car in our driveway right now."

"Are you in immediate danger?" His tone almost invited her to say yes, to give him a reason to turn the car in her direction.

"Dante, if we're right about this guy, I've been in immediate danger for twelve years. But we're ready for him—as ready as we can be. We didn't know to look for him when he managed to get into the safe room, but he won't get in a second time." She spoke confidently, either to convince herself or him. In the end, the case had to be the priority. They couldn't just sit and wait for the killer to come around again. The investigation could lead them to him on *their* terms, and that had to come first.

He cursed. "If Bamford is there, you're as covered as you can be. Keep the doors and windows locked, and don't answer the door. I mean it, Lei."

Lei laughed softly. His precautions were nothing more than what she and Emma did on a daily basis. It hadn't been enough to protect their fortress from being breached before, and she was no longer confident it would again. But hugging Dante to her like her favorite security blanket, using his presence to chase away the dark . . . She couldn't do it. She couldn't ask him to drop everything and run to her just because she didn't feel safe. "We'll keep everything locked down until you're back."

"If anything changes, call me and I'll come. I promise."

She found herself smiling despite the situation. "I will. Call when you're done with your stuff and on your way?"

"I will."

"Bye." She didn't know why she didn't just hang up, but Lei clung to the illusion of safety Dante's presence offered for a few seconds longer.

"Good-bye, Lei."

She hung up and slipped the phone back into her pocket. When she turned, Emma was looking at her strangely. "What?"

Her friend shook her head. "Nothing. You just . . . You really like him."

She started to protest, but they didn't lie to each other. "I don't know what I think. No, that's not true. I do like him. That's about as far as it goes." Given time, could it turn into something?

Lei didn't know how to be in a relationship. She didn't even know what a healthy relationship looked like. Her parents were still married, but their arguments that devolved into cold wars had been part of what drove her into Travis's fire. She'd misjudged *what* caused his fire, but that didn't change the truth—Lei didn't know how to do any of this.

But what she did know was that she liked Dante's strength and the way nothing seemed to dispel the calm that came off him in waves. There was a hint of intensity beneath that, though, and it intrigued her despite herself. "I like him."

Emma's brows drew together. "You already said that."

She gave herself a shake. "Sorry. It's not important right now." She grabbed a hair tie off Emma's desk and pulled her hair back into a ponytail. "Where are we starting?"

"Travis's known associates at the time of the murders." Emma made a face at the list scrolling in front of her. "It's too long—too many possibilities. Even if we take out the women—which I'm not sure we can at this point—there are over a hundred people on this list. And that's just the *known* associates. He could have been secret murder friends with someone he never interacted with publicly. That means we'd have no reason to look at them."

If she thought too hard about it, she'd get so overwhelmed that they'd never start. Lei grabbed Emma's cup and took a sip of her coffee. She made a face. Even if everything had changed about her friend after that night, her sweet tooth managed to prevail. "Jeez, Em, did you put an entire carton of sugar in here?"

Emma rolled her eyes, letting Lei dispel the hopelessness permeating the room. "We're going to start with a simple Google search. Even you should be able to manage that. We can cross off anyone dead or out of the country, and if they're not in this general area of the country, we'll flag them to be put on a secondary list to check if they traveled here for some reason."

It sounded like a whole lot of tedious work, but if the cops were focusing on the connections to the current victims, they weren't looking hard enough at the past. The theory that there was a second person set Lei's teeth on edge, but that didn't mean it was wrong. It would make sense. Travis had killed his way through twenty-one women over the course of eight hours. It was more than possible he'd done it alone—the prosecutor and the jury obviously thought so—but it was equally likely that he'd had an unseen partner.

She trusted Britton with her life. His instincts had been spot-on from the first moment he'd shown up in California to assist on that case. Combined with the fact that Dante obviously believed him, and she couldn't discount the theory just because she found it reprehensible. "I can manage that."

"I know." Emma gave her a tight smile. "Go pour yourself a cup of that black shit, and we'll get started."

CHAPTER EIGHTEEN

Dante picked Tucker Kendrick up at the airport. A big man with a shock of red hair, his keen blue eyes missed nothing despite the easy smile he usually wore. No smile covered his face as he tossed his bag into the backseat and took the passenger spot. "This case is one of the ugly ones."

"It is." Dante checked his blind spot and merged into traffic departing the airport. "You read the file."

"Yeah." Tucker stretched out in the passenger seat, his long legs hitting the dashboard. "Fuck, Young, did they have to give you a clown car, or did you request it special?"

"I requested it special. Obviously. I knew how much you'd enjoy it."

Tucker grinned. "It's good to see you, man. It's been too long."

They'd come up in the academy together, and both had been brought into the BAU at the same time. They saw each other semi-regularly in Quantico, but since they both ended up working with other partners, it wasn't as often as either of them would like. Dante shrugged. "Wish it were under better circumstances."

"You can say that again. I've studied the file, but Britton said you met with the ME again this morning."

Dante filled him in as they wove through traffic in the direction of the university. Even with the information Detective Smith's team had gathered, there wasn't much to tell. They didn't know enough, didn't have so much as a single string to tug on to see where it led. It felt a whole lot like they were chasing their tails while the unsub laughed his ass off, and Dante despised always being several steps behind.

Tucker crossed his arms over his chest and stared out the windshield, his gaze a million miles away. "And now Clarke is missing."

"They've put a separate team on that. We might suspect it's connected, but we don't know for sure, and so they're operating as if it's not." Dante felt pulled in a thousand different directions. He couldn't run around searching for Clarke door-to-door. He didn't even know where to start. He didn't know Seattle and the surrounding area the same way these cops did. If Dante got in the middle of their investigation, he'd be more hindrance than help.

He knew serial killers, and so he'd keep pushing forward on *that* case. He had to trust that Smith's secondary team knew what they were doing.

But where Clarke was concerned, it was a leap of faith he wasn't quite prepared to make.

Tucker cursed softly. "Britton is giving them all of twenty-four hours before he pulls every single agent who's not actively on a case and brings them here to help—and that's twenty-four hours from when she went missing." He checked his watch. "Which means they should be booking tickets right about now."

Hope unfurled in Dante's chest. Rationally, he knew Britton didn't have godlike powers to make everything okay just by his mere presence on a case, but his success rate was higher than any agent Dante had ever come across. He was the best out there, even if he wasn't in the field nearly as often as he used to be. If he was coming to Seattle to search for Clarke, the chances of her being found increased significantly.

If she's not already dead.

He tried to dislodge the thought, but it struck deep at the heart of his fear. If she hadn't been taken by the unsub, she might have been dead this entire time, and the search would only turn up her body—if it turned up anything at all.

"They'll find her," Tucker said. He squeezed Dante's shoulder. "She's tougher than all of us combined, and she's a fighter. Don't give up on her." His voice wavered ever so slightly, but Dante didn't call him on it.

Clarke was a friend to both—of course Tucker was just as torn up about this as Dante was. He sighed. "Before Britton flies in here like an avenging angel, we need to get these interviews taken care of. Detective Smith's people already talked to all the family and friends, but I want a crack at the two sorority girls who didn't live in the apartment."

"College girls might not tell their parents everything they've been up to, but sorority sisters? They'd know."

"Exactly."

Tucker watched the street signs. "Remind me, Young—did you pledge when you were at that fancy college? You know, before you broke your parents' hearts and rebelled by joining up with the FBI."

Dante snorted. "No. Fraternities weren't something that I ever found tempting." Much to his mother's disappointment. She'd pledged when she was in college and was still an active alumna of her sorority. It would break her heart to know what happened to these girls; it would strike a little too close to home. "Even the good ones were more of a time commitment than I wanted to deal with. I didn't need a brotherhood. I needed a degree."

"And yet a brotherhood is what you ended up with." Tucker frowned. "That's probably sexist. Sisterhood doesn't work, either. Siblinghood? Doesn't have quite the same ring to it."

It felt good to chuckle, as if it broke some of the tension that had been building in him for days. Tucker had always managed to find the humor in any given situation, and he used it to deflect as much as he used it for good. Dante didn't mind, because it gave him something to do besides obsess over ways he could have saved Clarke, or found those girls before the unsub managed to kill them, or been faster and caught the goddamn unsub himself when he'd broken into Lei's house. He let out a long exhale. "I misjudged this whole thing."

"You were playing the cards you had at the time." Tucker shrugged. "Contrary to how Britton operates, we're not all-knowing. You didn't make mistakes any more than you can say Clarke fucked up by going to that rest stop. This guy sounds like he had this whole thing planned down to the smallest detail." He pressed his lips together. "Actually, the only thing that *doesn't* fit is Clarke's disappearance. No way that guy knew you would be on the team assigned to this case. She went to college online, and she's got no link to the survivors or the sorority. She's the anomaly."

Dante was inclined to agree—and so was Smith. It was why he'd assigned a second team unconnected to the first. "We can't assume she's connected."

"I know. Fuck, I know," Tucker growled. "I hate this shit. I know she didn't take an unnecessary risk, but I still want to throttle her ginger ass for getting jumped and scaring the shit out of both of us."

Dante decided then wasn't the moment to point out "ginger ass" would apply to Tucker as well. He double-checked the address and took a right down a curving road. The girls they were meeting were both freshmen, so they lived in the dorms. "These girls will probably be skittish."

"Don't worry, Young. I've got my charming face on." Tucker smiled, and all the hardness disappeared from his blue eyes. It was a skill he'd possessed ever since Dante had known him, and it was a useful one, especially when it came to dealing with witnesses. They wanted to be comforted, and while Dante could usually soothe rattled nerves, when Tucker walked into the room, it was like standing in the middle of a summer day. He chased away the shadows, and people cleaved to him in waves.

He'd have made a killing as a celebrity or an evangelical minister.

Or a cult leader.

Dante parked the car and turned off the engine. "Let's go."

Ten minutes later, they were seated on an uncomfortable single bed opposite the two girls. Lacy Sanderson and Theresa Miller could have been sisters. They shared medium-brown hair that faded to blonde at the ends, and they were both swallowed up by oversize sweaters—Lacy in blue and Theresa in gray. Most of all, they wore identical expressions of awe when they looked at Tucker.

Tucker leaned forward and propped his elbows on his thighs, letting his hands lace loosely between his knees. "We just have a few questions, and then we can let you ladies get back to what you were doing before we came. Can you tell us if any of the other girls in the house had boyfriends? Especially if they were new?"

Theresa shook her head. "We were too busy to date. Luna had a guy back in Nevada, but they'd known each other since they were in diapers. The other girls went to parties and sometimes hooked up with guys."

"And girls," Lacy muttered.

Theresa bobbed her head. "Sure, and girls. But no one was seeing anyone seriously."

Tucker's smile widened, inviting them to confide in him. "Come on now. You're beautiful ladies, and your sisters were, too. You *never* dated?"

Lacy rolled her eyes. "You aren't that familiar with sororities, are you? We organize half a dozen different events through the school year, have to keep GPAs above 3.0, and we volunteer on top of all that. We aren't being dramatic when we say there literally wasn't time to date."

That made sense, especially if the unsub was a throwback to the first sorority murders. It also meant they needed to look at this from a different angle. Dante sat back. "What about teachers?"

Lacy frowned. "What about teachers?"

"Or not just teachers. Older guys. Any of them come sniffing around in the last couple weeks?"

Lacy shook her head, but Theresa frowned. "There was one guy. You remember him, Lacy. He was at the adoption fund-raiser, and he chatted up Jennifer. She made that joke about daddy issues." As soon as the words were out of her mouth, she blanched. "God, I can't believe she's gone. They're all gone. It doesn't even seem real."

Dante gave them a few seconds. "Can you describe the guy?"

"Sure. He was old." She scrunched up her nose. "Not *old* old, but way too old to be hanging out at a college fund-raiser."

Which could put him anywhere from thirty to sixty. "Okay, what else?"

"Dark hair."

Lacy shook her head. "No, he was blond."

"I think I'd know a blond if I saw him. Blond is my type—even if he was at least as old as you two." Theresa shot them an apologetic look. "It's not that I think you're old. It's just that . . ."

"Would you say he's older than me or younger than me?"

She shrugged helplessly. "I'm terrible at guessing. Lacy?"

"Close to the same age?" She didn't sound confident, though.

"Okay." Anywhere from thirty to sixty, with either blond or dark hair. Dante repressed a sigh. Eyewitness testimony was notoriously questionable. People tended to see what they expected to see, and that colored their perception. "Any identifying features? Tattoos? Something noticeable?"

Lucy shook her head, but Theresa frowned. "He was wearing another college's sweatshirt. A faded old hoodie that looked ancient." She closed her eyes and frowned harder. "I know those colors. Blue and yellowy gold." She snapped her fingers. "UCLA. He was wearing an old UCLA shirt."

UCLA.

Where Berkley and Lei and Emma had attended. It couldn't be a coincidence. Dante would bet good money that the unsub had picked that sweatshirt solely because college kids were more likely to focus on that than his face. *Maybe it's even his own sweatshirt if he went to school there around the same time as the original murders.* "He talked to Jennifer. Did it go any further?"

Lucy shook her head. "I don't think so. Jennifer was big into religion. She was saving herself for marriage, so she didn't so much as hook up with guys at parties or anything like that. I don't know what they talked about, but she went out with us after the fund-raiser and didn't mention him."

Dante had assumed hooking up meant sex, but apparently its definition was fluid. That was neither here nor there. Both girls looked exhausted, as if they'd run a marathon instead of been talking for fifteen minutes, so he nodded and stood. "I think that's about it for now."

Tucker's smile brightened. "Thanks for taking the time to talk to us. If you think of anything else, give me a call." He passed a card to both of them. "Have a good night, girls."

They stayed silent as they walked through the halls and out to the parking lot. It was only when they had safely locked the doors and pulled out of the parking lot that Tucker spoke. "Smart move on his part with the sweatshirt."

"Yeah, though it doesn't tell us a whole lot." Dante drummed his fingers on the steering wheel. "We know he staked out the sorority beforehand. He was probably at other events leading up to the murders, but something about Jennifer made him approach her."

"Didn't get far, did he?"

"Doesn't sound like it, but . . ." Dante shook his head. "If she was that vocal about waiting, she wouldn't have told the other girls if she *had* done something. That said, it doesn't sound like seduction is this guy's thing. That was how Berkley figured out his way into the house." Through Lei. "This one is sneakier. He's a stalker—he likes to watch from afar. Take his time and plan everything out to the smallest detail before he acts. I bet he knew everything there was to know about those girls before he made contact."

Tucker shifted, letting his head rest against the seat. "Does the Seattle PD have feet on the ground canvassing the neighborhood? I don't care how good he is—someone had to have seen him if he was stalking these girls for any length of time."

"They do, but if they found something, Smith hasn't updated me yet." The man's resources were strapped, but even coming up with nothing was important—it meant the unsub had stalked them electronically, and *that* could be tracked. No matter what it seemed like now, this guy wasn't a ghost, and he sure as fuck wasn't perfect. He'd made a mistake somewhere along the line. They just had to find it. "You ready to talk to the original survivors?" *To see Lei. To make sure she's really okay.*

"I think it's about time for that."

Dante looked askance at his friend, but Tucker didn't meet his gaze. He turned back to the road. "You sound like you have something specific in mind."

"Everyone's been treating those women with kid gloves. I have a few questions for them that haven't been covered yet. Now's as good a time to ask them as any."

CHAPTER NINETEEN

Four hours into Emma's exhaustive list and Lei couldn't handle it anymore. She rose without a word and marched up the stairs to change into her running clothes. She tossed on her holster, took the time to ensure her gun was loaded and the safety was on, and then tucked it back into the holster. Two minutes later she led Saul outside and sprinted for the tree line.

Selfish not to have told Emma where she was going.

Reckless not to have called Isaac first.

Stupid, selfish, reckless.

She didn't care. All the checking in. The fear. Having her every movement tracked and questioned. She couldn't handle it a second longer. Lei just needed some fucking space, and she'd deal with the consequences once she ran the restlessness out of her blood and made it back to the house. *And if the killer comes after me?* She touched the butt of her gun.

Let the bastard come.

Saul trotted next to her, his tongue hanging out of his mouth in a happy doggy smile. He hadn't liked being cooped up any more than she had. They needed motion and action and freedom. There had been little enough of that since the first murders happened.

She picked up her pace, eating up the distance. She wouldn't go more than three miles, well within the coverage of the cameras Emma had set up. The killer might be able to circumvent them, but Emma would realize he was doing it and be able to narrow down her location from there. *Sure. Whatever you have to tell yourself to justify what you're doing.*

Lei kept her gaze on the trees around her. She never brought headphones on these runs because wild animals were a possible threat, and surprising a deer could be just as dangerous as a cougar, so she kept her ears peeled for anything out of the ordinary. The forest around her felt too quiet, but that was as likely to be her nerves talking as anything else.

Still, it paid to be wary.

She hit the marker for a mile and a half and turned back the way she'd come. "Home, boy."

With every step, Lei expected someone to lurch out of the trees and come for her, but she made it back to the house unmolested. Isaac's car was nowhere to be seen, but she recognized Dante's rental. She smiled before she caught herself, and slowed to cool down. The screen door slammed open, and there was the man himself, his expression stormy. "You left." He didn't raise his voice, but in the sudden quiet of the space between them, he didn't have to.

"It was only a run."

If anything, her dismissal pissed him off further. He stalked down the steps, crossing the distance separating them in several long strides. "You can't take risks like that." He reached out like he'd grab her arms but dropped his hands at the last moment. "Anything could have happened."

"I was fine." She sounded defensive, but she couldn't help it. "I can't live locked up, Dante. I'll go crazy. I just needed to clear my head."

He raked his hands over his head. If he'd had much hair, he might have yanked it right out in sheer frustration. It came off him in waves, and she took a step back before she caught herself. He went still. She could actually see the professional FBI agent sliding back into place over the man beneath, and part of Lei mourned the loss. "I would never hurt you."

"I know." She studied him, taking in the layer beneath the frustration. *Fear.* He'd been scared for her. And why not? Last time she went on a run, she'd found the evidence the killer had left for her. Clarke was missing, maybe connected to this case. Of course Dante would assume the worst when he arrived and found her gone. "Did Emma show you the monitors?"

"Yes." He looked away. "But the unsub has already proven he can tamper with them."

"Dante . . ." She stepped closer and tentatively touched his chest. "I'm sorry I scared you."

He scrubbed a hand over his face. "This case has gotten to me. *You've* gotten under my skin. I care about you, and not just because you're part of this case. I care about *you*."

"Dante, I—"

"I know. It's too much and highly inappropriate and—"

"I care about you, too," she blurted. He didn't move, but she still had words bubbling up inside her, needing to be voiced, for the truth to be told. "I'm broken. I might have been broken even before that night, but I most definitely am now. I don't know how to do any of this, but I . . . I like how you make me feel. I like *you*."

He stepped to her and carefully took her hands. "It has to wait until the case is over."

"I know." Lei smiled up at him, but the feeling of peace shattered as the front door slammed. She glanced past Dante to find a large red-headed man leaning against the front porch post. Even if he hadn't had a badge clipped to his belt, she would have known him for a Fed. It was in the watchfulness of his blue eyes, the way he held himself, as if ready to spring into motion at any moment, the way he seemed to take one look at them and recognize that there was something deeper going on than just talk about the case.

He caught her looking and smiled, and she actually rocked back on her heels in the face of the charm she could almost feel. "Whoa."

Dante sighed. "That's Tucker—Agent Kendrick."

"Does he practice that look in the mirror? How does he keep from being mobbed by adolescent girls?" she murmured.

He laughed. "You'll have to ask him."

Maybe she would. Though, as Lei headed for the front door, the reality of the situation crashed down around her shoulders. The Feds weren't there because they were friends—not even Dante. He might be interested in starting something up with her—*after*. Right now, they were there to help catch the monster hunting Lei and Emma. And one of their number had already gone missing. *It's like something out of a horror movie. The killer is circling, and nothing we do can get ahead of him.*

She stopped in front of Agent Kendrick and held out her hand. "Lei Zhang."

"Agent Tucker Kendrick. I'd say it's a pleasure, but the circumstances kind of make that a lie." He had a good handshake, warm and firm. "I'm a fan of your work."

She blinked. "I didn't realize my work lent itself to having fans."

"Well, maybe not the usual type, but plenty of us Feds look at cadaver dogs and their handlers as something downright magical." He gifted her with another of those heart-stopping grins.

"That's all Saul." She glanced down to find her dog staring at Tucker in adoration. Seeing that, she relaxed a little. Saul's people instincts weren't always spot-on, but if he instinctively disliked someone, she always paid attention to it. Nine times out of ten, it eventually came out that the person had skeletons in their closet. The remaining one had just been a dick, but that still wasn't the type of person she wanted to waste her time on.

"May I?"

If she had any doubts about liking Tucker, they disappeared in that moment. "Sure. Saul, say hello."

Saul rushed forward and licked Tucker's hand as the man crouched. He allowed Tucker to pet him and then about bowled the big man over with his wiggling. She sighed. "You're such a sap, Saul."

"Nah, he's good pup." Tucker spent a few more minutes telling him what a good dog he was.

Dante stopped next to her. "The blanket?"

She wrapped her arms around herself, a protective gesture she couldn't stop from making. "Yes." She took a deep breath and charged on. "Isaac came in and bagged up the blanket to pass along to the Seattle police for processing, but I don't think the killer left anything behind. He's been too clever up to this point."

"I'm inclined to agree with you, but we'll check nonetheless."

Tucker gave Saul one last pat and straightened. "I had a couple thoughts I wanted to run by you and Emma."

Thoughts. It was a delicate way to say he was going to question them again. She nodded, because there was no other choice. Lei had racked her brain for anything and everything that could possibly be connected to Travis or the current killer, and there was nothing new that hadn't been there last week, or last year, or ten years ago. She'd trotted out every single moment she'd spent with Travis for both the prosecuting and defense attorneys, until it felt like *she* was on trial. If there was something more to remember, she would remember it.

Wouldn't she?

She realized both men were staring at her and nodded. "Sure. Let's get Emma and we can talk."

They found Emma exactly where Lei had left her, curled up in a blanket in front of her computer, Prince at her feet. Prince gave Tucker and Dante a stern look and laid his head back down, taking his lead from Saul.

Emma, on the other hand, was so furious she was practically shaking. "What the hell were you thinking?"

"I already got this talk from Dante. I don't need it from you, too." She hated feeling like an idiot—she courted that sensation enough on her own while she was running—and getting lectured for the second time in an hour was too much to take. "I went out. Nothing happened. I know it was stupid, but it happened and it's done, and I don't want to talk about it anymore."

"You don't want to talk about it? Well, that's just too damn bad." Emma shoved to her feet, sending Prince scrambling. "I don't know what I'd do if something happened to you, and you seem to have a fucking death wish. You can't do that, Lei. You can't put yourself in danger like that. I can't . . . What would I do . . . ?" She gasped in a breath, and her shakes got so bad the blanket fell from her shoulders.

Fuck. She's having a panic attack.

Lei guided her back into the chair and turned to Dante. "Xanax is in the cabinet closest to the back door." He nodded and wasted no time leaving the room. Though she was conscious of Tucker watching them, she ignored him for the time being. "Breathe, Emma. I'm here. I'm safe. I'm sorry I worried you. You know how I get when I'm stressed. I should have talked to you before I left."

Emma grasped her hands hard enough to make her bones grind together. "I can't lose you, too, Lei. I won't survive it."

That's what she was afraid of. "You didn't lose me, Em. I'm right here."

Dante reappeared with one of the little blue pills. Lei took half a second to make sure it was the right one and then handed it to Emma. "Here. Take it with your coffee."

It took ten minutes for her shakes to settle and her breathing to come normally. Her blue eyes took a slightly hazy note, and she shivered. "That was a bad one."

"It was." Lei pulled the blanket higher around her friend's shoulders and tucked her back into the chair. She was just glad it had only taken one pill to derail the panic attack. On the days it took two, Emma usually ended up taking an impromptu nap on the couch in her office, and they needed her to answer questions with Lei. Once she was sure her friend was okay, she sank into the other office chair.

Dante and Tucker both had carefully blank expressions on their faces, but she wasn't naive enough to think they hadn't filed away what had just happened. At least they didn't pity her or Emma. "Your questions?"

Tucker exchanged a look with Dante and leaned forward. "There's one thing about this whole case that just doesn't make sense to me."

She braced for whatever he was about to say. It was her fault. It had to be somehow. No matter how irrational it seemed, it was her fault all the way down the line to when she'd let Travis through that window and released him on a houseful of unsuspecting women.

And that was it. Her deepest, darkest fear.

That she'd somehow released *this* killer as well.

Tucker continued, his blue gaze jumping from her to Emma and back again. "All that stuff happened in California. If we're following Britton's theory about there being another person in that house—which is a solid theory, though we can't discount that Berkley worked alone—then his hunting grounds were in California. And yet you're in Washington now, and he's managed to stay ahead of this entire investigation from the beginning, and he's jumping all over the place between here and Seattle as if he's familiar with the area."

Emma shrugged lethargically. "Twelve years is a long time. Maybe he *is* familiar with the area."

"That's precisely my point." His sunny smile was completely at odds with his stillness. "When did you ladies move up here?"

Lei frowned. "Um . . . eight years ago?"

"It was eight years ago," Emma confirmed.

The trial had been drawn out, and then they'd both chosen to stay at UCLA to finish their degrees. Through those years, it had been as if she'd had her neck on the block and was waiting for the sword to fall and finish everything. Emma was so heavily medicated, she'd almost needed a keeper just to get through her day, and Lei's aggression was off the charts because she expected an attack to come from every corner.

Eventually they'd realized that they couldn't continue on in that way. Their families didn't understand. Emma's mother wanted to jam her back into the mold of the person she'd been before that night, and when Emma didn't—couldn't—comply, she'd punished her with cold silences and, eventually, those fucking cards. Lei's parents would have had her committed if they thought for a second an institution could hold her. Her mother's favorite hobby became diagnosing her with new disorders until Lei had been forced to cut off all but the smallest amount of contact.

They had no friends left except each other. There was nothing to do but leave town—leave the entire state.

Tucker nodded as if they'd said more than they had. "And why did you pick Stillwater?"

Lei opened her mouth but stopped. She didn't know. They'd been looking at a couple of different options before Emma found this house, but there were other houses in other states. Tennessee and upstate New York had topped the list, both meeting the requirements and giving them plenty of space to pursue the cadaver-dog angle Lei had chosen for her future. "I'm not sure."

"There was a price drop on the house." Emma shifted deeper into her cocoon of blanket, pulling it tightly around her. "We had almost settled on the New York house, but the owners of this one dropped the price by twenty thousand, which meant we could settle in and make all the required changes in one fell swoop."

Yes, that was it. Lei nodded. "We had—have—money, but we donated a large amount to a victims' advocacy group after the trial. The rest we tied up in investments and whatever—a trust. It left enough to buy a house, but not much more." Still plenty of money. It had seemed a great stroke of luck that the housing market was doing poorly enough to require that kind of price drop, but neither she nor Emma had questioned it overmuch. Why would they?

Now, considering the direction of Tucker's questions, she wondered. "You think that was him."

"I don't know what to think."

Dante was nodding, a bemused look on his face. "So he herded them here and then waited for the right time to spring his plan." He caught Lei's look and shrugged. "It's not out of the realm of possibilities any more than our other theories are at this point. If we operate under the assumption that the simplest explanation is most likely the truth—which is simpler? That he guided your choice to live in a place of his choosing and was already set up to watch you before you arrived? Or that he has somehow stumbled or hacked his way into your systems after having recently found you?"

When he put it like that, it *did* make more sense for the killer to have herded them to Washington. The thought left her cold down to her very bones. All these years, she'd been living in as close to blissful happiness as she was capable of, thinking that the only things she had to fear were her memories. But, if Dante and Tucker were right, the killer had been there all along. She shuddered. "Stillwater isn't a large community. If there was a stranger there, everyone would be talking about it."

"There are a lot of far-flung houses situated in the forest. We checked the property records for all of them, but with money or the right connections, that sort of thing could be faked." Emma spoke as if in a dream. "If he bought the house with an LLC and went a town or two over to shop—or ordered online . . . People would gossip, but they wouldn't gossip to *us*." She gave a strange laugh. "Or to you. They don't say much of anything at all to me."

Because Emma never left the house.

Lei shoved to her feet. "I need . . . Give me a minute. I just need a minute." She rushed out of the room, her breath coming too fast, her thoughts a frenzied buzz inside her head. He'd been here all along, and for all her smug feelings of superiority and being a survivor who called people on their bullshit, she hadn't known it. She hadn't sensed it. She'd been just as blind now as she had been twelve years before.

Oh, God, I'm destined to repeat history over and over again.

"Lei."

Dante's steady tone brought her up short, every muscle in her body shaking from the effort to keep from sprinting out of the house and into the night. She needed something to feel in control again, but she'd never had control. It was all a lie. "I just need . . ."

"A minute. I know." He didn't touch her, just waited for her to face him. "This doesn't negate all the good you two have done in the last eight years. It changes nothing."

She wished she could believe him. "It changes everything." They'd been living on borrowed time all these years, and the devil was finally calling due on that debt.

CHAPTER TWENTY

Dante let Lei walk away. She obviously needed time to come to terms with the potential bombshell Tucker had just dropped, and he wasn't going to help by following her around like a dog nipping at her heels. He headed back into the office. "Can I get you something, Emma?"

"I'm going to check on Lei." She stood, weaving a little, and left the room.

Tucker shook his head. "I'm cursed."

"What the hell is that supposed to mean?"

He shot Dante a look. "Exactly what I just said. In all the years I've known you, I've never known you to get twisted up over anyone related to an active case. You're the pillar of strength and calm and whatever the hell you want to call it. That woman"—he jerked his thumb toward the ceiling, where the sound of a shower being turned on reached them—"has you twisted up in knots."

Denying it was pointless, so he shrugged. "It isn't affecting how I do my job."

Tucker wandered over to the papers spread across the desk next to Emma's, and Dante followed suit. It was a list of names, some crossed off, some highlighted. He flipped through the pages, and it was only then that he noticed the second column, with titles like *UCLA football* and *Physics class*. "They're tracking Berkley's known associates."

Tucker raised his eyebrows. "Lot of people."

"The guy was popular and rich—telling combo." He wasn't the only killer to have those traits, but he'd been a beloved member of both the college and Westside LA society. The kind of guy who knew everyone and was generally well liked. In nearly every character-witness testimony, they'd all uniformly said that he had the world at his feet and a bright future ahead of him.

"You know what else I don't get? Travis Berkley." Tucker set the papers down in the exact spots they'd been. "You know how Britton said there were two distinct styles of killing going on in that house?"

"Yeah. Stabbing, and the strangling with rape. Both are intimate ways to kill a person, but different flavors."

"Mmm-hmm." Tucker moved to look at the monitors. "Did you notice that Berkley himself seems to fit two profiles?"

Dante shrugged. "He's a sociopath. He likes to play games, and that means he takes on different roles depending on the situation." He eyed Tucker and shifted gears. "Britton thinks there was a partner. I'm inclined to agree with him at this point, because the unsub being a fan doesn't fit any longer."

"The partner theory, I get. What I don't get is why sometimes Berkley was coming across as an alpha predator, and sometimes he comes across as a submissive version of that."

"It could all be to play the game, but he's in prison. Even if he has something to do with what was happening now, there was no reason to play the submissive partner. If anything, his ego should be clamoring for him to take credit, even where credit isn't due." They hadn't really taken the possibility of a partner into account until recently, and that meant he and Clarke hadn't had a chance to question Berkley about it when they spoke with him.

Clarke.

For a second he'd been so caught up in theorizing with Tucker, he'd almost forgotten that she was in danger. He pressed a fist to his chest. They'd find her. He had to believe that. In the meantime, he would do his damnedest to find the unsub before that bastard hurt another woman.

Before he hurt Lei.

Because that's where this was headed, where it had always been headed. Emma was also part of the endgame, but Lei was Berkley's way into the house that night, and she was the one he'd targeted for weeks leading up to the night of the massacre. *She* was the one Berkley had information about in his jail cell, about her job and about the general location where she lived. She was also the one he'd set the series of hoops to jump through with the missing dead girls.

Yeah, Lei was the main fixation. Emma was secondary. If the unsub was able to get into the house at any time, he could have killed Emma before anyone could stop him. He hadn't. He'd terrified her enough that she'd called Lei to run home to rescue her, keeping the focus on her friend and on the fact that he'd tainted a place she considered safe.

He shook his head and forced himself to focus. "You think it's all part of a bigger picture?"

"I don't know what to think. Seems like every time we nail one of these profiles down, a new kind of monster comes along and makes us doubt everything we thought was true."

"Berkley isn't a new kind of monster. He's textbook." But that was part of the problem. If he followed the profile Britton had put together as closely as everyone claimed, he should have reacted differently to Clarke and Dante when they met him in prison. He'd been almost lackluster and bored, rather than agitated and delighted to fence verbally with them. If prison was one thing for a guy like Berkley, it was boring. Any new stimulation was something to be coveted and played with. He hadn't done either. He'd sounded like he was reading from a script provided by someone else, which had lent credence to Dante's question about him possibly being the submissive partner.

But that would mean Britton's profile was wrong, and so was everything in Berkley's life leading up to the point when he committed those murders. The other option would be that he was drugged, but the prison would have told them if that was a possibility.

No, something else was going on.

And he had a feeling only one person really knew the full score. Dante sighed. "We're going to have to go back to California."

"I'm coming with you."

He looked up to find Lei standing in the doorway, her hair still wet from the shower. She'd changed into a pair of jeans and a plain gray T-shirt, and she looked ready for anything. Maybe she even was. That didn't change the fact that he'd spare her from this if he could.

That was the problem, though—her presence at that interview might mean the difference between more girls turning up dead and stopping this guy once and for all right now.

◆ ◆ ◆

Lei couldn't believe what she'd just offered. She desperately, *desperately* did not want to see Travis again. The thought of sitting down across the table from him made her skin crawl. Even worse was the suspicion that this had been his plan all along.

It would be different facing him like that than it had been in the courtroom. More intimate. More dangerous, though she didn't truly believe that he'd try to physically hurt her. Even if he could with the shackles. It wasn't about physical pain—that would have been preferable to the games Travis played.

"Lei, no," Emma whispered.

"Yes." The word came out more like a question than a statement, so she cleared her throat and tried again. "I'm going. You'll get more out of him if he thinks he's winning, and that's what it will feel like if I'm the one to show up." She didn't have a choice. Her mental well-being didn't balance out against the potential for more deaths. For *Clarke's* death.

The more time passed since Clarke disappeared, the surer Lei became that her disappearance was connected with the killer. It was too damn coincidental that there were *two* monsters hunting in the area. As they'd just talked about, the simplest explanation was the most logical, and the simplest explanation was that the killer had somehow gotten to Clarke. *How* was a mystery, but there were a whole hell of a lot of mysteries right then.

Tucker studied her. "You'll have to run it by Britton, of course. He can get you clearance to attend that meeting, but if he says no, that's it. You can't go around him."

She wanted to argue, but it would just be another mark against her. "Let's call him, then."

Tucker glanced at his watch. "He should have landed by now, so that works."

Landed. She frowned. "I thought he didn't go into the field that much these days."

"Only when a case is fucked-up beyond all reason." Tucker grimaced. "There seem to be a lot of those lately. One of his people is missing, so he's bringing in the cavalry. He takes this kind of thing personally."

That, she got.

If Britton was here, she could almost believe that everything would be okay. Dante might have a soothing personality that made her feel safe, but Britton's ability to put people at ease was almost supernatural. She'd bet it came from a lifetime of learning how best to manipulate people and situations, rather than some kind of voodoo, but that didn't make it less effective. "Let's call him."

Emma cleared her throat. "Lei, can I speak with you a moment in the hallway?"

There was no getting around this. If Emma freaked over her going for a run, she wasn't going to be excited at the thought of Lei heading back to see the man who'd set their lives on their current nightmarish course. That was just too damn bad, though. Lei couldn't hide out here until this all blew over or he finally got tired of playing around and came for them directly. It wasn't her nature, and if one more person died while she sat on her hands in helpless frustration, she'd start chewing through the walls. Emma might thrive within these four walls, but they felt like a tomb to Lei.

She glanced at the agents. "Go ahead and call Britton to fill him in. I'll be a few minutes." She walked out of the office and shut the door behind her. They could hash it out right there in the hallway, but it didn't feel right. This conversation meant something, no matter how frustrating she found it. Lei skirted Emma and headed for the kitchen. It was shaping up to be a long evening and an even longer night, so Lei went through the familiar motions of putting on a new pot of coffee.

"You can't go see him."

She focused on counting the scoops. "I'll do whatever it takes to put an end to this, up to and including sitting across from him and telling him whatever he needs to hear to give us the information *we* need."

"He won't, Lei. You know he won't. He's too smart to give up something unless he already planned to do it, and this is what he's wanted all along."

It wasn't anything she hadn't thought to herself, but somehow hearing it out of Emma's mouth irritated the hell out of her. Lei slammed the coffeemaker lid shut and stabbed the button to get it brewing. "You think I don't know that? I'm the one who's had to field request after request to see him or talk to him or answer his fucking letters. I know the only reason he wants me there is to play out some sick little game he's been fantasizing about since we got him locked up. *I know*, Em. I can't change any of that."

"Then why are you going?" Emma looked about ready to burst into tears, her full lower lip quivering, her blue eyes a little too shiny beneath the harsh overhead light. "Why are you doing this?"

"I don't have a choice." Maybe she'd never had a choice. It didn't matter now. Nothing mattered but seeing this through. She'd deal with the fallout once the immediate danger had passed and the dust had settled. "Please don't make this harder for me than it's already going to be."

Emma opened her mouth like she was going to keep arguing, but deflated. "I'm scared, Lei. I'm so scared. Every time I think I'm as scared as I can possibly be, the bottom drops out, and a new wave of terror rolls over me, and I don't know how we're going to manage to walk away from this alive."

"Don't do that." She crossed to her friend and gripped her shoulders. "Look at me, Em. *Look at me.*" She waited for Emma to obey. "He's playing a sick game, and it might not be the same as last time, but he doesn't get to win now any more than he won then. We will stop him. We will put this sick son of bitch behind bars just like we did to Travis."

Emma made a visible effort to nod. "Okay."

"He doesn't get to win. If we stop fighting, that means he wins. If we give in to fear, then he's going to walk. I can't live with that. Can you?"

"No." This time the word came out stronger. Surer.

"That's my girl." She gave Emma's shoulders one last squeeze and straightened. "If Britton doesn't give his full support of this, I won't go. I want this to end, but that doesn't mean I'm going to make rash mistakes." She caught her friend's look and sighed. "*Any more* rash mistakes. I did apologize about earlier."

"I know." Emma sighed. "I'm sorry. I know I'm not the steadiest under the best of circumstances, but I'm turning into a complete basket case."

"Considering how things are going lately, I think you're holding up remarkably well." It was more or less the truth, too. Emma might be on the verge of a nervous breakdown—they might both be—but she hadn't curled up in a ball and given up. She was still fighting, albeit in her own way. "We'll get him, Em."

"Promise."

"I promise." Even as she said the words, she hoped to God she wasn't lying.

CHAPTER TWENTY-ONE

"Are you sure this is something you're willing to do, Lei?"

Dante held the phone on speaker between them. Half of him wanted Britton to tell Lei this was a mistake and that under no circumstances was she to go to California to talk to her ex, the serial killer. The rest of him knew better than to try to make this decision for her. As much as he wanted to wrap her up and tuck her away somewhere safe until this was all over, that wasn't the way of things. She had a part to play, whether he liked it or not, and she wouldn't forgive him for trying to keep her out of it.

It didn't make it any easier to see her blanch. "I'm sure. I think he'll say things to me that he wouldn't say to your agents."

"I'm inclined to agree with you. There always was a connection between you and Travis. I know it's not a comfortable thing, but most serial killers move on even if their victim gets away. They rarely take the time and effort to track the survivor down and attempt to finish the job, let alone orchestrate something of this magnitude. While I do believe Emma's walking out of that house irked him, his true focus has always been you." Britton didn't say it like he was apologizing—it was simply a fact.

She wrapped her arms around herself. "If I can help, I'm helping, Britton. This is bigger than my fear. This is about making sure no one else has to identify another girl in the morgue. I'm the only one who can do this, and you know it."

Britton didn't sigh, but the sound came across in his tone all the same. "I don't like it, but there are a lot of things about this case that I don't like. I'll book your tickets for tonight."

Tonight? Lei mouthed.

Dante took over. "I'll get us on the flight. I have an updated report for you once you're settled, but Tucker can deliver it."

"Dante, please take me off speakerphone."

He exchanged a look with Lei and shrugged. What Britton wanted, Britton got. Dante obeyed and put the phone to his ear. "You're off speakerphone."

"Good. I'd like Tucker to stay at the house. The local police are stretched thin as it is, and frankly, they're not going to do much good parked just out of sight down the driveway. In addition to that, Tucker's got a way about him that might prompt Emma to share whatever information she's been withholding to this point."

"Why do you think there's information being withheld?"

"Because she's Emma. Neither of these women deal well with feeling helpless, though they work through it in different ways. Lei sprints toward confrontation, just as she's doing by agreeing to speak with Travis. Emma, on the other hand, hoards information like a squirrel storing nuts in preparation for winter. It makes her feel more in control, and while I don't think she'd hold back anything important to this investigation, I can't guarantee it. Tucker has a better chance than anyone else of getting her to talk about it."

While Dante didn't disagree with that, he couldn't imagine Emma would be okay with the idea of a man staying in her beloved house—especially a man she'd just met. "I'll see what I can do."

"I spoke with Detective Smith about Clarke. Her rental car was spotted heading south toward Portland. His response has been less than comforting—he would believe Clarke decided to take an impromptu trip—but I've sent two agents down there to see what they can find."

"Clarke wouldn't leave an open case, let alone without a word to anyone."

"I know that. You know that. Everyone who's ever come in contact with her knows that. Unfortunately, our good detective is overwhelmed, and I think this is the straw that broke the camel's back."

He didn't give a fuck about Smith's being overwhelmed. Clarke was in *danger*, and that bastard was willing to pretend it wasn't an abduction because *he* was stressed out. "I'm glad you're here" was all he said. Britton might be a father figure to half the agents in the BAU, but Dante knew better than to spew his emotional bullshit all over his boss. There was no denying how comforting it was to know the man was in his corner—in Clarke's corner. Britton might not let emotions get the better of him, but no one would accuse him of not caring about the agents under his command.

"I'll forward you the information about your flights."

It was a dismissal, so he hung up and turned to Lei. "I guess we're doing this."

"I guess we are." She looked like she might be sick at any moment, but she made a visible effort to straighten, a lean sapling standing in the face of a gale-force wind. *Bend or break.* Lei glanced at the doorway leading into the office where Emma and Tucker waited. "The longer I wait, the more I'm going to second-guess my sanity. I know in my heart of hearts that this is the right choice, but it doesn't mean it's an *easy* choice." Something flickered through her dark eyes, and she shivered. "I'm not whole, Dante. I might fake it really well, but there are parts of me missing that I'm never going to reclaim. I'm not even sure I want to at this point."

He didn't blink at the apparent change in subject. She'd said something in that vein earlier in the yard, and he hadn't directly addressed it then. "No one is really whole. We're all carrying some kind of baggage."

Her lips quirked up. "Even the perfect unruffled FBI agent?"

"Maybe especially him."

Knowing she'd be facing the object of her nightmares would be dredging up shit she might have thought was long buried. He offered her information like a life preserver. "I've been accused of being a robot more times than I can count. Or Spock. Or more of a sociopath than the monsters I hunt."

Lei's eyes went wide. "What?"

"I never set out to emulate my father—the brain surgeon—but whether through conditioning or genetics, holding people at a distance is just what I do. It's my default. It isn't because of damage—my childhood was mundane enough despite growing up affluent. It's just the way I am."

"I *like* the way you are." She held his gaze for a long moment and then looked at the ground. "I don't think you're broken. Not like I am."

Dante shifted closer to her and waited for her to look up at him. "Are you telling me this as a warning for the meeting with Berkley? Or are you trying to warn me off *you*? Because I'm not sure if you got it from our earlier conversation, but that ship has sailed, Lei."

She bit her bottom lip, her brow furrowed. "You know, most guys just meet people online or something. They don't use a murder investigation as a dating service."

"Don't. Don't do that. Don't cheapen this or make it sound like I'm just out to bag a freak show or whatever fiction you're currently constructing in your head. I'm interested in you, Lei. More than interested. I would be if we'd met on the street." He raked a hand over his head.

"I'd rather we'd met on a street, because it'd be a whole hell of a lot less complicated than escorting you to California to have a meeting with your serial-killer ex." He grimaced. "That came out wrong."

Against all reason, she burst out laughing. "God, you're right. This is like some kind of sick sitcom. All we need is a damn laugh track and we're in business."

As happy as he was to see her looking surer of herself, Dante couldn't let things stand between them as they currently were. "I do want to see where this goes. After."

"After," she agreed. Lei touched him almost hesitantly and ran her hands up his chest. "It's not just one-sided. I don't know what to do with this feeling. I don't exactly have the best track record."

He covered her hand with his. "We'll take it one day at a time." It was all he could offer her. They couldn't be sure of tomorrow, and he wouldn't do her the disservice of promising something he had no control over. Dante would do everything in his power to keep Lei safe. Beyond that, it was out of his control.

Doesn't matter. I'll figure it out.

She took a steadying breath and smiled. "Life is weird sometimes."

"Like is most definitely weird." He kissed her because being this close and *not* kissing her was as unnatural as breathing underwater. Lei melted against him and slid her arms around his neck, letting him take the lead. Dante kissed one corner of her mouth and then the other, savoring the way her body quivered in response. Her tongue darted out and licked his bottom lip, and that was all the encouragement he needed to turn and press her against the wall.

Lei was fire in his arms, her body lean and strong and in constant motion. She arched against him at the first touch of his tongue to hers, her fingers digging into his shoulders, a silent demand for *more*. He wanted more, too. He craved hours spent exploring each other and learning what it would take to re-create the little whimper she made when he rolled his hips against hers.

He kissed along her jawline and dragged his mouth down her neck. Dante inhaled deeply, taking in the clean scent of her, and closed his eyes. "We can't do this now."

"I know." She panted lightly, her fingers making little kneading motions on his shoulders. "I know," she repeated, sounding slightly more in control. "As tempting as it is to drag you upstairs . . ."

He rested his forehead against hers. "I want our first time to be somewhere you're comfortable enough to let loose. To not have to muffle your moans because you're afraid of someone overhearing. I don't want anything holding either of us back. I want it all."

She shivered. "God, Dante, you're too tempting for my own good. Yes, I want that. I want all of that." She took a shuddering breath. "Though I think now might be the time to remind you that we have cameras set up all over this place, so we more than likely have an audience. Again."

Damn it. He knew that. He *did* know that. He'd just forgotten in the midst of Lei.

Dante took a breath and then another. "Right. I suppose I should let you off the wall, then."

"I suppose so." She sounded amused and totally unafraid for the first time since he'd arrived today, so that was a win even if the situation was less than professional. *It hasn't been strictly professional since I met Lei.* He stepped back enough to let her slide down his body. She'd wrapped her legs around his waist at some point, and he mourned the loss of the squeeze of her thighs against his hips.

Lei started to move away from him, but paused. "Dante . . ." She seemed to brace herself. "This isn't just a convenient sexy distraction. I mean, you're offering me comfort in the middle of a pretty traumatic situation, but that's not all this is."

"I know."

She smiled. "Good."

◆ ◆ ◆

Things went quickly after that. Privately, Lei would have liked to talk this damn situation to death, if only to keep from having to *do* what she'd promised for a little longer. But the decision was made, the tickets were purchased, and she had packed an overnight bag into her Jeep. Emma remained closeted in her office—she'd never been one for good-byes—but Tucker stood on the porch, watching her and Dante closely. "You sure about this?"

"Too late to worry about it now." Lei double-checked to make sure she had everything she needed in her wallet.

For his part, Dante had been quiet since they'd made out in the hallway like horny teenagers. She flushed to think of it. She was used to handling stress, though admittedly she'd never been under quite as much stress as she had been lately, and Lei had never thrown herself at a man the way she kept throwing herself at Dante. The only thing saving her pride was the fact that he couldn't seem to control himself any better than she could.

That he wanted *more* as much as she did—in a way that had nothing to do with sex.

She glanced at him, but he was having some kind of silent communication with Tucker. Taking a hint, Lei climbed into the Jeep and closed the door, giving them the illusion of privacy. She glanced at her phone and found a text from Emma. I'm no good at good-byes.

She typed out a quick response. It's only for twenty-four hours. I'll be back close to this time tomorrow.

I feel like something bad is going to happen.

She stared at her phone. It would be easy to say something pat or comforting and push off Emma's fears. It was something she'd done time and time again over the years. Emma let fear dictate her moves . . .

But hadn't Lei done the same thing, if using a different method? She might not hide, but she was reactionary when it came to something that made her afraid. In the end, who was the smarter of the two?

She didn't have an answer to that any more than she had comfort to give Emma right now. The same dread apparent in her friend's text had been building in her ever since she'd volunteered to see Travis again. Rationally, she knew he was locked up, but that hadn't stopped him from reaching across time and distance to strike at them here in Washington. It didn't matter if it was his hand doing the damage or not—he was behind this. No one could convince her otherwise.

Still, she needed to respond. If it does, we'll deal with it. Stay safe.

You too.

She set her phone down as Dante rounded the front of the Jeep and slid into the passenger seat. Lei glanced at him. "Everything okay?"

"Yeah. Tucker's not too impressed with my lack of professionalism with you. I might be written up for it once Britton finds out, but . . ." He shrugged. "It's worth it."

She didn't know what to think of that. No, that was a lie. A wisp of pleasure coursed through her at the realization that he was effectively putting her before the job. Even knowing him such a short time, she realized what a novelty that was. Dante was so by the book, it would have been funny under other circumstances.

As they turned off her driveway and onto the narrow highway, he pulled a laptop out of his bag. "I have to write an updated report with the information we have from the last twenty-four hours."

"Go for it." She was talked out, to be perfectly honest. Round and round and round they'd gone, over and over again. None of it made any difference. What did it matter if Travis wasn't acting according to his profile? He was behind bars. He might be responsible, at least in part, but the profile they needed to be focusing on was the current killer's.

She let herself relax as much as she was capable of as they drove through the winding pass and down into the greater Seattle area. The tickets were on Dante's phone now, so she headed straight for the airport. *Straight for Travis.* Lei's skin crawled, but she ignored the sensation of tiny ants marching across her arms as best she could. The choice was made. Now all that was left was to live through it.

Dante didn't talk much as they parked and made their way into Sea-Tac airport. Lei wasn't exactly a nervous flier, but there was something about going through the extra security that set her teeth on edge. She hated feeling like she'd done something wrong, but that was her issue, not the TSA's.

For all that, the security line moved quickly enough, and they made it to their gate with plenty of time to spare. Lei dropped into an open seat and sighed. "At least that's over until the flight back tomorrow."

"How are you doing?"

She glanced over to find Dante actually looking at her for the first time in almost two hours. "I could ask you the same thing. You're kind of checked out."

He hesitated, and she could actually see him considering whether to let her in or not. Finally, he sat next to her. "I'm worried about Clarke. Detective Smith isn't taking her disappearance seriously for whatever damn reason, and even with Britton in Seattle, he can only do so much without local police support." He glanced out the window at the plane currently taking off. "Every hour a person is missing heightens the chance they end up dead. If she's not already . . ." He shook his head. "Clarke and I have been partners for three years. We're friends. I trust her with my life, and she does the same with me—and I wasn't there when she needed me."

He'd been with Lei instead. She reached out and laced her fingers through his. Comfort wasn't her forte, whether physical or verbal, so she tried to picture how she'd want someone to talk to her if their situations were reversed. "The chance this isn't connected is a whole lot less than the chance that it is."

"I think so, too."

She tried to picture the timeline. "It's possible he left the house and started back for Seattle but changed his mind for some reason and turned around." That rest station was twenty minutes from the house, maybe a little more. Honestly, it didn't make sense that Clarke had stopped there instead of pushing through. She frowned. "Why was she at the rest station to begin with?" Maybe that was a more important question than how the killer had known she'd be there.

"I don't know. She called me when she was in her car, but I don't know more than that."

They could fill the oceans with the things they didn't know about this case. "That's probably something Britton should be focusing on in addition to where her car is, don't you think?"

Dante's dark gaze went distant. "Yeah, you're right. Give me a few."

A woman's voice announced preboarding for their flight, and Lei straightened. The sooner they got this over with, the better it would be. It was the lead-up that was the worst. She'd built this confrontation up in her mind, buoyed by too many years of fear. At the end of the day, Travis Berkley was just a man, and he was no longer a danger to her.

By the time she made it to California, she might even believe it.

As if giving the lie to her thoughts, her phone buzzed, drawing her back to the present. She frowned. She and Emma had already said what passed as their good-byes. Her friend should be back to the search through Travis's known associates, and Lei didn't exactly have other friends.

But when she brought out her phone, it was a text from an unidentified number. An invisible band squeezed her chest as she used numb fingers to bring the message up. "No." She hadn't realized she'd spoken aloud until Dante was there, kneeling in front of her.

"Lei, what's wrong?"

She passed him the phone, watching his lips move as he read the words on the screen.

I'm coming for you, Lei-Lei.

CHAPTER TWENTY-TWO

In Lei's weak moments, when fear threatened to take hold and drag her down permanently, she imagined Travis chained in some dark and dank dungeon, screaming for mercy. It was nothing more than he deserved—his own personal purgatory before death took him to hell once and for all.

In reality, the prison where he was locked up was remarkably . . . normal. Mostly clean, not particularly dark, definitely not dank. She studied everything as she followed Dante inside and went through the motions of being searched.

She didn't make a habit of hanging out in prisons, but this was underwhelming in the extreme.

They were eventually led down a brightly lit hallway to a series of doors. The guard stopped in front of one. He looked at Dante and then focused on her. "Do not touch the prisoner. Do not lean over the table. Take your seat and do not move from it. We have cameras set up, but we can't protect you if we can't see you."

And they couldn't ensure she didn't slip Travis something if she was close to him. The thought left her sick. Her fingers itched to touch the reassuring weight of her handgun, but it was probably for the best that she'd left it back in Washington. If she walked into that room armed, she couldn't say for certain that she wouldn't unload an entire clip into Travis's chest.

Maybe then she'd finally be free of the nightmares.

Lei realized the guard was waiting for a response and nodded. "I understand."

The guard turned to Dante. "Thirty minutes, max."

"Got it."

And then there was just a door between her and the monster she'd spent twelve years trying to get past. Lei touched the door handle and froze, every muscle locking in place. She'd imagined this moment, had envisioned in living color what it would be like to face him without a judge watching or someone standing in witness, filing every word she said to be used in Travis's next appeal.

A good portion of the time, those imaginary conversations happened with her holding a gun, but that was neither here nor there.

"You don't have to do this." Dante at her back, his solid presence steadying her even as he offered her an out.

"Yes, I do." She opened the door and walked into the room.

Travis Berkley, her own personal bogeyman, lounged in a chair on the other side of the table. His hands were cuffed to the middle of the table, and she could see his ankles cuffed to the floor as well. He was skinnier than when she'd seen him last—an appeal five years ago—but the weight loss only seemed to sharpen his attractiveness, turning it from the good old American boy into something significantly more dangerous. Or maybe it was just revealing what he was all along.

He looked up and his lips split into a wide smile. "Lei-Lei."

Hearing him using his private nickname for her actually made her knees buckle as every muscle in her body screamed at her to get out of that room as fast as she could, but Dante was there, pulling out a chair for her. She didn't take her eyes from Travis as she shuffled forward and sank into the chair. It put them too close, but scooting back would telegraph just how freaked out she was, and she couldn't afford to show weakness.

Even if it meant she was almost within touching distance.

For his part, Travis was studying her just as closely. "You look different than I imagined."

She touched her shorter hair and then forced her hand down. "I'm here. This is what you wanted, wasn't it?"

He shrugged. "I guess it was."

He seemed almost . . . disconnected. She stared into his cornflower-blue eyes. They were grayer than she remembered, but the glint of cruelty was still there, buried beneath the act. Lei tucked her hair behind her ears. "In all the time I've known you, I'd never have guessed that you'd willingly play second fiddle—even to a fan."

Travis chuckled. "Lei-Lei, always so fierce. Don't you know that sometimes it's better to let someone else play the game? I'm a bit limited in here." He motioned with his hands, making the chain rattle. Lei refused to flinch, and his grin widened. "Games with the other prisoners get old fast. They're creatures of base needs. Sometimes a man finds himself craving something of a . . ." He eyed her. "A softer nature."

Lei sat back, staring at him. There was something . . . She couldn't quite put her finger on it. Something off. "Travis, you were always a fan of walking down memory lane. You remember that night?"

"Of course I remember that night. I relive every detail during my many hours in solitary."

Dante might as well have not been in the room for all the attention Travis had paid him. It was just as well. The more he focused on her, the more likely he was to forget himself and let something slip. *Like he let something slip before he murdered all your friends?* No, she couldn't think like that. "Tell me about your partner?"

He burst out laughing. "Is that the story you're running with now? Silly Lei-Lei. You know there was me and only me that night. I climbed through that window, I beat your lovely ass black-and-blue, and then I played with your friends until they bored me. End of story."

Something clicked in her head, something she wasn't quite able to put into words. She changed tactics. "Why did you stop writing to me?"

Something flickered through his eyes, there and gone in an instant. If she hadn't been watching him so closely, she would have missed it entirely. *Confusion.* Travis laughed again, but this time it sounded forced. "Like I said, I get bored easily."

He's lying to me.

He didn't even bother to do it well, either. It was there in the way his gaze flicked to her and away again, how his nostrils flared, how he shifted imperceptibly, as easy to read as the weather. She'd learned a lot in the last twelve years, but even in hindsight, she'd never been able to read Travis.

What the hell is going on?

A suspicion formed in the pit of her stomach, growing stronger with every breath. A horrible, terrifying, impossible suspicion. Lei shifted forward again—careful to keep well back from the table—noting how Travis did the same, mirroring her position. As if he couldn't help himself. "Travis," she murmured.

"Yeah, Lei-Lei?"

"You remember our first date?"

"Of course I do."

Her stomach tried to crawl out of her throat, but she kept her tone even and her expression inviting. "You remember how you picked me up in your daddy's Porsche and took me out to that fancy dinner."

"You wore the blue dress. I always liked you in blue." He smiled. "It was a good night."

Holy mother of God. Lei pushed back her chair and rose. "I think we're done here."

Surprise widened his eyes, but he covered it quickly enough. "You haven't bothered to ask me about the dead girls. You always were cold, Lei-Lei, but I never figured you were *this* cold."

She didn't answer, just turned for the door and waited for the guard to unlock it. Her heart beat faster than a hummingbird's wings in her throat, blocking her ability to speak. It was just as well. What she had to say wasn't fit for these walls. It was crazy. Crazier than crazy. Impossible.

Dante took one look at her face and guided her through the doors to collect their things. They signed out and walked through the doors into the late-spring California heat. Still, Lei couldn't make herself give voice to the truth lodged in her chest. She slid into the passenger side of the rental and pulled her knees to her chest and wrapped her arms around her legs.

Dante locked the doors and turned on the engine to get the air-conditioning flowing. They sat in silence for several long minutes as the car cooled perceptibly.

Say it. Open your damn mouth and say the fucking words.

She swallowed hard. "Dante . . ."

"You don't have to say anything if you don't want to. I can go back in and question him now, or I can drive you back to the hotel and then come back here. You don't have to do anything but keep breathing. We'll figure it out."

He thought she was upset over seeing Travis. She twisted to face him and grabbed his hand, needing something to anchor her in the midst of this insanity. *It can't be possible. It's* not *possible.* And yet . . .

"Dante," she repeated. "That isn't Travis Berkley."

He blinked. "What?"

"I don't know who that man is in there, but that's not Travis Berkley. He didn't pick me up in his daddy's Porsche on our first date. His dad wouldn't let him touch that car, let alone drive it. I did wear a blue dress, but Travis had a picture of that up on social media. That guy"—she pointed at the prison—"that's not Travis."

◆ ◆ ◆

What Lei was saying *was* impossible.

Dante considered how best to explain that to her, because it couldn't be clearer that she was sure she was correct. "Maybe you're misremembering."

"Oh, please." She sat back and took her touch with her. "I know it sounds crazy, but don't insult me by telling me I don't remember in vivid detail every single moment I spent with Travis and every word we exchanged. I've searched my memory time and time again to try to figure out where the red flag was or what lies I must have missed." She pointed at the prison again, her hand shaking. "He lied to me in there, and I instantly knew. He never wrote those letters to me, but whoever *did* write to me *was* Travis. He knew things that only Travis could know, and his handwriting was identical."

He chewed on that for a few moments. "Travis Berkley doesn't have any siblings, and his DNA and prints were taken when he was arrested. Both matched those found on the girls who were raped."

"I'm aware," she bit out. "I don't know how it's possible—I just know that it's the truth."

"I'm not doubting you." He was just trying to figure out how it could be possible. It seemed like something out of a spy thriller—a switch between an innocent man and a guilty one.

Except . . . what if it wasn't a switch at all?

They had assumed Berkley had a partner, and the partner was the one doing the murders now. What if . . . What if the partner was the one in prison, and *Berkley* was the one murdering girls now? "Was Berkley good with computers?"

Lei made a sound suspiciously close to a sob. "He was decent, but that was twelve years ago. If Emma can become a hacker whiz, I don't see why Travis couldn't. But I can't say for certain that he was or wasn't back then." She pressed her hands to her chest as if trying to regain control of herself. "You're thinking about it."

"You're right—it does sound crazy. But we can at least make a few phone calls and see what falls out. We're here, after all." Berkley's parents were still local, and they might not want to talk to the Feds, but Dante wasn't going to give them a choice. If anyone knew how it was possible that what Lei was claiming was the truth, it would be Mr. and Mrs. Berkley.

"And then?"

"And then I'll pay another visit to whoever the hell it is serving Travis Berkley's sentence." He put the car into gear and pulled out of the parking lot toward the exit. "I'm going to have to drop you at the hotel before I go talk to them."

"I'd rather wait at a coffee shop or something like that." She shuddered. "I can't . . . I don't want to be alone right now. I'll go crazy if I sit in a hotel room. At least if I sit and drink overpriced coffee, I can just . . . I don't know. Process."

It was a lot to process. They couldn't make a straightforward accusation against the man in the prison. Either it would make Lei look crazy, which would work against her in any future appeals Berkley attempted—and there would be more appeals—or someone would actually listen and the man in that cell might walk free.

If he *wasn't* Berkley, then he had to be . . . an identical twin?

Maybe an identical twin named Trevor?

Dante shook his head. It defied the laws of probability. If the Berkleys were hiding an identical twin, they would have trotted him out the second Travis went on trial. If they were truly identical, their DNA would be the same, which would account for the tests not raising any red flags—*but* it would be nearly impossible to prove that one twin was the killer while the other was innocent. Instant reasonable doubt. "We have to handle this very, very carefully."

"I'm not crazy, Dante. I know this sounds nuts, but I'm right."

He merged onto the freeway heading south. "Call Emma. Can she track Berkley's birth records?"

"She should be able to." Lei grabbed her phone and started dialing.

Meanwhile, Dante had his own call to make. He hit the button to call Britton. As expected, his boss answered almost immediately. "What have you found?"

"Are you sitting down?"

A long pause. "Tell me."

"We talked to Berkley, but Lei is claiming that, whoever the man in that prison is, it isn't Travis Berkley. He looks like him, talks like him, but isn't him." Knowing Britton would want all the facts, he started at the beginning and went through the entire interview and what Lei said afterward. In the grand scheme of things, it wasn't much.

But all Britton said was "Hmm. It would explain the inconsistencies we've found."

"Identical twins might have the same DNA, but they don't have the same fingerprints . . ." But Berkley's hadn't been taken until he was arrested, and he hadn't been allowed bail, so the switch had to happen before that. *Bet some of those fingerprints they couldn't match to people* did *match the real Travis Berkley.* "This kind of shit doesn't happen in real life, Britton. It sounds like something out of a movie."

But he couldn't quite explain how Berkley would have a personality transplant and misremember key details about his time with Lei. Prison changed people, but Dante had studied Berkley's profile extensively. If he was as hyperfocused on Lei as all evidence supported, he would relive the time they spent leading up to the murders, if only to get the satisfaction of knowing he'd played her so thoroughly. It was confirmation of his superiority, proof that he was an unmatched predator.

Small details might fall by the wayside over the years—at least theoretically—but something as big as the car wouldn't.

"Don't discount the impossible just because it seems impossible. Talk to Travis's parents—specifically his mother. I'll call ahead so she knows to expect you."

He didn't ask how the lead FBI agent in the case who'd sent this woman's son away would still be in contact with her. It was such a damn Britton thing to do. Someone unassuming would guess that it was because he was just that likable, but the truth was more complicated. Britton lived by the truth that he never knew when a connection could become useful. There was no reason to burn a bridge he might need to cross in the future, and apparently the Berkleys numbered among those bridges. Naturally. "Thanks. I'm heading there now." The sooner they got to the bottom of this, the sooner they could get back to Seattle.

Because the end of this thing, however it went down, would be in Washington. Every instinct he had pointed in that direction, and he had no doubt they were correct. The man in prison hadn't committed these murders—whoever was free had.

If Lei is right . . . Travis Berkley is free, and has been this entire time.

"Keep me updated."

He hung up and looked over to where Lei stared down at her phone. "Lei—"

"Travis was the one who climbed in my window that night." She spoke so low, it was almost a whisper. Dante wasn't sure if she was trying to convince him or herself. "I'm sure of it." She shook her head. "I don't understand any of this, Dante. I don't understand how this is possible, how everything got so fucked-up so quickly. I've spent the last twelve years operating under a truth, and I feel like the rug just got swept out from under me."

He reached over and laced his fingers with hers. "We don't know for sure yet, but we'll get to the bottom of this."

"*I* know the truth. Everything else is just confirmation."

CHAPTER TWENTY-THREE

"That's impossible."

Emma scanned through the birth records at all three hospitals within reasonable distance from where the Berkleys lived. She knew Travis's birthday—of course she did—but to be safe, she expanded the search to a month beforehand and after. When that brought up nothing, she expanded by a year.

"Hmm."

Tucker leaned over the back of her chair. "What does *hmm* mean?"

"Stop lurking and I'll tell you." She pulled up the file and read it. "Bethanny Berkley was admitted a year before Travis's birth with a miscarriage in process. They lost the baby." There was even a death certificate for a girl baby, so there was no way in hell that was Travis. "But there isn't a record of him being born."

"Maybe they had a doctor deliver him at the house."

She shot him a look. "You've never met the Berkleys, have you?"

"Why would I?" When she just stared, he sighed. "No, but I read the file."

Of course he had. The file. It was always the file. Every single one of the cops, Isaac included, thought they knew what she and Lei had gone through because they'd read *the file*. There were horrors that words couldn't describe, and they included plastering herself between the wall and the couch, praying to any god who'd listen that Travis wouldn't notice she was missing. That none of the other girls would shake off their shock and reveal her hiding place. Of holding her breath every time the door opened and pressing her hand so hard to her mouth that she had half-moon cuts from her nails as she listened to him take yet another one of her friends out of the room, never to return.

Hell was those three hours when there was no one left in the room but Emma, and she still couldn't make herself move because she was convinced Travis stood in the doorway, just waiting for her to reveal her hiding spot.

Her body shook even thinking about it, and she pulled the cuffs of her sweatshirt down over her hands. She couldn't change the past, and she couldn't escape it, but she could educate the man standing over her. "Bethanny Berkley is old East Coast money. Gerald Berkley—Travis's dad—is also old-school money. I'm not saying that they don't have a private doctor on call, but Bethanny's mom died in childbirth with Bethanny's sister. It created a kind of unhealthy need to go to the hospital for every little thing, because she was sure a *real* doctor could have saved her mom."

He stared. "How the hell do you know that?"

"Lei dated Travis for, like, four months. She went to dinner at their house, which was where Bethanny grilled her about any future babies they might have and how she had better get herself and Bethanny's grandchild to the hospital when the time came and not be stupid enough to try for a home birth." It had seemed crazy at the time, and that was before they knew Travis was a freaking monster. "Girls talk, Tucker. There is no way Bethanny Berkley had a baby outside a hospital. Even if she *did*, she would have gotten her ass into an ambulance that would have taken her to the hospital immediately after, which would result in a birth certificate. A birth certificate we don't currently have." She grabbed the phone and thrust it at him. "Here, you need to call."

He blinked. "What?"

"Keep up, please. I don't do the phone—social anxiety—but there's a slim chance that the birth certificate never got filed electronically for some reason. You need to call and check on it." She jiggled the phone as she waited for him to take it. "We can't call the courthouse. They have one on file there, but that's different." Emma frowned. "I guess it's not technically a birth certificate that we need as much as a certificate of live birth. Proof that Travis Berkley came from Bethanny Berkley."

"If he didn't, then he was adopted, and that opens up a whole realm of possibilities." Tucker took the phone and pressed the "Call" button. He moved to the other side of the room, and it was like a different person had slipped into Tucker's skin. His posture became . . . looser. His smile brighter and less serious. Even his tone lightened and gained an "Aw shucks, ma'am" kind of thing.

It was freaking terrifying.

Emma turned back to her computers, her mind awhirl with Lei's news. She couldn't process it. She didn't *want* to process it. The only thing that got her through day after day was knowing that, no matter what scars marked her soul, Travis was serving the sentence he deserved behind bars.

If that wasn't true . . .

She shuddered hard enough that her fingers skittered across the keyboard. Emma didn't have a frame of reference for a world with Travis still moving through it. If he was free . . .

He's been in our house. Again. He's stood on the other side of the door to my office and tapped, probably smiling that sick smile and getting off on the fact that he scared the shit out of me.

Her vision blurred, and she curled her body into as small a spot as she could manage. She couldn't even comfort herself with the knowledge of the panic room, because he'd tainted that as well. The safe room wasn't safe, and neither was the house, but leaving was out of the question. Not now. Not without a plan and a place where she could start the process over from scratch.

Except . . .

Would she ever really feel anything resembling safe again? She had here, at least most of the time. She and Lei had spent years making this place into a small fortress, resting assured that no one could breach their defenses unless they let them. If, after all that, they hadn't really managed to do anything but create a secure place for him to get to them . . .

She closed her eyes and concentrated on the coaxing tone of Tucker's voice as he spoke to someone at the hospital on the phone. The words didn't matter as much as his presence in the room with her. He wasn't evil. He was here to keep her safe, even if only for a little while.

The rest she and Lei had to do themselves.

Emma inhaled and exhaled through the tightening in her chest and throat. She could breathe. It was just a panic attack. She couldn't take another Xanax because she needed to focus on finding the information Lei needed to figure out what the hell was going on.

She was safe.

Mostly.

With one last inhale, she straightened and opened her eyes. Tucker stood watching her, a contemplative expression on his face. She glared. "What are you looking at?"

"There's no record of Bethanny Berkley ever giving birth to a baby, aside from her miscarriage, but the nurse I spoke to was an old gossip, and something Bethanny did all those years ago pissed her the hell off. She let it slip that Bethanny *can't* have children because of complications that arose when she had the miscarriage."

Dante left Lei at a Starbucks with her laptop and phone, then headed into the extensive neighborhood that the Berkleys lived in. He wasn't big into the various subcommunities of Los Angeles, but this one reeked of understated wealth. All the houses were situated well away from the street, their fences and gates as classy as they were forbidding. Definitely not the kind of neighbors that would pop over to ask for a cup of sugar.

He knew, because he'd grown up in a neighborhood strikingly similar to this one, albeit on the opposite coast. It was all so damn . . . wasteful. The money, the politics, the jockeying for position by spending money that could actually make a difference in someone's life. Throw in the fact that his parents had the wrong color skin to ever truly fit in with their suburban McMansion neighborhood, and it was a lesson in futility.

It wasn't for him.

He found the correct address and turned into the driveway. It took all of thirty seconds after he gave his name to be admitted inside, and Dante couldn't help thinking that the generic white Toyota he was driving had something to do with that. *Mustn't let the neighbors see. What would they think?* He worked his way to the house, taking in the heavily manicured lawn, the mansion built in the same brick as the fence surrounding the property, and the garage that was nearly as big as the house. *Family likes their toys.*

He parked and headed for the front door, but it opened before he could so much as knock. Bethanny Berkley herself stood there. She wore a pair of slacks and a classy blue shirt that perfectly matched her eyes. Whatever lines might have been present on her face had been Botoxed away, giving her a vaguely surprised look. She took him in with a single visual sweep, her pale-pink lips twisting. "Please come in."

She led him through the first doorway on the left. Even though he knew better, he couldn't help comparing this sitting room to Lei's. Whereas Lei and Emma's was slightly cramped with mismatched furniture that spoke of eccentricity and character, this room could have come out of a catalog. Dante sank gingerly onto the tiny couch, half expecting it to shatter beneath his weight. "Thank you for meeting me on such short notice."

"I don't know what you expect me to be able to tell you. My only child is locked away on the say-so of those two sorority girls. Women like to bring down powerful men. It's what they do."

He could spend a whole lot of time picking apart that sentence, but Dante didn't have time. He had a burning question, and the only person who might be able to shed some light on the impossible situation sat perched on the chair across from him. With the information Tucker and Emma had found, he knew there was more than a possibility that Lei really was right. There was no record of Travis's adoption, but for people with money, like the Berkleys, that didn't actually mean anything. Private adoptions weren't something people talked about often, but they still happened—and they'd happened a whole lot more often thirty-some years ago.

He leaned forward. "Mrs. Berkley, I want to know about Travis's adoption."

Her jaw dropped, and her mouth gaped open like she was a fish out of water. "Excuse me?"

He'd meant to handle this more smoothly, but it was too late now. All the pressure of the case and the danger to both Clarke and Lei and the lies compressed inside him. This woman might not have set her son on the path to kill women, but her lies had facilitated him all the same. "Travis. You adopted him as a baby. I need to know what agency that went through, and I need the agent's name."

"This is outrageous. Travis is *mine*."

He met her gaze steadily until she looked away. "I never said he wasn't, though if I were you, I don't know that I'd be so quick to claim him. Not my place to judge you for that, but I will be needing that information."

She tried to stare him down for the second time, and for the second time, she looked away. "You don't know what it's like, Agent. Even now, when we're supposed to be so enlightened and equal, nothing is really equal. I was a Berkley and couldn't give my husband an heir. He was going to leave me for one of his young things that he thought I didn't know about. I didn't have a choice."

He squelched the pity threatening to rise. This woman had stood by her son against the mounting evidence against him. She didn't deserve pity. "Ma'am, I'm not here to judge you for that. I'm here for the contact information."

For a long moment, it looked like she'd argue, but she finally sighed. "I don't suppose it can hurt the family's image after all this time. Once Travis was convicted, we were ostracized from our social circles, and even a decade later, people actually turn up their noses when they see me." She gave a half-hearted smirk. "At least it's slowed my husband's indiscretions. Women don't trust him anymore, thinking the apple doesn't fall too far from the tree. If only they knew."

He had nothing at all to say to that. Twenty-one girls had died that night, and she was more concerned with her social standing than she was with the loss of the victims' futures and their grieving families. *Maybe some of Travis's disconnect was actually learned behavior.* Something to ponder later. All he said was, "I appreciate the information."

It took her twenty minutes to track down the code to the safe and pull out the relevant name and number. "I couldn't begin to guess if they're still up and running after all this time."

He glanced at the scrawled name and number on the card—the Lynburn Agency. "It's a place to start. Thank you for your time."

It was only when she had seen him out the door that she frowned. "Why do you need this?"

"No specific reason, ma'am. Just following up some leads for a case in Washington."

Her interest flickered out. "Oh. Well, then. Have a nice day, Agent."

She was most definitely heavily medicated, and he might have felt bad about it—about the awfulness of being married to what appeared to be a serial philanderer or mother to a serial killer—but Dante had larger things to worry about than yet another victim of Travis Berkley's actions. He walked directly to his car and drove off the Berkleys' property. A quick text to Lei had him ensuring she was waiting when he pulled up.

Lei took one look at his face and nodded. "She has that effect on people."

"You're taking this whole thing rather well."

It came out sounding a little accusatory, but before he could apologize, she shrugged. "I think I'm a little in shock. Too much has happened in too short of a time. I'll be freaking out as soon as it all sets in."

He held out a hand, and she took it. The contact steadied him, and he nodded to where he'd set the card in the center console. "That's the information. Make sure Emma shares it with Tucker, too." He could be sure Tucker would keep Britton updated. There hadn't been any word on Clarke, and he had the completely irrational fear that if he called Britton yet again, he'd learn she'd been found dead. It didn't make any sense, but an invisible clock counted down to a confrontation that promised to defy expectations. This wouldn't be an unsub who got pulled over during a routine traffic stop. This wouldn't be a sting organized after months of investigation.

No, there was only one way this ended, and it was with someone's death.

He was determined to do whatever it took to ensure that death wasn't Lei's, Emma's, or Clarke's.

CHAPTER TWENTY-FOUR

The trip back to Washington was almost anticlimactic. They landed with little fanfare and headed for the parking lot where Dante had left the car . . . Was it only yesterday? Lei swayed on her feet, exhaustion threatening to take hold. A person's system could only take so many shocks in such a short time, and she was well over her limit. She wanted her bed, she wanted Saul, and she wanted to just shut out the world for a few hours.

But they had one more stop to make before they went back to her place.

Dante drove them to a little hotel situated on the outskirts of Seattle. It was maybe an hour from Stillwater, but close enough to get to the local precinct without too much trouble. *Smart.*

She'd thought she was prepared to see Britton again after all this time. They'd talked on the phone semiregularly over the years, but he'd never had cause to visit, and she hadn't given him the excuse. Larger-than-life Agent Washburne had listened to her when no one else would. Had *believed* her. She'd always been afraid to meet him after the insanity of the trial and the aftermath had died down, to recognize that he was only a man, and an infallible one at that.

And yet when they walked out of the elevator and into the lobby, her heart swelled at the sight of his familiar broad shoulders and kind eyes. His skin was a shade darker than Dante's brown, and he was a few inches taller. *Still larger-than-life.* Britton saw her coming and gave a tired smile. "You look well, Lei."

She had to force herself to stop and not throw herself at him. He'd hugged her exactly once, but it had been a defining moment in her life. Lei's father didn't hug. He patted. Physical intimacy of any flavor was something to be avoided, and it was something she'd always craved despite herself. That single hug from Britton had been what she'd imagined a father's hug should be—all-encompassing and comforting.

Get ahold of yourself. Britton isn't here to feed your daddy issues.

Lei settled for a smile. "Hi, Britton."

He nodded at Dante. "The others are out, but you can update me in the conference room. I've taken the liberty of ordering for us."

As suspected, when the food arrived, it matched perfectly—a burger for Dante, a salad for Britton, and a french dip sandwich for Lei. She shook her head. "It's been ten years. How the hell do you still know what I eat?"

"Call it a hunch."

Dante snorted. "Call it magic. No one can figure it out, but he's never wrong. Best I can tell, he keeps files on everyone he might ever come across, and updates them regularly."

She smiled, but let the expression fall away almost immediately. Britton watched her. He hadn't so much as picked up his fork, which was as good as inviting her to start in. "You've heard."

"Tucker is with Emma right now while they dig into the history of the Lynburn Agency. They were a private adoption agency that functioned for about fifteen years in the eighties and nineties, though they haven't been active in nearly twenty years. If they have the records somewhere, it will take a court order to get to them."

Too much time. She wanted to rail and scream that Travis was coming, and all these hoops just meant they wouldn't be prepared when he did. It wouldn't change anything. Lei and Emma might skirt the edges of the rules sometimes, but Britton wouldn't. It was one of the things that made him who he was—and brought him to head his own division of the FBI.

He needs a court order, but Emma doesn't. If she could find a reason to send Tucker and Dante away for a little bit, Emma could track down their files, if they'd been digitized. She wouldn't be able to risk it with an FBI agent looking over her shoulder, but she *was* capable of it. Britton and his people would get it the legitimate way that would hold up in court, and, meanwhile, they wouldn't be stuck sitting on their hands longer than necessary.

Satisfied, she reached for her fork. "How did we miss this?"

"No one expected an identical twin." When Dante raised his brows, Britton nodded. "We'll have to wait for confirmation, of course, but that's the logical assumption. Travis—or his twin—was tested for DNA samples when he was taken in, and he wasn't released on bail, so there was no opportunity to switch him out with another person. While DNA technology has come a long way in a decade, there's no reason to think it was a mistake back then."

"His mother doesn't know."

Lei nodded. "If she knew, it would have been public knowledge. She pulled every ploy she could when Travis was on trial. An identical twin would have been enough to get him released." She went still. "Wait, does this mean that trial is null and void?"

"It's not that simple. Travis Berkley was convicted of twenty-one counts of first-degree murder. In order to get that sentence overturned, he would have to prove that the trial was unfair—not that he was innocent."

Dante picked up a fry. "What I don't understand is why he didn't come forward with the knowledge that he was a twin. It should have been enough to create reasonable doubt and result in a not-guilty sentence."

Lei's stomach twisted in on itself. "Unless Britton was right all along, and they were both there that night. The only way reasonable doubt works is if the court doesn't know which twin is guilty. If they're *both* guilty, they both go to jail, just like normal people. If Travis was the dominant partner, he could have convinced his twin to take the fall for him—especially since the twin was going to be convicted anyway." She didn't doubt for a second Travis was capable of it. He had been an expert manipulator, and getting other people to do what he wanted was his forte. Lei didn't know how the twins had found each other, and the chances of *two* sociopaths in a single family . . . She didn't know the odds, but they had to be astronomical.

That meant Travis must have convinced his twin—Trevor?—to participate in the murders, and then he took it a step further and let him take the fall.

What the hell did you say to him to make that happen? Was it a long, drawn-out process?

Or did he already have the same urges imprinted in his DNA, the same as you?

She had no answers.

While she was lost in thought, the conversation had moved beyond her.

Britton nodded to Dante. "Our priority right now is catching Berkley. Then it will be up to the courts to decide how to handle the twin. If it's as I suspect and the twin was actually in the house that night, he'll have a separate trial. It's a moot point at the moment."

Focus on finding Travis.

More likely that he's going to find me.

"Lei."

She glanced at Dante and found him looking at her with those soulful dark eyes. "Yeah."

"We will find him. We'll put a stop to all of this. It will be okay."

She wished she could believe him. It was so easy to say that of course it would be okay and the good guys would win and vanquish the evil monster lurking in the dark. That wasn't how life worked—not always. Sometimes the monster won. Sometimes the good guys fell in the line of duty, and sometimes cases went unsolved for decades.

Sometimes they went unsolved forever.

As if she needed more proof of that than finding long-since-decayed bodies with Saul, there was Emma's software. Thousands upon thousands of missing persons. Just as many Jane and John Does. Both data banks increasing daily.

She wanted Dante's comfort as much as she'd wanted a hug from Britton. But both were ultimately a lie. They couldn't guarantee her safety and get Travis captured, or they would have accomplished it by then.

And what about Clarke?

How did her disappearance play into this?

She managed a smile for Dante but turned to Britton before she could get distracted. "Do you have any news about Clarke?"

"Not enough." Britton leaned back, his salad untouched in front of him. "We found her vehicle abandoned in Portland, but we can't guarantee that she drove it down there. It's not far in the grand scheme of things, but I'm inclined to think it's a red herring to make us look south instead of here in Seattle. It would have been easy enough for the unsub to drive it down there, ditch it, and catch a train back north. All in the space of a day, even."

Which meant they had a whole lot of nothing to show for all their searching.

She forced herself to take a bite of her sandwich, chew slowly, and swallow. "You said unsub. Are you using that as a generic term, or do you think it's the same unsub who is killing the girls?" *Do you think Travis did this, too?*

There wasn't a damn doubt in her mind that Travis was behind this. She'd suspected it from the start and almost convinced herself that it was really all in her head, only to be vindicated in the end. That was the problem, though—she hadn't *wanted* to be vindicated. She wanted to be proven wrong, to go back to her assurance that she could face down whatever the world threw at her because she'd already survived the worst there was.

Except she hadn't survived—not yet.

He was coming for her.

Britton was talking, his even words drawing her back to the table and the discussion. Again. "While it's entirely possible that we're dealing with two perpetrators, I think he knew Clarke would be in that spot at that time, and he planned for it."

Dante draped an arm over the back of Lei's chair. It was a casual move that he did while his mind was obviously a thousand miles away, but she saw Britton mark it with the slightest raising of his eyebrows. Dante tapped his finger against the chair. "Have you checked her phone?"

"Of course. There were half a dozen calls to and from numbers we've traced back to local restaurants. All were busy during the lunch hour of the day she was taken, so they don't remember if they spoke to her or not. On the surface it would appear she was trying to order lunch, which I highly doubt, since Clarke liked fast-food burgers and the no-nonsense of a drive-through, but we have no way to confirm why she would be calling those places or why they would be calling her back."

Covering his tracks.

Travis always was too smart for everyone else's own good. "They're all within walkable distance of each other."

"They are." Britton took a drink of his iced tea. "We're working on getting security footage, but it's difficult without support of the local police."

From what she understood, they hadn't been really helpful from the start. Lei understood, even if she didn't forgive it. The LAPD hadn't wanted to believe that there was a monster lurking locally, either. There was a rumor for the first night or so that a drifter had broken into the Omega Delta Lambda house and murdered those girls, and Lei and Emma were so traumatized by it that they were making up crazy tales about it being an upstanding member of society.

Dante's thumb touched her back, an offering of silent support. He nodded. "Detective Smith isn't so bad, but he's in over his head, and he's not reacting well to that fact. You'll figure it out. You always do."

Lei's phone trilled. She started to apologize but frowned when she saw it wasn't Emma calling. It was an unknown number. It took her two tries to get her shaking under control enough to answer. "Hello?"

"Lei-Lei." He said her name as if relishing the taste on his tongue. It had been one of the things that drew her to him in the first place, because one thing twenty-one-year-old Lei Zhang had wanted more than anything in the world was to be *relished.*

She couldn't move. Couldn't speak. Couldn't breathe.

Travis.

The bogeyman shouldn't be able to take form enough to place a call, and yet here they were. A hand closed over her shoulder, an arm pressed against her back, and suddenly Dante's crisp scent wrapped around her. She closed her eyes and inhaled. Knowing he was right there didn't calm her racing heart, but it gave her the strength to form words. She took the phone from her ear and put it on speaker. "Travis."

Instantly, Britton and Dante were both on high alert. Britton took out his phone and started texting furiously, and Dante's grip on her tightened ever so slightly. He was there. She was safe. Travis wasn't going to burst through the wall and drag her off to whatever hell he'd been living in for the last twelve years. *I'm safe.*

"It's been fun watching you run around chasing me, but that's over now. I'm done playing." He still sounded downright happy, even though a dangerous edge crept into his tone.

There wasn't enough air in the room. Hell, there wasn't enough air in the entire city to compensate for the poison dripping from his voice into her ears. She closed her eyes. *No. This isn't who I am anymore. I am not his fucking victim. I am a goddamn survivor.* She gritted her teeth. "If you wanted me, you should have just come for me and been done with it."

"Where's the fun in that?" He chuckled. "I enjoyed my walk down memory lane. Omega Delta Lambda will always hold a special place in my heart."

Her stomach lurched, threatening to rebel, and she was suddenly glad she hadn't managed to eat much. "I'm going to stop you."

"I invite you to try." Another chuckle. "But I have to say, your reputation with that mutt of yours made me think you'd be more of a challenge now than you were back then. That's not really working out that well, is it?" Wind whispered in the background, crackling across the line.

Where are you, you son of a bitch?

She found herself leaning forward, trying to concentrate on anything that would give away his position. Something came over the line, distant and indistinct. As the silence stretched on in their standoff, it slowly formed into a noise she recognized.

Dogs barking.

Saul barking.

Lei gripped the phone so tightly, it was a wonder it didn't come apart in her hands. Her entire world narrowed down to the warm plastic and glass pressed against her hand and the man breathing lightly through the speaker. She couldn't beg. It wouldn't do anything, and

Travis would only get off on it. Threatening him wouldn't work, either. Despite all evidence to the contrary, he wasn't actually pissed yet. *You will be before I'm through with you.*

No, there was only one way to play this to potentially get through to him, and she didn't know if she could stomach it.

She didn't have a choice.

"Travis." His name tasted like sludge on her tongue. "You know I've always been the goal. I'd say I'm flattered, but we both know that would be a lie." She met Dante's eyes and made a writing motion. He grabbed a hotel stationery pad and a pen, and she scrawled out *He's at the house.*

Dante's eyes went wide, and then he was up and scrambling for his phone, presumably to call Tucker.

They'll be ready for Travis. We'll get him this time.

She just had to stall him a little longer.

"My Lei-Lei, always speaking the truth."

She was losing him. She swallowed hard. "Come get me, Travis. I'll walk out of here right now. No police. No Feds. Just me. Isn't that what you want?"

"Of course. That's what I always wanted." He hummed faintly. "You know, I was thinking about marrying you. It would have made my mother happy."

She blinked. Of all the things . . . *He's insane. More insane than I could have anticipated.* "You murdered twenty-one women, Travis. *Twenty-one.* You can't possibly think I'd marry you after that."

"I left little Emma alive for you. That was my gift to you. You can't honestly expect to be in a relationship without some compromises."

The roaring in her ears drowned out Dante and Britton's low conversation. It drowned out *everything.* The world shifted and realigned itself, and up was down and down was up. "Emma escaped you."

"Because I let her." He took on a gentle chiding tone. "I know how to count. Even with Trevor playing second fiddle to me, do you really think I would have forgotten that Emma was in that room? She was your best friend."

Trevor.

His twin's name is Trevor. The note wasn't a mistake after all.

Lei shook her head. Focus. *He's threatening Emma. But . . .*

She had a specific narrative of what had happened that night, and Travis seemed determined to turn it on its head. "You tried to kill *me*!"

"Don't be dramatic. I needed you out of commission and above suspicion. None of your injuries were life-threatening. It's not my fault you decided to jump off the damn roof." He sounded so normal, as if they were an old married couple and she'd done something unforgivably silly. Maybe in his mind, it all equaled out. Sure, he'd murdered an entire houseful of women, but he'd left her best friend alive, so the scales must be balanced.

Focus, Lei. You can freak out about Travis being in love with you later.

"Come get me, Travis," she repeated, trying to get them back on track. "That's what this is all about, isn't it? Or did you put your twin—Trevor—in jail just for shits and giggles? I'm sure he'd love to know that."

"All in good time."

"What are you talking about?"

"You didn't think it would be that easy, did you?" There was a thud in the background, as if he'd dropped something heavy. "I gave you Emma's life last time, and you didn't appreciate it. If you want to save her this time, you have to work for it. Good luck, Lei-Lei."

CHAPTER TWENTY-FIVE

Emma took a quick shower in an effort to get her head on straight. Her hands ached from all the typing, and she had a piercing headache starting behind her left eye from all the screen time. Or maybe it was stress. At the end of the day, it didn't matter, because she'd needed to get a little alone time away from the pacing FBI agent in her office.

He meant well, probably, but he had too much energy for her space. It exhausted her and wore on her last nerve, so after she'd gotten her searches rolling, she'd retreated to the relative solitude of her bathroom. She washed her hair twice just to give herself something to do, but guilt wouldn't let her linger under the scalding spray.

Lei needed her.

And if she was right . . . Emma shuddered. As much as confirming Lei's suspicions would create a nice, pat little answer to who was committing these atrocities, it also meant that *Travis was free*.

It was something she'd tried again and again not to think too hard about, because she would . . . what? Run? The thought of leaving the house filled her with such dread, her entire body trembled. Locking herself in a safe room was no better. He'd proved he could get to her there, even if she and Lei had changed the code. If he'd found it once, he was capable of finding it again.

She couldn't lock herself up and wait for all this to blow over. Lei needed her. It was still possible that Travis had some kind of psychotic break in prison, and *that* was what her friend was picking up on. It was actually more likely than Travis going on a killing spree with his long-lost identical twin and then letting said twin take the fall for him.

But Lei had been right about him being adopted, which was something that had never come up before. There'd been no reason to look into it—the cops had Travis in custody, and his parents weren't clamoring to blame him being a crazy killer on genetics that weren't theirs. They *claimed* him, even after it became glaringly obvious that he was guilty.

Emma shut off the water and grabbed a towel. She instinctively reached for her phone and frowned when it wasn't on the counter. *Must have left it downstairs in my rush to get the hell out of that room.* It didn't matter. She'd be down there in a minute or two, and if something important happened, Tucker knew where to find her.

She still picked up her pace. Emma pulled on a pair of yoga pants, a sports bra, and a long-sleeve shirt. After considering for half a second, she yanked a sweater over her head, too. A pair of thick wool socks and she was as ready as she was going to be.

She opened the door to her bedroom and paused. The house felt . . . eerily empty. Not a single sound came from downstairs. Not dog nails clicking on the hardwood, not Tucker's pacing, not even the steady hum of her electronics.

Oh, God.

She reacted on instinct, stepping back into her room and slamming the door shut. Her hands shook as she engaged the lock, but it wasn't enough. If someone else was in the house, the flimsy lock on her bedroom door wouldn't slow them down in the least.

If someone *wasn't* in the house, then she could have a good laugh about it later.

She turned and slammed into something hard. Some*one* hard. Emma bounced back a step and hit the door. It took her eyes precious seconds to adjust to the low light and recognize the man standing in her room. Her brain took even longer. "No."

"Hey, Emma," Travis Berkley said. "Long time, no see."

◆ ◆ ◆

Dante flew through the dark pass, pushing the car faster than was wise. Tucker wasn't answering his phone. Neither was Emma, or Sheriff Bamford, who had been on duty, last they'd heard. Lei sat still and silent in the passenger seat, locked in her own personal hell. He didn't know what to say to reach her, didn't know if he should even try.

But he couldn't *not* try.

"Britton will be behind us shortly. He'll bring the team members he's got here, and they'll raise both the Seattle PD and the little local towns surrounding Stillwater. He won't get through the net."

"He's already through it." Lei didn't look away from the road blurring under the car's tires. "He wouldn't have called me if he thought for a second that we could get there in time. Travis doesn't play fair. He never has. Emma is already gone, and probably whoever else was in or near that house, too."

Emma wasn't dead. Dante wouldn't say it and give her false hope, but Berkley wouldn't have put this much time and effort into getting Lei exactly where he wanted her just to disappear again. If she thought for a second that Emma was still alive and in danger, she wouldn't stop long enough to come up with a plan—she'd just throw herself into danger, and to hell with the rest. "Promise me that you won't react until we have all the information."

"Like hell I won't." She wrapped her arms around her small frame. "I can't promise that any more than you can promise you'll be logical where Clarke is concerned."

Travis hadn't said anything about Clarke. It might be all part of his sick game, but Dante couldn't help thinking that maybe they were wrong all along—that Clarke's disappearance was completely unconnected to this case. The thought left him empty and sick. "We'll wait for backup."

"Sure." She didn't bother to sink any meaning behind the lie.

He didn't call her on it. They wouldn't know what they were walking into until they got there, and any speculation was pointless. He drove as fast as humanly possible, the tension in the car rising with each mile they moved closer to Lei's house.

He was going so fast, they almost missed the turn. Dante slammed on the brakes and hit the gravel in a skid. The car rolled to a stop and he exhaled. "Sorry."

"Don't be." She bounced her leg as if considering bolting out of the car and running the rest of the way to the house, so he crept forward, hoping the momentum would be enough to keep Lei in the car. They drove the quarter mile through the forest, the trees seeming to crowd closer than they ever had before. Dante was all too aware of the way the headlights left them blind to everything not directly in their path. Berkley's MO didn't point to him as a sharpshooter, but they couldn't take anything for granted anymore. "Lei, sit back." He knew without asking that telling her to put her damn head down would be met with resistance.

"Don't tell me to—"

He let the car roll to a stop. The sheriff's cruiser sat in the middle of the driveway, the driver's side door open and the dome light on. "Stay here."

"No way." She opened the door before he had a chance to argue, her handgun flashing in the low light.

"Damn it, Lei." He followed her, drawing his own gun and keeping an eye out for an ambush. They reached the cruiser in seconds, and he tensed, half expecting to find the sheriff's body.

It was empty.

She let out a shuddering breath. "Let's keep going."

It would take too much time to move the cruiser and drive the last couple of hundred yards to the house, so he just shut the door and followed her through the darkness. Every step of the way, Dante was sure Travis would melt from the shadows and strike.

Nothing happened.

They reached the house safely, and Lei opened the front door and stepped inside. "Emma? Tucker? Saul? Here, Saul!"

The silence in response was deafening. Dante grabbed her elbow when she went to move forward. "Don't you dare." He pulled her back and nudged her behind him. Dante pointed to himself. "Federal agent." He pointed to her. "Civilian. Stay behind me, and we'll clear the house."

Her lips thinned, but she finally nodded. "Okay."

They moved through room after room. Empty. Empty. More empty. With each missing sign of people, Dante's worry grew. Tucker was a big man and trained in multiple ways to take out a suspect and defend both himself and anyone around him. Berkley shouldn't have been able to get the drop on him. If he had . . .

It didn't bear thinking about it.

Both the women's rooms and the spare were empty. Dante looked askance at Lei. "Safe room?"

"We have to check."

He didn't imagine Berkley was huddled in the safe room, waiting to strike, but Dante still kept close as Lei keyed in her code, and then he wrestled the door open. Something moved in the darkness, and he had his gun halfway up when Lei shoved his arm to the side. "Saul!"

"And Tucker," came a groan from deeper in the shadows. "And Prince."

The dog whimpered, his tail wagging and then not, as if he wasn't sure of his welcome. Dante waited for Lei to go down on her knees and wrap her arms around the animal before he skirted around them to where Tucker was. He pulled out his phone to get a better look at his friend and winced. "Fuck, Tucker."

"Got the drop on me." One of Tucker's eyes was completely swollen shut, and he had a nasty gash down the other side of his face. He didn't seem hurt otherwise, but Dante was careful helping him to sit so he could cut through the zip tie around his wrists. "Did you get a look at him?"

"It was Travis fucking Berkley." Tucker shook his head and rubbed his wrists. "Like being attacked by a ghost. I went for my gun, but I hesitated because he surprised me."

Lei let go of Saul. "Where's Emma?"

"He took her." Tucker lumbered to his feet. "That bastard took her." He pointed to the still-active monitors. "He didn't drive off, though. He went through the woods. North, I think."

Lei nodded. "That monitor shows the running trails leading north."

The same trails where she'd found the purse a couple of days ago. *Was it only a couple of days ago? It feels like a hundred years.* Too much had been crammed into too few hours.

Dante helped Tucker stand but had to work to keep the big man from tilting over. "Concussion?"

"Not sure." He touched his eye gingerly. "I think I lost consciousness for at least a minute or two, so probably."

"Let's get you downstairs." If he was still dizzy, then Dante wasn't going to leave him to navigate the narrow stairs alone. "Lei, I'll be right back."

"I'll be down behind you." She knelt next to Saul and ran her hands over his big body, probably checking for injuries. Prince nudged her shoulder, whining. "I know, boy. I know."

"Okay." He watched her for a long moment, but the eerie calm that had fallen into place when Berkley had called hadn't so much as faltered. She was poised to explode, and Dante had to make sure he was there to protect her when she did. "We'll find her."

"I know." Still too calm. She should be screaming or shaking or *something*, but she just kept checking the dogs and not looking at Dante.

There was nothing for it. He had to get Tucker downstairs, and he had to call and update Britton so his boss knew what they were walking into. *At least Berkley hadn't killed Tucker.* He could have. He *should* have, if only to keep from being followed before he was ready.

That he hadn't meant Tucker served more purpose alive than dead. *Slowing us down,* Dante realized. Berkley had every reason to believe Lei would tear after him the second she got there and realized Emma was gone. Even if he'd been haunting the forest around this house, Lei had spent eight years traipsing all over it while training Saul and the other dogs she'd worked with. She *knew* the area in a way no one else could.

"What did he look like? Berkley?"

Tucker grunted as he sat in the kitchen chair. "I didn't get a good look, but he looked normal. The kind of guy normal people nod to on the street instinctively."

It lined up with both what he'd seen of the man's pictures and interviews and the surviving sorority girls who saw him at that fund-raiser. They hadn't thought he was creepy or deranged-looking—just *old.*

Which supported the suspicion that Berkley must have been living a life somewhere in Seattle or a nearby area this entire time. He hadn't been camped out in the forest while he stalked Lei. He'd been accumulating his technical knowledge so he could hack past Emma's firewalls and security setup.

And *that* meant Lei and Saul would have the advantage in the forest.

Dante glanced at the stairway, but she hadn't followed them down yet. "Call Britton and tell him what's happened." He didn't *think* Lei would scale the outside of the house with Saul in tow, but he couldn't trust that she was thinking clearly right then.

Dante found her in her room. He stood in the doorway and watched as she slid a large knife into her boot sheath and stuck three ammo clips onto a belt she hadn't been wearing before. Handguns were checked and double-checked and then went into the shoulder holster. "Lei."

"If you're going to tell me that we have to wait for Britton, you might as well save your breath. Travis set this up on purpose. I'm not going to risk Emma's life while we wait for the FBI, and then wait some more while they bicker with local police on the best way to track a serial killer through the woods. I can do it. I was always meant to do it." She straightened, and he realized Saul had a vest on now. The dog sat at her feet, waiting attentively. "We've trained for years for this."

"You train to track cadavers. Emma is still alive."

She gave a bitter smile. "You underestimate our paranoia. Just because Saul is good at tracking corpses doesn't mean he can't track live people. We already covered that with the last search." She moved to the bed and picked up three tank tops that he hadn't noticed before then. Two went into a pouch at her waist, and the third she kept a hold of. "What will it be, Dante? Are you going to try to stop me? There isn't a damn place in this house you can lock me up to keep me from following them. She's trusting me to save her. Emma is all I have left in this world, and I'll be damned before he takes her from me, too."

She's not the only thing you have in this world.

He didn't say it. Couldn't say it.

Lei was right. She was better equipped than any of the agents currently rushing this way. There was also the added fear that if they took too long and didn't play by Berkley's rules, he would kill Emma.

If Dante let Lei do this, Berkley might kill them all. "Lei—"

"There's something else." She walked to her dresser and picked up a simple white envelope. Without another word, she handed it to Dante and waited.

He wouldn't like whatever it held. He spent one eternal moment arguing with the part of him that wanted to throw it away, toss Lei over his shoulder, get in a car, and drive as fast as they could away from this horror show.

That wasn't who he was. It wasn't who *she* was.

There was no turning away from this.

He opened the envelope. Inside were two Polaroid-like photos. One depicted Emma, a thin rivulet of blood trailing from her temple, her blue eyes wide and mindless with terror. Her hands were tied in front of her, and she wore a similar outfit to the one she'd had on yesterday when they'd left.

The other picture was of Clarke.

CHAPTER TWENTY-SIX

Lei should have prepared Dante for the shock of seeing Clarke tied and bloodied in a photograph obviously left by Travis. She *should* have told him the second she realized Travis had left the dare behind, the taunt written in his bold hand. *Tag. You're it.*

There were a lot of things she should have done.

But she saw the way he was leaning and knew that he'd err on the side of safety and waiting for reinforcements. It was the wrong call—the call that would get both Emma and Clarke killed. *If they hadn't been already.*

No, she couldn't think like that.

He slid the photos back into the envelope. "It could be an old photo."

"It was taken in my kitchen. It's not an old photo." She shook her head. "You have to follow protocol. I understand that. *I* don't. Please move out of my way."

She stepped toward him, but the look on his face stopped her. It was like staring in the center of a hurricane, his rage and frustration threatening to suck them both down. Dante blinked and leashed it, but she was struck again by this man's hidden depths. She would have liked to have spent time exploring them, getting to know his ins and outs and what made him tick.

So fitting that Travis had managed to ruin yet another good thing in her life.

Finally, Dante stepped back. "I'm going with you."

"Dante—"

"If you think I'm going to let you walk into those trees alone, then you're thick in the head. Tucker can stay here and monitor our progress so Britton and the rest of them can follow when they get here."

"Fine." Easy enough to agree. It would be over by then. "But we leave now."

Dante took a quick detour to get Tucker and Prince set up in Emma's office, which was just fine. She needed a few minutes with Saul before they got moving. Lei led him outside and in the general direction Travis must have taken the women. Clarke hadn't looked like she was in good shape, but he'd still have his hands busy trying to herd both her and Emma. It made it less likely that he'd stash one of them somewhere.

He knew she'd track him—track Emma.

It was most definitely a trap.

Lei didn't give a fuck. Let him spring the damn trap. No matter what he thought, no matter what research or stalking he'd engaged in over the years, he didn't *know* her anymore. He might think he did, but she'd prove just how dead wrong he was.

She went to one knee before Saul, his cue that it was time to work. He sat, nearly quivering with excitement. Lei held out the first dirty tank top she'd pulled from Emma's hamper. Saul knew Emma, but if they were tracking a specific scent, she needed something fresher and more specific than *Find Emma*. "Find."

She heard Dante come out the front door and pad down the stairs to stand behind her. She let Saul sniff his fill and stood as he turned in the direction of the north trail. Lei glanced back at Dante. "Stay behind me. The trail is fresh, but it might get confused at some point. Just . . . follow me."

"I'm here." Just that, the steady truth that he'd have her back no matter where this trail led.

And maybe even after . . . if there is *an after.*

She turned back to her dog. She was putting him in danger by bringing him on this search, but she didn't have his nose, and she was only a passable tracker—and only during the day.

It felt like fate spinning out before her, every decision she'd made bringing her to this point, to this search. To one final confrontation with Travis. One of them wasn't walking out of the forest today, though she couldn't begin to guess who would prevail. *He won last time. He won't win again. It ends here. Now.*

"Search, Saul," Lei said, never taking her eyes from the path. *I'm coming for you, you son of a bitch.*

Saul took off on his active searching pace. The scent trail was strong and true here, with little to distract from it. If Emma had spent any time at all outside the house, Lei would have started the search at the trailhead where it left the grass, but there would only be one scent trail from her, and it would be the one that started tonight when Travis dragged her from the place she'd spent the last eight years.

Lei couldn't think about how scared Emma was—how scared *she* was. Instead, she focused on Saul, her own personal compass. No matter what else was going on, her dog only cared about following the trail to its natural conclusion. Between him leading her forward into the darkness and Dante's comforting presence at her back, she could almost believe that good might triumph over evil tonight.

Almost.

During the day, the jogging path felt almost spacious, the sunlight filtering through the trees overhead and continual sounds accompanying every footfall and breath.

Tonight, there was none of that. The darkness hid potential threats, and the entire forest seemed to be holding its breath. Every shadow promised danger, and the interlaced tree limbs overhead didn't let in nearly enough of the waxing moon.

Lei did semiregular practice searches with Saul at night because they rarely knew what conditions they would walk into when they were contracted. Most of the time, searches could be scheduled during the daylight hours, but sometimes that wasn't possible for one reason or another. Lei was a big fan of being prepared for any given situation.

I wasn't prepared for this.

No one could have been prepared for this.

Saul paused, his nose a few inches off the ground, and Lei held up a hand to let Dante know to stop. Saul started moving back and forth, looking for the scent cone. *Travis must have taken her off the trail here.* Lei took her eyes off Saul long enough to check the surrounding area. They'd made good time, moving well past the point where she'd found the purse before.

The darkness disoriented her, making it hard to gauge distances, but she thought they must be nearing the edge of their property. She usually turned before this point to loop back around for her five miles.

Saul pawed the ground, his sign that he'd picked up the scent again. She shifted nearer, following him off the path. The trees grew close enough together that she had to turn sideways to get through them, and Dante had to actually squeeze, but once they were through the copse, the space opened up again. It was hard to see in the low light, but . . . "This is another path."

Dante held up a hand and moved farther down the path while they waited. He disappeared for a couple of seconds, and then he was back, his expression grim. "Hard to tell in the dark, but it looks like it runs parallel to the one we were just on."

Their property ran tall and narrow, stretching roughly five miles north and northwest and maybe two miles wide. They bordered state land to the west, which gave Lei plenty of ground to cover in her practice searches with Saul, so she was careful not to trespass on their neighbors to the east. The trees were thick enough that she'd never seen anyone on her runs or when she spent time outside, but it sure as hell looked like this trail was used to mirror hers.

So someone could watch her.

So *Travis* could watch her.

She swayed, anger warring with terror. Saul shifted restlessly, reminding her that the search wasn't over and they hadn't found their target. *Emma.* She had to keep it together for Emma. "Stay close," she whispered. Lei had anticipated a long and drawn-out search when they first started, but now she was suddenly sure that danger was so much closer than she could have dreamed.

Saul led them along the second path, turning almost directly east at the point where Lei suspected her property stopped, and down a sloping decline in the direction of the highway. *If he managed to get both Clarke and Emma into a car, that's the end of it. Saul is good, but no dog can track* that.

But Saul didn't head for the highway. He looped south again, still following the trail, and picked up his pace. *We're close.*

The trees gave way unexpectedly, and she dived for Saul, grabbing his vest and hauling him back. "Hold, boy."

Before them stretched a perfectly manicured lawn. It was twice as large as Lei and Emma's, and there was what looked like a pool lurking a couple of hundred yards to the south, next to the house situated in the middle of the open ground. It wasn't insanely large, but even at this distance she could tell it reeked of money. Bright lights poured out of the floor-to-ceiling windows that showcased an immaculately decorated living room in what could only be called mountain chic. A large fireplace dominated the room, and oversize furniture practically screamed that a manly man lived there, even if he wasn't the type of man who actually knew a damn thing about roughing it.

And in the center of the room, hanging from the roughened wood chandelier by a rope tied to her wrists, was Clarke.

◆ ◆ ◆

Dante took two steps forward before he caught himself. They had no backup, no knowledge of what they were walking into, and with Clarke obviously set up like the lure in a trap, Berkley had to be counting on them to react first and worry about the rest later.

Which was exactly what he'd been about to do.

He touched Lei's back and jerked his chin toward the trees. They needed a plan, but more important, they needed to convey their location to Tucker and Britton. Once they were safely out of sight of the house, he shifted close enough that she could hear him while he spoke barely above a whisper. "I got turned around back there. Where are we in relation to your house?" He was used to navigating cities and occasionally small towns. Everything looked the same in the forest, and the forest at night? Forget about it.

"Um . . ." She closed her eyes, obviously retracing their steps. "The property to the east. Maybe northeast. We were close to the highway at one point, but then we looped south, and so directly east is the best bet."

He slipped his phone from his pocket and sent a group text to both Britton and Tucker. He only had one lonely bar of service, but after considering it, the texts went through. He replaced the phone before Britton sent an order demanding they stand down and wait for reinforcements.

Clarke's location was most definitely a trap, but Dante couldn't leave her hanging there while he waited for the safe route. She wouldn't hesitate if their positions were reversed, and Lei sure as fuck wasn't going to stop now that the end was in sight.

He clasped her hand, squeezing it to get her to focus on him. "First Clarke. Once she's secure, we'll search the house and find Emma."

She hesitated, but nodded. "Okay."

"This time, you stay behind me."

Another hesitation, shorter this time. "Let's go." She murmured a command to Saul that had him taking a position six inches to her right, his stance alert.

Dante drew his gun and waited for Lei to do the same. Then they worked their way across the open ground, avoiding the large pools of light. Just because they were walking straight into this trap didn't mean they had to be idiots about it. He constantly scanned the area, but the light made him night-blind. Berkley could be standing in a pool of shadows, and because of the damn lights in the living room, Dante wouldn't see him until it was too late.

He aimed for the back door that seemed to lead directly into the living room. On the first try, it opened in his hand. *Definitely a trap. He might as well have laid out a welcome mat for us.* Dante's phone buzzed, but he ignored it as he eased open the door and slipped into the house, pausing to give his eyes a moment to adjust. From his position, it looked like Clarke's chest was moving in slow exhales and inhales, but he couldn't be sure.

Lei joined him in the house and motioned to Saul to sit. She closed the door and locked it. *Smart. Ensuring Berkley can't approach from that direction.* She motioned for him to head to Clarke while she covered him, and Dante didn't hesitate.

He crossed the room with a handful of long strides and lifted Clarke from the hook that had been hung from the bottom of the chandelier made of reclaimed wood. She was slight in his arms, a vivid reminder of exactly how human she was. Her skin was a rainbow of bruises, and she'd rubbed her wrists raw against the rope binding her. *Always fighting, no matter how long the odds.*

She stirred, her head lolling against his arm. Clarke blinked blue eyes at him, confusion warring with relief. "Dante?"

"I'm here. You're safe now."

"Trap," she breathed.

"I know."

The lights went out.

A thud had him spinning to where Lei had stood, but he couldn't see anything except starbursts of light as his eyes tried to adjust. Saul yelped, and then terrifying silence descended. Dante rushed to the back door, only to find it hanging open.

Lei was gone.

CHAPTER TWENTY-SEVEN

Lei fought against the arms that pinned her against a solid chest. *Travis's chest.* He dragged her out of the house and around the corner toward the front. "Stop fighting or I go back in there and shoot your fucking dog," he growled against her neck. "And I'll carve up your boyfriend while I'm at it."

She'd lost her one gun in the shuffle, and he used her moment of surprise to grab the other from her holster and fling it into the darkness. "Now, Lei-Lei, are you going to play nice?"

"Where's Emma?"

He ignored that. "Answer the fucking question."

She could try to fight. She might even be able to get away from him long enough to go for the knife in her boot. But as capable as she was, Lei didn't like her chances against Travis with only a knife between them. Not with Emma's life in the balance. Not when Dante was at a disadvantage because he had Clarke in his arms. Not with Saul hurt and . . .

Can't think about any of that. Focus on the now.

It took her two tries to speak past her dry throat. "I'll play nice." The words tasted of poison on her tongue, but he had all the advantages in that moment. The only chance she had was waiting for his guard to go down and striking then.

"Good girl." He hauled her around the side of the house as Dante's roar cut through the night. "Quite the animal you have there, isn't he?"

She didn't dignify that with a response. But when Travis towed her to the front door, she froze. "What are you doing?"

"Inside. Now." He glanced over her shoulder and shoved her inside. She barely had time to catch herself on the wall before Travis was there, grabbing her upper arm and forcing her up the stairs. Lei could hear Dante yelling her name outside, but without light or Saul, he wouldn't be able to tell if Travis had taken her back to the woods or somewhere else. He wouldn't even think to look back inside the house.

Lei sure as hell wouldn't have.

They kept moving, going down a long hallway and up a third set of stairs. It wasn't until Travis shoved her and turned to haul the stairs up behind him that she realized he'd brought her to the attic.

Lei didn't think. She grabbed her knife and went for his back.

He turned just as she brought the knife down and caught her wrist. "Ah ah." Travis squeezed until the blade went flying and twisted, forcing her around and her arm up between her shoulder blades. "You aren't the only one who learned a thing or two in the last twelve years." He steered her deeper into the attic, past furniture covered with white sheets and a mirror that almost reached the ceiling above them.

There, in the back corner, lit by a low lamp, was Emma. She was slumped on her side, her blue eyes closed. "Emma!" Lei started forward, but Travis yanked her back.

"Not yet." He buried his face in her neck and inhaled, low and deep. "God, I missed you, Lei-Lei."

Every single hair on her body stood on end. There wasn't a single way to interpret that move but sexual, and her mind went blank in terror. *I can't, I can't, I won't. Get off me.* She moved on pure instinct, slamming her heel into his foot and twisting out of his grip when his hands went slack with shock.

Stuck between flight or fight, there wasn't a real choice at all. *No knife. No gun. But I still have me.*

She punched him in the throat, and then she did it again as he bent in half. "Choke on that, you fucking monster." She tried to knee him in the balls, but he turned his hips at the last moment and she only hit his thigh. Lei settled for kicking his legs out from underneath him. He hit the floor and she backed away, frantically searching for something resembling a weapon.

Down below, Dante's bellows got quieter.

He was moving away from the house.

Travis groaned and rolled to his hands and knees. Lei stared. He wouldn't stop. She didn't have a single thing to fight him with, and he was stronger than she was. If he stopped long enough to realize that all he had to do was threaten Emma, this would be over before she had a chance.

Lei kicked him in the face, flipping him onto his back. She sprinted back toward the stairs, but she could hear Travis cursing behind her. It would take too long to figure out how to get them to descend again.

No, her only hope was the window leading out onto the widow's walk. If she could get out there, she could signal Dante and lead Travis away from Emma at the same time.

Lei scrambled over a covered chair and unlatched the window. It was new enough that it swung open easily when she pushed it, and she climbed up onto the windowsill. Every instinct demanded she run and hide, but she had to keep Travis chasing her. She forced herself to hold still, to wait until she heard his pounding footsteps and saw his shadow reaching for her to slip out onto the roof.

Her feet slid, and the past slammed into her with the strength of a body slam. Just like that, she was twelve years younger, weaving over the roof of the sorority house, trying to scream for help past her hoarse throat. She'd fallen, whether from vertigo or the concussion Travis had given her.

She wouldn't fall now.

Lei forced herself to keep moving, to put a little distance between her and the window. The roof incline was steep enough that she had to crawl to reach the peak, but she managed. She twisted, searching for movement below, but there was nothing. "Dante! Dante, I'm here!"

A hand closed around her ankle. "He's not coming for you, you dumb bitch." Travis yanked her off her feet, and it was only his hold on her that kept her from falling headfirst down the slope of the roof. Lei scrambled against the shingles, trying to get a hold even as she kicked at his face. Her foot made contact with his shoulder, and he released her, sending her sliding down the side of the roof.

She caught herself on a gable halfway between the window and the thirty-foot fall, but Travis was too quick. He flipped her onto her back and forced her arms above her head. "I had plans for you, but I guess this will do. I'll let Emma know that every cut she receives is because you weren't good enough to stand in her place. She'll curse your name before she's dead." He shifted his grip on her wrists to one hand and pulled out her knife with the other, raising it over his head. "Good-bye, Lei-Lei."

A gunshot rang out through the night, and Travis jerked. His blue eyes went wide as another shot hit him, and he slumped to the side, caught in the angle between the gable and the main roof. Lei snatched the knife from his limp grip and scrambled back out of reach. Her hands shook, but she forced herself to hold still and watch as the light bled out of his eyes. Even then, she could barely trust that Travis was, in fact, dead.

He's dead. It's over.

Oh, God, it's finally over.

"Lei!"

Dante.

She slid back a foot and then another, until she was at the edge of the roof. Still keeping one eye on Travis—Travis's body—she leaned over to see him standing in the middle of the lawn. Clarke was at his feet, and he had a gun braced in both hands as if he couldn't quite believe the threat had passed, either. "Dante." She didn't yell, but he heard her all the same.

"Are you okay?"

"No." She swallowed hard. "But I'm alive."

He nodded. "Watch him. I'm coming up."

◆ ◆ ◆

Things happened quickly after that. Dante left Clarke in the living room with Saul and a gun—the dog was injured, but alive—and made his way into the attic. He found Emma still unconscious on the ground, but she seemed relatively uninjured.

By the time he made it to the roof and Lei, sirens screamed through the night. *Britton with reinforcements.* Dante checked Berkley's pulse, but he already knew the man was dead. He'd shot to kill. They'd leave the body there for the medical examiner to deal with. It was the survivors who mattered.

He helped Lei to her feet and then over to the window. "Did he hurt you?"

"A little." She said it like it didn't matter, and maybe it didn't. She lived. Emma lived. Clarke lived. Beyond that, any injuries could heal. She knelt next to Emma. "Em, honey, talk to me."

The blonde moaned a little, and her eyelids fluttered, but she didn't wake. Dante crouched next to her. "Drugged, I bet. I've got her." He scooped her up, stood, and waited for Lei to precede him down the stairs.

Dante followed her down to where he'd left Clarke. She took one look at them and gave a weak grin. "Dante, the savior."

"Not this time." He might have shot Berkley, but he couldn't take credit for saving the day. If Lei hadn't managed to yell his name, he might have blundered right into the fucking woods and left her at Berkley's mercy. By the time he'd figured out his mistake, it would have been too late.

He set Emma next to Clarke and checked her pulse again. "Steady," he said to Lei.

And then she was in his arms. He squeezed her as tightly as he dared, letting the feeling of his body wrapped around hers calm his racing heart. It had been so fucking close. If he hadn't heard her. If he'd been on the wrong side of the house when Berkley had gone after her with the knife. If, if, if.

We're here. We're alive. We made it.

The front door burst open beneath a boot, and then FBI streamed into the house. Dante recognized Vic Sutherland and his wife, Maggie, and a few others, but it was Britton he looked for. He met his boss's gaze. "He's on the roof."

Britton nodded and started issuing orders. Two agents were dispatched to watch over the body until the medical examiner arrived. Two more were to search the house, and the remaining two were to set up a perimeter. Only then did he approach.

He knelt in front of Clarke and touched her knee. "I'm glad you're okay."

"You know me. Can't get me down." She didn't have quite the same brazen tone that Dante had come to expect from her. Whatever Berkley had done to her had left its mark beyond the bruises marring her face. He wanted to ask, but Britton was better equipped to deal with it. At least for now.

Britton nodded as if she'd said more than she had. "Humor me by accepting an ambulance ride so the hospital can look you over."

"Okay."

That, more than anything else, confirmed that she was more injured than she looked. Dante met her gaze over Lei's head, but she glanced away before he could divine her thoughts. Britton turned to him. "Emma?"

The woman in question stirred but didn't wake. "Unconscious. Maybe drugged." It was the only way to explain why she hadn't woken yet.

"He would have had to in order to get her out of the house." Lei lifted her head. "We found Isaac's car. Is he . . . ?"

"He was stabbed and left in the trees just off the road from where his cruiser was. He's in critical condition, but he's alive." Britton narrowed his eyes. "Are you injured, Lei?"

"No." When Dante gave her a little squeeze, she amended, "Not seriously enough to need a hospital. He only had me for a handful of minutes when all was said and done."

It hadn't felt like a handful of minutes. It had been a small eternity as he rushed out of that house and into the darkness, Clarke's labored breathing in his ear, finding no sign of Lei and knowing Berkley had her. Realizing he might never see her again. That if he didn't move fast enough, she would be reliving her worst nightmare, and this time she might not make it out the other side. Seeing her on that roof, watching Berkley jerk her legs out from under her, that frantic slide down the incline . . . Dante held Lei closer, not caring that they had an audience, not giving a damn about anything but the fact that she was whole and safe in his arms. "You're okay. It's okay."

"I know." She shivered. "Or my brain knows. It's taking my body a little bit to catch up."

Her dog gave a soft woof, and Lei slipped out of Dante's arms. "Saul." She knelt next to the dog and smiled when his tail slapped the ground. He lay on his side, his breathing a little funky. Lei touched his side and cursed. "He's bleeding. I think Travis kicked him."

"We'll get him in the ambulance, too."

If anyone thought the paramedics might have a problem with Britton's pronouncement, no one argued. As if on cue, the front door opened again, and more people poured into the house. In a matter of minutes, both Clarke and Emma were strapped to stretchers and removed from the building, quickly followed by a lone paramedic carrying Saul. Next came the Seattle PD, along with Dr. Franco.

Detective Smith stopped next to them, not looking any happier now than he had the first time Dante met him. "It's over, then."

Dante nodded. "It is."

"Thank Christ."

He kept his arm around Lei. She leaned on him more and more as time went on, her shivers becoming more pronounced until he leaned down and spoke softly in her ear. "Why don't we leave before your legs give out and Britton calls the paramedics back to haul you into the hospital?"

"Good plan."

He let go of her long enough to pull his boss aside. "I'm taking Lei to a hotel. Questioning can wait until tomorrow."

Britton's eyebrows inched up. "It seems cut-and-dried enough, but we'll have to take statements in the morning so that it's all on record. Go take care of her."

It took an hour to find a suitable hotel, and Lei didn't let go of Dante's hand through the entire check-in process. If he had missed how affected she was by what happened tonight, that would have been a huge clue. He let her set the pace up to the room, and he threw the dead bolt as soon as the door shut. "Come here."

"God, Dante. Just . . . God." She clung to him, letting him walk them back to sit on the bed. That's when the shakes started. "I was so scared."

"Me, too." He gathered her up into his lap and held her close. "I'm here. You're here. We made it. We saved Clarke and Emma." Maybe if he said it enough times, the truth would sink in. He closed his eyes, and the image of Lei sliding headfirst down the roof slammed into him. "We're here."

"He's dead."

"Yes."

She shuddered harder. "After all this time . . . He's really gone. The threat is really gone." She twisted and pressed her face against his chest. "Thank you. If you hadn't . . . Thank you."

He smoothed her hair back from her face. "Let me hold you for a while. I don't know if I can sleep tonight, but I think we both need this."

Her lips twitched in something that was almost a smile. "Your timing might be a little suspect, Agent Young."

"I meant what I said before—I do want to take you out when the dust has settled. I like you, Lei, and I admire you a whole hell of a lot."

This time, her smile actually made an appearance. "Dinner and a movie might be kind of anticlimactic after hunting down my serial-killer ex-boyfriend."

He chuckled, his amusement eating away at the fear still lingering along the edge of his awareness. They were safe. They actually had a chance at the possibility of a future because the threat was gone. "I was thinking more along the lines of a shooting range, or you can show me one of the hiking spots around here I keep hearing about." He pressed a kiss to her temple. "And while we're out, after kissing the hell out of you, I'll give you my pitch on why you should join the FBI and the BAU."

She tilted her head back, a clear invitation. "I think I might be able to be persuaded."

"Don't make it too easy on me."

"I wouldn't dream of it." Lei kissed him, sliding her hands up to cup his face. Every touch, every taste, was confirmation that they were alive. They'd won. They'd beaten the monster and had lived to fight another day.

And it was all because of the woman in his arms.

CHAPTER TWENTY-EIGHT

Six months later

"We find the defendant, Trevor Addams, guilty on all charges."

Lei sagged against Dante, relief taking all the strength from her body. Six months ago, when Travis had died, she'd hoped that the nightmare was finally over.

Today, that became the truth.

Trevor Addams, identical twin to Travis Berkley, had been entitled to his own trial in the deaths of twenty-one Omega Delta Lambda sorority girls. It should have been an open-and-shut case, but he'd pleaded not guilty. It had been like traveling to the past, although this time, instead of using the defense of a good boy who'd taken a wrong turn, the attorneys chose to blame everything on Travis and try to prove that Trevor had been just as much a victim as the dead girls.

They'd failed.

The only good thing about the damn trial was the closure it offered. The answers.

Trevor had been the one to hunt down his twin's location and identity when he was sixteen, and a twisted friendship had formed as a result. There had been the typical starter crimes—fires, killing animals, stalking—as they worked up to what happened that night. Travis was most definitely the dominant partner, but best she could tell, Trevor had been more than willing to go along for the ride.

Dante pulled her closer and pressed a kiss to her temple. "How are you doing?"

"I'm okay." It was the truth. Trevor Addams might be able to count his time served toward his sentence, but when there were twenty-one life sentences with no possibility of parole, he wasn't going anywhere anytime soon. He'd been a foster kid, and it didn't appear he had any other family to speak of. "Let's get out of here."

He kept his arm around her as they headed out of the courthouse through the side door to avoid the circus of reporters camped out on the front steps. It wasn't until they were safely tucked into his rented sedan that she breathed a sigh of relief. "It's really over."

"It is."

She twisted in her seat to face him and took his hand. Her heartbeat kicked up at the casual touch that still felt anything but, even after half a year of talking to Dante almost regularly and seeing him as often as they could manage. Her phone buzzed, and she smiled at the sight of Emma's name. "Hey, Em."

"They found the bastard guilty."

"They did."

Emma exhaled, as if she hadn't dared believe it. "I'm glad. How are you holding up?"

"Pretty good, actually." She stroked her thumb over Dante's knuckles. "How's the new office?"

"It's good. I have an assistant now, and she's not totally terrible. She spoils Prince, though." For all her grumpy words, her tone was as happy as Lei had ever heard. The move across the country had been good for both of them. Emma had picked out a condo in DC that put her at a nice central location to contract out with the FBI as they needed her and still continue to work on her missing-persons program. She didn't leave her home now any more than she had before, but she was allowing herself to become a little less isolated, a bit at a time.

As for Lei, she'd taken Britton's offer of a job.

She smiled. "You'll train her up right."

"That I will." Emma laughed. "It's good having Saul here while you're traveling. Prince misses him when he's gone. Where are you off to now that the trial's over?"

She glanced at Dante. He showed no signs of listening to their conversation, but she had no doubt he heard every word. "Arizona—Scottsdale. There's a triple homicide that may or may not be a serial killer, so Dante and I were called in to consult."

"Tell D hi for me." Dogs barked in the distance, and she cursed. "I have to go. I'll catch up with you soon. Love you."

"Love you, too." She hung up and set the phone in the cup holder. "I think we should move in together."

Dante's hand tightened around hers, but his face showed no expression—until she got to his dark eyes. All the emotions he kept bottled up lingered there, a window to the very depths of him. "I don't want to rush you."

She laughed, feeling free for the first time in as long as she could remember. Feeling like the old Lei. Except she *wasn't* the old Lei. She wasn't the postmassacre Lei, either. These days, she was something else altogether. Still broken. Still very much a work in progress. Too proud, too willing to jump straight into danger to prove she wasn't afraid, too prone to wake up from nightmares, her scream caught firmly between her clenched teeth.

Lei pulled their interlaced hands to her face and kissed his knuckles. "Dante, we spend most of our time on the road, living out of hotels. We already *are* living together, as far as our current lifestyle is concerned.

I don't want to spend our limited time in DC apart. I want to be with you."

His slow smile was like the sun emerging from behind a cloud. "Let's move in together." He stopped at a light and leaned over to capture her mouth in a soul-searing kiss. "I love you, Lei Zhang."

"You damn well better." She spoke against his lips. "Because I love the hell out of you, too. Now let's go catch us a serial killer."

ACKNOWLEDGMENTS

Thank you to Krista Stroever for helping me make this story in the Hidden Sins series into the best version of itself. Big thanks to the team at Montlake for your amazing support!

Thank you to Lauren Hawkeye and Piper J. Drake for being my go-to support team. Writing books feels like a much less solitary journey when I can chat with you two!

As always, thanks to John Nave for not taking my random research questions as grounds to throw me into the back of a cop car. I swear I'm not burying bodies in the woods—and this book is my evidence!

Hugs to the support team at home—Kristen Nave and Hilary Brady. You two keep me sane and help me remember to take a day off every once in a while! Thank you!

Last, but never least, to Tim. Thank you for brainstorming great ways to fictionally murder people, for never complaining about pulling more than your fair share of dinner duty, and for keeping me anchored no matter how crazy life gets. Kisses!

ABOUT THE AUTHOR

New York Times and *USA Today* bestselling author Katee Robert learned to tell her stories at her grandpa's knee. *The Surviving Girls* is the third book in the Hidden Sins series following *The Hunting Grounds* and *The Devil's Daughter*. Her 2015 book, *The Marriage Contract*, was a RITA Award finalist. When not writing sexy contemporary and romantic suspense, she spends her time playing imaginative games with her children, driving her husband batty with what-if questions, and planning for the inevitable zombie apocalypse. Visit her online at www.kateerobert.com.